ROCK PAPER SCISSORS

ORDINARY MAGIC STORIES

ALSO BY DEVON MONK

Ordinary Magic:
Death and Relaxation
Devils and Details
Gods and Ends

Shame and Terric:
Backlash

House Immortal:
House Immortal
Infinity Bell
Crucible Zero

Broken Magic:
Hell Bent
Stone Cold

Allie Beckstrom:
Magic to the Bone
Magic in the Blood
Magic in the Shadows
Magic on the Storm
Magic at the Gate
Magic on the Hunt
Magic on the Line
Magic without Mercy
Magic for a Price

Age of Steam:
Dead Iron
Tin Swift
Cold Copper
Hang Fire (short story)

Short Fiction:
A Cup of Normal (collection)
Yarrow, Sturdy and Bright (Once Upon a Curse anthology)
A Small Magic (Once Upon a Kiss)

ROCK PAPER SCISSORS

ORDINARY MAGIC STORIES

DEVON MONK

ISBN: 978-1-939853-10-3

Published by: Odd House Press
Art by: Lou Harper
Interior design by: Indigo Chick Designs

TABLE OF CONTENTS

DEDICATION

For my family, and all the readers who asked for a little bit more Ordinary.

ROCK CANDY

Just an Ordinary Halloween...

POLICE OFFICER Jean Reed doesn't normally mind pulling the graveyard shift in Ordinary Oregon, the sleepy little beach town where gods vacation and monsters reside. But October in Ordinary is anything but normal. One mob of cursed gnomes, one haunted harbor festival, and one chilling visit from Death makes this October stranger than most.

But it's Jean's boyfriend, Hogan, who really has her flustered. With their six month anniversary ticking down to Halloween, she wonders if their time together is anything more than a casual fling. When she discovers Hogan has been keeping secrets, Jean must decide if their relationship has been nothing but a trick or if it's been the one treat she's always wished for.

CHAPTER ONE

LATE. I, Police Officer Jean Reed, was late. I threw my controller onto the chair next to the couch and jogged to the bathroom. The alarm on my cell shouted the Venture Bros. theme song from somewhere in the pile of discarded clothes at the side of my bed. I hadn't done laundry in a week because I hated doing it, so my room was a bit of a mess. I had three minutes to shower (made it in two), one minute to get into my uniform and boots (nailed it), and half a second to kiss the very sexy man lounging on my couch.

Hogan mumbled against my lips and slid a little sideways, crookeding up our mouths as he simultaneously tried to look past me at the screen where he was a tiny rock with a knight's helmet and sword on a quest to fight a paper dragon.

"Watch for the sand pit, boyfriend," I said.

"Got it."

"Don't stay up too late." We were still kissing, our words tumbling between our lips.

"Got it."

"Don't go in the scissor forest without me."

"Got it."

"Watch the hammer hail!" We both broke the kiss. I was still leaning over him, my knee between his spread legs, one arm braced on the back of the couch. His pliant body went tense and alert beneath me.

It was sexy as hell.

We both stared at the screen while he totally shielded up and threw his sword into the clouds. Sunlight broke through and melted the storm of hammers.

I exhaled. "Nice."

He paused the game. "Come here." His hands slid over my hips and he tugged at me, drawing me down. He had that warm hungry look in his clear-blue eyes, his dark features softened to a dusky purple from the glow of the game.

"No. No way." I pushed up, loving the slow friction of his palms resisting as I tried to get him to release me. "I am late. You need to go home and go to bed so you can wake up early and make me spicy maple bars, baker boy."

"Pumpkin glazed cinnamon buns, actually. They can wait."

It would be easy to stay, to wrap up in the mellow low tones of his words, to tease out of him the slight Jamaican accent he'd inherited from his mother.

But I *was* late. And super responsible. And...Hogan lifted up to press a kiss at my collarbone.

What was I saying? Oh, yeah. I was a police officer. Badge, duty, and justice for all, etc., etc.

"I think," I said, as I finally pushed onto my feet, "that you better lock the door behind you and remember to put your cup in the sink this time."

Hogan shifted until he was fully sitting. Such a fine-looking man, tall with nice wide muscular shoulders, a long torso that tapered to narrow hips. He had thighs that made me envy his jeans, and a butt I couldn't keep my hands off.

But more than his ample physical aspects that drew me to him, he also had this deep, quiet gentleness that had surprised me when we first started dating after meeting on a gaming forum. His steady eyes and heart never missed anything, but he didn't feel the need to talk all the time. Didn't feel the need to judge, to declare, to order.

He was like tides, rolling in and out with an endless calm, with grace, with beauty.

It was no wonder he ran a bakery like a boss in our little seaside town where gods vacationed and monsters worked and lived. Not only did he have an amazing talent of teasing out the best and most unexpected combinations in pastries, breads, cakes and cookies, he also had a way of teasing out the best in his customers.

And in me.

That was a startling thing I still hadn't come to grips with.

We were just dating. This was a casual thing. Fun. Fleeting.

And yet...

And yet Hogan had come over after his early shift ended and before my late shift began for five months now. Five months was almost half a year. I'd never dated anyone for so long.

I'd never wanted to until now. It scared the pants off of me.

"Ah, now you're doing it."

"Doing what?" I asked.

"Thinking too hard about us."

"Like there's anything to think too hard about. *Us*." I tried to make it sound flip, but it came off as a question. Darn it.

"Go to work." Calm, easy.

His smile said other things. His eyes said other things. And when he stood and kissed me, his lips said oh so much more: Yes, there was an us. Yes, we were still good. Yes, this thing was going to last another week, another month.

Yes, this was good and he was here, a part of this strange little life I lived in this strange little town I helped take care of.

Yes, all that, all me, was still enough for him.

I wanted to hear that from him. Wanted to know that he knew we were something that would last. Wished we had a promise between us, a pledge. Because I worried. Hogan had traveled. He was smart and successful. There was no place in the world where he couldn't belong.

Sometimes I wondered if he could really be satisfied living here. Happy being here. Not just with this little town, but with me.

Experience told me the odds were not good on that. Most of my ex-boyfriends had left town the first chance they got. Had left me.

But there was a part of me that hoped this would be enough for him. That he'd stay here, and live here for a very long time.

He cupped my cheek with his palm and kissed me again on the forehead, a benediction, a habit, a good-bye ritual he'd done ever since I'd been hit by a car a month ago. "Be safe."

"At my desk? Not a problem." I patted his butt, because who could resist that? Certainly not I. "Hatter's going to take the graveyard shift patrol. It's all good."

"I know." And that smile. That *smile*. It was secret, joyful, open, reckless. It was somehow all these things, all these *Hogan* things, all the parts of him I wanted to hold. All the parts of him I wanted to keep.

"That grin is so much trouble," I said.

He chuckled and gave a passing effort at innocent eyes. "I like your hair all orange and purple." He drew his fingers through the long wet strands of it.

"Flatterer. You better clean up the dishes and don't forget to hit a save point before you switch over to river travel."

He didn't need me to tell him any of that. But I hoped he heard the things I had tried to wedge in between my words.

That I liked him. A lot. That I wanted him to stay in my life. Maybe for a long time.

I'm not a shy person. I never have any problem telling someone my opinion or giving them advice. I laugh things off, poke at the rules until they dent and bend, and generally act like life is not to be taken too seriously.

Being the forever-baby sister of the town's infamous Reed sister trio has its perks. We are police officers like our dad was. Delaney, my eldest sister is the bridge for god powers. She is the one and only way gods can step into town, put their powers in storage, and vacation like mortals.

My middle sister, Myra, is serious about her book studies. Most of those studies involve the wisdom and arcane knowledge in the ancient texts Dad left in her safekeeping, just as his dad left them to him. She has a knack for always being in the right place at the right time.

And me? Well, I have the family gift of knowing when something really bad is going to happen. A month ago, that feeling was the only thing that gave me a split-second warning before a car had come barreling toward me.

I could have died instead of just been banged up a little.

So it's a good talent to possess, but it isn't as important as the things my sisters do and the gifts they possess.

Also, my gift isn't without cost. Not that I've ever told anyone that.

"Jean." Hogan rubbed his hands down my arms. Long, strong fingers caught to weave between mine. "What's wrong?"

Nothing. That was the truth I wanted to believe. So I held onto it with both hands and all my heart.

"I'm late because some sexy son-of-a-bun is holding my hands like he's going to ask me to go steady." I grinned at him and batted my eyes.

He shook his head, but there was nothing but smile in him. Sunshine and warmth. Like a hearth fire. Like home.

Was I that for him too? Despite my bravado, I couldn't work up the nerve to ask.

"I'll see you soon." He gave my hand one more squeeze, then flopped back down on the couch.

And just like that, the moment to ask him if he wanted the same thing I wanted: for our five months of dating to turn into something more, for us to agree that we needed each other for more than a week, a month, a year, had passed.

I could hear the clang of the rock knight cutting his way through the cardboard cliffs before I'd even gotten halfway across my living room to the door.

CHAPTER TWO

ORDINARY'S POLICE station was a small one-story building tucked off the main coastal road: Highway 101. It had a screen of trees to one side, wetland at the back, and a parking lot on the other side.

Myra's perfectly clean cruiser and Delaney's old Jeep were both parked by the station. I parked my truck facing the wetlands instead because I loved how the trees and brush had gone brown and orange.

Autumn. My favorite time of year. Fall came early on the Oregon coast, trees shedding down to their bare bones only to be wrapped in heavy fog and draped in gowns of grey and rain. The wet had settled in for the long winter months, storms rising and falling between wedges of pale yellow sun breaks. Showers, drizzle, rain, downpours, would all take their turn rolling through from now until spring.

The air was filled with the smells of fires on the beach, rain in the pines, moss, green, dirt, and salt. And between all that floated the sweetness of coffee roasters, bakeries, and pumpkin spice.

Pumpkin spice everything.

I could see how some people couldn't wait for Thanksgiving, for that warm, cozy comfort of family and food and familiar faces. I liked Thanksgiving just fine too.

But my holiday, the one I checked off the days on my calendar for, the one that I intended to start decorating for tomorrow, was Halloween.

I loved it as a kid. I loved seeing the monsters in town dress up as things they really weren't, and loved it even better when they came out as their real selves. Loved it when they went all-out giving candy, running haunted houses, and hosting pumpkin carving contests. I loved it even more when the gods in town got into it. One year Frigg threw a costume ball so crazy and fun, I had never found the bra I'd been wearing.

I loved the witches, hexes, ghosts and ghouls. I loved the Halloween movies and cartoons that played non-stop from October first to October thirty-first. I loved the old silent horror movies, and the newer, much more screamy, bloody ones. I was a sucker for pumpkin patch hay mazes and apple bobbing and just…everything.

Halloween was my jam, and I celebrated it every single day through October.

I got out of the truck, ignored the drizzle, and made my way into the station. As soon as I stepped through the door, I knew I was in trouble.

Every person in the room had their finger on their nose.

"You all look ridiculous." I took off my coat and tried not to let my panic show.

Something was going on. It must be a bad thing since every person on the force was acting like a three-year-old.

"Hey, baby sister," Delaney said in her not-boss voice. "We have a little job for you."

I waved my hand at all of them. "You can stop grinning and pointing at your noses. I get it. I'm pulling crap duty. Bring it on."

"No argument?" Myra raised one of her sculpted brows. She was always so put together, and she totally owned the rock-a-billy look.

I snuck an extra glance at Delaney. She'd been shot with a vampire-killing bullet about a month ago. Even though she had tried to pass it off as no big thing, that had been the second bullet she'd been on the wrong end of this year.

Her recovery had taken time. Ryder Bailey, her boyfriend who was standing in the corner of the room looking all rugged and handsome as our reserve officer, had moved her in with him. As far as I could tell things were going good for them.

Really good.

That made me happy in a way nothing had for a long time. I mean, I'd been waiting forever for them to finally catch a frickin' clue and see how good they were together.

Ryder and Delaney had known each other nearly all their lives. In second grade, I'd caught Ryder making a wish on a dandelion fluff. He'd been really quiet when he'd done it, his voice just a whisper. But he didn't know I'd been there, right around the corner, digging a hole I was going to fill with water so I could make mud monsters.

His wish? He wanted Delaney to love him like he loved her.

And I'd heard it.

Everybody knew if you heard a wish someone else made, that wish wouldn't come true.

Which, yeah, maybe that wasn't how it worked. Wishes were tricky magic, and I certainly wasn't someone who knew all the ins and outs of that.

But when I'd been seven, I'd known three things: Ryder loved my sister. I'd heard him wish for her to fall in love with him, which meant it couldn't come true. Therefore, I had to do everything I could to make sure his wish came true.

And I had. Of course Ryder had waffled between throwing longing looks her way and ignoring her completely all through high school. Delaney had done the same with him. And no matter what I tried, they never seemed to both be in the longing stage at the same time.

Then Ryder had gone out of state for six years of college, and I figured all those years of me finagling to get them together were wasted.

But he'd come home almost two years ago now.

And look at them: in love.

Hatter snapped his fingers. "Jean?" he said in that Texas accent that I thought he just put on so people would buy his long-and-lanky, easy-going cowboy vibe. "I think we broke her."

"Please." I rolled my eyes. "Like anything about this job can break me. What is it, what do I have to do?"

"You do know what day today is?" Hatter asked.

"September thirtieth?"

Shoe snorted a laugh, which was all the laugh that man could make. Shoe had been Hatter's partner when they'd been on the force up in Tillamook before we'd stolen them for the force here. He was Hatter's opposite in just about every way. Short, wide, reticent, suspicious, and seemingly humorless. Seemingly, but not actually without humor. Get a few drinks into that man, and he was a hoot.

"Try again," Hatter suggested. He waggled his eyebrows and bit down on a juicy grin.

"It's the first," Delaney said, totally squashing his fun. "October first, Jean. Tonight, when the sun goes down in three hours, you'll need to be ready."

I heard her, but the only words that registered were the date. October first. Already? Yes, of course, already. I'd just been admiring the autumn leaves and reminiscing about Halloween.

How had I forgotten the horror we had to deal with every October?

"Jean?" Delaney said.

Hatter snapped his fingers again.

I glanced up at him. At her. At all of them. Felt the fear crawl over my skin with prickly feet. "The gnomes."

It came out as a rough whisper.

Shoe snorted again.

"We hear it's a problem," Hatter drawled. "You folks have to deal with them every October? That right?"

I tried to talk, but my throat was too dry. So I swallowed and tried again. "It's more than that."

"It will be fine," Delaney said. "I did it the year before last. No big deal."

"If you call that slimy disaster no big deal," I said.

"You're being dramatic."

"We were scrubbing pixie puke off the highway for weeks."

"Pixie puke?" Ryder asked.

Yes, he'd lived in Ordinary all his life, but he'd only recently found out about the secrets it held. He always jumped in and asked questions whenever we mentioned a new kind of creature that he didn't know lived here.

Delaney had made us swear not to clue him in to any of the supernaturals because she liked to make him figure it out on his own.

Frankly, I thought she used that knowledge in exchange for kinky sex or something.

"The papers said it was a hag fish spill," Myra supplied.

Ryder frowned. "So pixies look like snot eels?"

"Not at all," Delaney said. "But when gnomes make an entire swarm of pixies puke, it gets pretty slimy. All over the highway. All over half a dozen unfortunate cars. Smells like rotten fish. And takes days to clean up." At the look on his face, she smiled. "Aren't you glad you know that little factoid, Mr. Bailey?"

"Uh, not really."

"Like I said," I said, "disaster. And before *you* say anything," I jabbed a finger toward Myra, "I have two words for the job you did with this last year: chocolate toilets."

Myra had the good grace to wince. "We took care of it."

Was she blushing? I hoped she was blushing.

"We *replaced* every public toilet in Ordinary, including the heads in half the boats docked in the bay. If I never see another stanky wax ring, flange, or flapper in my life, it will be too soon."

"Good band name," Hatter noted.

"Flange and Flapper?"

"Stanky Wax Ring."

I grinned at him. There was a reason he and I got along like sinner and sinnest.

"Are you done?" Now *that* was Delaney's boss voice.

"With?"

"Stalling to try to get out of this? I'm sending Hatter out with you."

"I can do it alone."

"You won't because I said you won't. I expect you to update me as soon as you make contact."

"Contact?" Hatter pulled a stick of gum out of his pocket and tossed it in his mouth, breath-freshening like an interviewee in suck-up mode.

"The head gnome," I grumbled. I stormed over to the little table in the hall that held the coffee pot and usually a few snacks. Nothing but dregs and crumbs. "I expect a fresh pot of this when I get back." I lifted the coffee pot. Shook it.

Four sets of fingers zeroed in on noses.

"Oh, for real?"

Delaney chuckled. "I'll make coffee before I end my shift. Call as soon as you find the leader."

And because she was my big sister, and because she sounded genuinely concerned, and because I knew just how dangerous this assignment could be, I nodded.

"Where have we last seen headless Abner?" I asked.

"Myra?" Delaney asked.

Myra shook her head and sat at her desk. She tapped a screen there. "Last we saw him, he was on the corner of Ebb and 4th."

"By the old fire hall?" I asked.

"That was last March. I drove by yesterday and didn't see him."

Of course she had. Myra was thorough like that. Responsible. Got things done in the proper order of doing them. Despite the milk chocolate toilet debacle.

"We'll start there." I grabbed my coat.

"What do they look like?" Ryder asked all casual, like he wasn't chomping at the bit to find out a little more about Ordinary's more unusual citizens.

"Gnomes? They look like gnomes," I said.

"So....red hats?" he ventured.

"You've seen gnomes, Ryder."

"All right," he said in a go-on tone.

I just grinned. "Maybe if you do something kinky for Delaney, she'll tell you all about it."

Delaney sighed and covered her face with one hand. Ryder let out a surprised laugh, but that look in his eyes as he watched her reaction was all lust and love.

"Maybe I will," he said quietly.

I gave him two thumbs up.

What could I say? I was a romantic at heart.

CHAPTER THREE

HATTER AND I drove past the old fire hall, which was a box of a building barely big enough to hold two parked cars and a can opener. The parking lot of a restaurant with mural of a disappointed crab stretched out east of the little fire hall. Short brown grass cut a small swath on the west side by the fire hydrant.

The building wore an indifferent coat of yellow paint, and the glass garage doors took up the whole face of it. There was a sign on the door saying the meeting had been moved to the community center. The sign was faded. I didn't think this old place had been used in years.

A perfect spot for headless Abner.

"You gonna let me in on this?" Hatter asked like he was wondering if I wanted to split an order of fries. And if he'd actually asked that I would have told him no, because, hello: fries are not for sharing. But this was about gnomes and gnomes were an all-hands-on-deck problem.

"I sometimes forget that you don't know everything about Ordinary."

"Does anyone?"

I shrugged and decided to drive around the block one more time just to make sure I had covered the hall from all angles. Gnomes were tricky.

Hatter fiddled with the vent. "I've done a fair share of pitching in when your father asked, but it wasn't all that often. He liked to play things pretty close to the vest about this town."

"He had a protective streak a mile wide. Delaney inherited it."

"Pretty sure all his daughters inherited it."

"Fair."

"So, gnomes?"

I sighed. "I don't know how it happened. Some people say it was a drunk witch. Others say it was a curse-happy harpy. I've even heard whispers that the local Jinn did it as a revenge-wish fulfillment. But whoever or *whatever* did it, we have to spend every day of October mopping up after that mess."

"Still don't know what mess we should be mopping. Gonna stop talking in circles any time soon, or should I pay for an extra ride?"

I gave him a short smile. "That wish, hex, spell, whatever, fell on all the gnomes in the town."

He frowned.

"The garden gnomes. The statues people put out in their yards and think are cute? Those gnomes."

"Oh." He sounded disappointed. "I thought we were talking living breathing sorts of people."

"We are. For the thirty-one days of October, the garden gnomes come alive. They are living, they are breathing, and they are pissed off little buggers."

He laughed. It was a squeaky, hissy sound that I liked. Hatter was fun to be around. He had a way of making things seem like they weren't as bad as one might think, and that there was room for a little fun shoved between all the responsibilities of this job.

"So we should be looking for something on the move?"

"Not until sunset."

"They only come alive at night? That's not creepy."

"Some of them are okay, I guess, or at least not creepy, really. But angry? Oh, yeah."

"What do they have to be angry about?"

"Spending eleven months out of the year frozen as stone? Hating that they have to wear the same dumb hats every day of their lives? Or, oh, here's a good one. That time they found out a gnome statue got the job for that travel commercial. A gnome statue that wasn't from Ordinary."

"Didn't go over well?"

"Ca-frickin'-lamity. We had to round them up into one of the storage units, and then red hat our way in to calm them down."

"Red hat?"

"It's a gnome thing. If you put on a red hat, preferably pointed, they'll think you're one of them."

"Even though I would, presumably, be taller than a garden gnome?"

"Yep."

"And human, and alive, and a cop?"

"It's like bats seeing with their ears. If a gnome sees a red hat, you're a gnome."

He grinned and snapped his gum. "I do not know why I didn't ask to be transferred to this town years ago. You have all the fun."

I gave him my evil laugh. "Oh, we'll see if you still think that when you're done with gnome duty, buddy."

"Bring it on, Jee-jee."

I flipped him a finger and scowled at the nickname even though I sort of liked it.

"We need to go on foot." I pulled into the parking lot next to the old fire hall.

"Statue, right?"

"Yep."

"Is there a reason you call him headless Abner?"

"He has no head, Hatter."

"Doesn't that make it difficult during negotiations?"

"He's good at charades."

"You're serious."

"As a...." I patted my chest and made my fingers into claws.

"Serious as an angry monkey? Mad monkey? Monkey Jean? Monkey in jeans?"

"Monkey? How did you get monkey out of this?" I repeated the motions. "Heart attack. It's heart attack. I'm as serious as a heart attack. You suck at charades. You are not allowed to handle the negotiations with Abner."

"All right then. I'll..." he pointed at his eyes, then tipped his fingers down and made scissoring motions, "follow your lead."

We started off toward the hall. As the dark of evening thickened into night, the chill of winter pinched goose bumps from my skin. I zipped my jacket and scanned the tall grass. It was possible someone had finally gotten rid of headless Abner. It was possible he'd been taken to the dump. I shuddered a little. Most gnomes that were thrown away stayed inert during

October. But there were...rumors. Reports we'd never been able to verify.

"Your face," Hatter said, as we rounded the corner to the back of the hall. "What are you thinking about?"

"Zombie gnomes."

He stilled, then his smile swept up wide. "Just adding 'zombie' on the front of a thing doesn't make it more frightening, you know. Watch: Zombie potato. Zombie turtles. Zombie accordion."

"Sure, you talk big now. See how hard you're laughing when a zombie gnome is eating your brains."

"Will it even know I'm edible if I'm not wearing a red hat?"

"Ha. Ha."

We'd finished the perimeter of the building and I paused, hands on my hips, scanning the damp grassy stretches farther down the road. It was getting too dark to see much without flashlights.

"Should I secure zombie-killing bullets? Or is this a hammer-and-chisel-to-the-heart kind of operation?"

"Look, smartass. We don't even know that there are zombie gnomes. I've never seen it, and neither has Myra or Delaney."

"So what you're saying is there is no danger."

"What I'm saying is, if there *are* zombie gnomes, and we have heard rumors that say it's possible, then we have no idea how to restrain or kill them. So laugh about that, why don't you."

And the jerk did.

CHAPTER FOUR

TURNED OUT headless Abner was a no-show. He wasn't in any of his typical haunts. He used to belong to a rental on Ebb Street, but it looked like the new rental agency had finally done away with him.

"So what's the next move?" Hatter asked.

It was super dark now, and we were parked on the corner of Anchor. Mr. Denver lived there along with his wife. Mr. Denver was a retired music teacher with hearing damage, and Mrs. Denver slept with a jet engine she insisted was a white noise machine. She also collected yard art. A lot of yard art.

Including a boatload of gnomes.

The little buggers were hiding in the bushes, stacked up the edges of the front steps, hanging on swings from the porch rafters.

A quick count gave me thirty of various sizes and accouterments. Some with shovels, some with buckets, some with lanterns, flowers, bunnies, mushrooms, and one with a gun.

I was keeping an eye on the one with the gun.

"We wait for them to wake up."

"Sun's down," he noted.

"Yep." I took a drink of my soda, didn't look away from the yard. "Any minute now."

"There some kind of strategy to this?"

I saw a branch rustle, grass wave. This was it. "Think like a gnome."

I pushed out of the truck and strode to the yard knowing there was no way Mr. and Mrs. Denver would hear us.

It was important to pick out the leader of the group. Not easy since they all looked pretty much the same. All the boy gnomes had beards, all the girl gnomes had braids.

"We going to see anything else come alive?" Hatter whispered as we came up on one side of the big rhododendron bush at the edge of the property. "Flamingos? That bear statue over there?" He waved toward the garage.

"Just gnomes."

I didn't know if there was a time-release on the spell, hex, whatever it was, but one minute they were statues, maybe a random shift or blink here or there, and then they were all alive.

I stepped out from behind the bush. "Is headless Abner still one of you?"

Three dozen gnomey heads turned. Three dozen sets of gnomey eyes looked up at me, lingered on my badge, then looked away.

Well, they all looked away except for one gnome. She was vintage, chubby, with happy round features and two long blonde braids falling from beneath her hat. She wore a long dress and a scowl.

"Gnice to see you, Officer Reed." She said in passable English, though there was a bit of an accent–nothing I'd heard from any creature except a gnome. I didn't know what it was, but it always caught at my ear, as if there was a silent letter in there somewhere I should be noticing. "Who's the gnew partner?"

"This is Officer Hatter. He'll be your secondary contact for the month."

She was still scowling, but wasn't looking at us anymore. Gnomes had short attention spans. Sometimes that worked to our advantage.

"Why are my apples purple?" She shook the basket hanging from the crook of her arm as if that would do something useful. The little stone apples clacked like a fistful of marbles. "Why are all my apples purple?"

This was bad. Gnomes were creatures of habit. If one found out someone had updated their paint colors with a little bit of whimsy, it did not go over well.

"They're plums," I said.

She glanced up at me, then back at her basket. "Plums?"

"Plums."

"Oh," she said with a quick smile. "How invigorating. Plums." She stood a little taller, tipped the knob of her chin upward. "I wouldn't suppose any of the other gnomes have plums in their baskets, do they?"

I had no idea.

"Absolutely not," I said. "You're quite the trendsetter. So, about headless Abner. Have you seen him?"

"Why would you think I had?"

"You're in the most heavily populated gnome yard in town. I just thought someone would have brought him this way."

"He's gnot at the hall?"

"No."

She turned around, a shuffling, rocking motion as if her legs were made out of flat-bottomed ice cream cones.

She made a show of looking at the gnomes who had all crowded up to stand behind her.

"He's gnot here," she said, as if just noticing.

"Right. Do you know where he is?"

"Gno?"

I waited.

She shuffle-rocked back around to face me. "He's gone."

"Gone, gone, gone," the gnomes whisper-chanted behind her.

Great. They'd gone from unalive to culty in ten seconds flat.

"We are without a leader."

"Leader, leader, leader."

"A gnew leader must be chosen!"

"Gnew, Gnew, Gnew!"

"Only the most worthy shall lead us. The most trendsetting." She reached into her basket and grasped a plum, then held it up over her head as if it were a torch. "She who holds the plums of prophecy!"

Hatter shifted, his hand lingering at his hip. "On a scale of one to get-the-grenades, how crazy is this?"

"Hatter, it's always get-the-grenades in this town."

Both his eyebrows rose slowly. "Want me to call for reinforcements?"

"Naw. We can handle this. Behold my power." I held out my hand, palm flat forward. "Red light."

Just like in the kid's game, Red Light/Green Light, every gnome went dead still and looked up at me. I had no idea why a kid's game worked on them, but I was glad it did.

If I'd never dealt with these little statue people before, it might be unsettling, those eyes of stone with a frightening kind of longing filling them. It might be a tad bit terrifying to realize that those eyes hungered for a life less fleeting than their own.

Gnomes weren't exactly stable. But we dealt with dangerous creatures every day.

We'd recently had a demon blackmail his way into town via stealing Delaney's soul. Also, he seemed to be way too interested in Myra. Whenever he and Myra were in the same room, they were arguing.

It would have been entertaining to watch Myra get all riled up–okay, who am I kidding? It *was* entertaining–but there was a lot about demons I didn't know and didn't understand.

There was no chance he was harmless. And I didn't care what Delaney said. He enjoyed getting Myra worked up a little too much for it to be passed off as just a 'demon thing'.

Because, seriously? I wasn't down with a demon who held one of my sisters' soul hostage, while he was making moves on my other sister.

Even if he was handsome, had a wicked disregard of the rules and had, shockingly, saved a couple lives in town.

For a price.

I wasn't into the bad-boy type. But there was no denying he had this...smolder, plus flashing eyes and muscles for miles.

Bathin was hard to miss, but he was not hard on the eyes.

I could see why Myra might not want to resist all that.

But before she made a move, before *he* made a move, I needed to know more about him.

What would hold a demon down? Chains? Spells? The Home Shopping Channel played backward to summon a portal into a dimension of unknown horror?

That was totally a thing. Do not try it at home, kids.

There had to be a way to find out what his intentions with Myra really were. Lock him in a cell in the middle of the night when Delaney and Myra were off shift? Handcuffs, zip ties, holy trinkets and chains? Oh, yeah. That would do it. I could make him talk.

Because I was good at that. Good at being everyone's friend. Good at being the one who was easy to talk to, the one who didn't ever let the world get to me. I laughed a lot, played a lot, and was never shy about giving my opinion.

I could be a hardass when I needed to be.

That was a side of me I didn't let out very often. A side of me I certainly hadn't let Hogan see yet.

Something like fear knotted my stomach, and I checked to see if this was a bad-feeling omen courtesy of my family gift.

Nope. It didn't have that edge to it that hit me like a javelin to the brain, then kept on digging until I felt like I was going to toss my cookies.

This was just regular old dread. Worry over the just-for-fun relationship with Hogan that was starting to feel like something just-a-lot more to me.

Something deeper. Something honest.

Being the youngest Reed meant I had two other siblings who were quick to take on any and every responsibility. Though I'd never asked for it, Delaney and Myra had always tried to shelter me from the harsher aspects of life.

I didn't want to be sheltered. The only way I'd convinced them of that was not letting them see how much my bad omen ability really affected me. So I smiled. I laughed. I joked. I didn't show them that I woke up with nightmares so real sometimes, it took me hours to stop shaking. I didn't tell them that once I knew something bad was going to happen, I carried it in me, the sounds, sights, smells, and touch of it as if it were happening to me, over and over.

I'd been determined to follow right in Dad's footsteps despite my family gift. And in my sisters' footsteps too. I'd become a police officer and, as a Reed, I'd become a guardian of Ordinary and Ordinary's secrets.

Somewhere along the way I'd decided it was my job as the youngest to make sure my sisters fell in love and lived happily ever after.

Even if that meant interrogating a demon behind my sisters' backs. Even if that meant scheming for years to get

Ryder and Delaney to finally look at each other and *see* what they could be.

But *my* love life? *That* I had always been determined to play easy-breezy.

Did it matter that Hogan and I were coming up on our six-month anniversary of dating?

Did I want it to matter? Yes, yes, I did.

"Ordinary to Officer Reed," Hatter said. "You are cleared for landing. Copy that?"

I blinked a couple times to focus. Gnomes all looking up at me with beady eyes. Hatter standing closer than he had been just a...however many minutes ago.

Still night. Still dark. Still a little drizzly. Still no headless Abner.

"You at full capacity, Reed, or should I call this in?"

"I just got a little derailed for a second there." I so didn't want him calling my sisters on me.

"You should install a brake on that brain of yours."

"What, and give up all the random scheming? You'd miss it."

"All right. Say I would. How about you scheme our way out of the thundergnome that's about to go down here."

I chuckled. "All alive gnomes of Ordinary," I started in an authoritative tone I'd heard Delaney use since I was six years old and she'd decided she was the boss of me, my stuffed animals, and our cat that, according to her, didn't like rides in the clothes dryer.

How did she know what the cat liked? She couldn't speak cat.

"You will not forget that, while you are alive, there are rules you must follow to remain in this town. You may not harm any human, creature, or god or else you will be exiled."

There was a collective gnomey gasp, and a whispered "gno!" though I couldn't tell who said it.

"You are a creation of Ordinary. A gift."

Ha! A curse, more like, or spell. But from their perspective, I had to assume they considered life a gift.

"Outside of this town, you will no longer be alive. You will be stone statues every day and night of the year. So I suggest you choose your new leader peacefully. Understand?"

They still stood there, staring at me. Oh, right. I had to say the magic words. One of them sort of *"meep"ed.*

"Green light."

And that's when the gnomes attacked.

Okay. *Attacked* might be a little dramatic. They were small. And shuffley and had flat teeth. But they were also armed with hoes and pick axes and purple apples and a gun, for chrissake.

For being such little things, they could carry a hell of a punch if they got in punching range.

When they all closed in as quickly as their little flat-cone legs could take them, they were a force to be reckoned with.

"Red light," I commanded.

Yeah, we were way past that. They just kept shuffling. At least they hadn't gotten to chanting yet.

"Whose gnight? Gnomes's gnight!" A brown-bearded fellow with a wheelbarrow said.

And yep. Here came the chant.

"Whose gnight? Gnomes's gnight! Whose gnight? Gnomes's gnight!"

"So I'm gonna go ahead and call for backup," Hatter said.

"Naw, we'll just round them up."

He looked down at the pointy hatted mob. "Don't think I have cuffs that small."

"These are gnomes, Hatter. Cuffs don't work." I reached into my jacket pocket, and pulled out two thin paper packets. I tossed one to Hatter.

He caught it, turned it between his fingers. Read the front. "Radish seeds."

I ripped the top off of my packet of carrot seeds. "Sprinkle like your life depends on it," I said with a chuckle.

Hatter took me at my word. He tore open the packet and sprinkled, casting out far past our shuffling hoard, while I did the same.

The tiny, and I do mean tiny, radish and carrot seeds tumbled into the damp grass.

As soon as they hit the ground the gnomes all cheered, "Seeds!"

And then: "Gno!"

As if a switch had been flipped, they suddenly started moving more smoothly and efficiently. They worked the wet, grassy soil with whatever tool they might have, or with their bare hands, tending the tiny seeds.

Hatter stood beside me watching the industrious little crew. Even the gnome with the gun was shooting tiny holes into the dirt, though I wasn't sure what good that would do.

"Huh. So this is a thing. You couldn't have given me a head's up?"

"It doesn't work every time, honestly." The annoyed look he gave me was awesome.

"Stop scowling. Most of these garden gnomes are actually garden gnomes. Their first instinct is to garden. They're going to track down, sort out, and replant every one of these seeds into neat little rows. Mr. and Mrs. Denver might have a nice little veggie garden if the seeds make it through winter. This should keep the gnomes busy until sunrise."

"And by then they'll be stone again."

"Not only stone, but by then, they will have forgotten all about this. Very short attention spans. They only remember one day at a time, though they have some kind of long-term memory that allows them to remember they're only alive in October, and during that time they have to live under the rules of Ordinary and follow what their leader says."

I strolled toward the truck.

"Now that Abner is gone, they don't have a leader," he said.

"I know." I got into the truck. Time to cruise the neighborhoods where other gnomes might be wandering. "That's why we need to find out who killed Abner."

CHAPTER FIVE

DELANEY ROLLED into the station before sunrise. I was at my desk, having already written up my reports. Hatter had left about an hour ago to get some sleep.

Hogan and I had been trading dirty texts since 4:00 am. Owning a bakery made Hogan an early riser. I hadn't been willing to give up the night shift for a couple reasons. One was that it gave me time to deal with my nightmares if they popped up. Another was that I liked Ordinary at night. Most of the time it was quiet as a cotton ball.

Every once in a while the nocturnal members of our town would be out and about causing trouble. I loved to see what the vamps, weres, ghouls, and other people got up to at night.

I'd been known to join in if it was a bit of fun.

I'd been known to tell them to knock it off, if it was illegal, too.

This morning I'd been trying to talk Hogan into bringing me donuts. It was the middle of the morning rush and he couldn't get away since it was only him and Billy manning the place now that all the barely legal high school labor had gone back to school.

"Morning." Delaney hung up her coat and headed straight for the coffee pot. "Anything I should know?"

"Headless Abner is missing. Dead or disposed of. The gnomes in Mr. and Mrs. Denver's yard tried to riot, and the Higgins's cow got out, ate a box of apples, and got stuck in their neighbor's pool."

She glanced at me.

"Empty pool."

She nodded. "So, just a normal night."

I threw the pencil I had been drumming on the desk edge at her. It missed because she knew how to dodge.

"The gnomes have no leader. It's a problem. No, wait, I got this." I spread my hands like I was envisioning a marquee in lights. "Missing Headless Abner Leaves Gnomes Head Less."

"Boo."

"You like it."

"Maybe it's time for the gnomes to get a new leader. You'll need to gather them up and walk them through the process."

"Right. Sure. Happy to. Except I don't know what the process is because there is no process."

She grinned at me and took a sip of coffee. "Like that's going to stop you."

I groaned and let my head fall back between my shoulders, eyes locked on the ceiling. "Why? Why me? Myra would be better at this. You would be better at this. I'm the worst choice for this job."

"Oh?"

I held up my hands and ticked off points on my fingers even though I didn't look away from the ceiling. "I'm impatient. Impulsive. Easily distracted. Blunt. Not the kind of person you want to guide a tiny terra cotta culture through a big political adjustment."

"You forgot something," she said gently.

I tipped my head down and met her sparkling gaze. She pointed at her own finger. "Dramatic."

"You suck and I don't like you anymore."

She laughed and leaned against my desk. "I'll let Myra know you need some suggestions on how to get a new leader in place. You'll need to get it done soon."

I covered my eyes, imagining the horrors of Halloween rolling out with a bunch of murderous gnomes roaming the streets.

"We could round them up. Lock them up, just for the month. It's not like they would remember what was happening from one day to the next." I knew, as soon as it was out of my mouth, that it was a bad idea. We didn't lock up a person, creature, or god simply because they were an inconvenience. There were laws in Ordinary. Rules.

And we Reeds followed them.

"What's going on?" Delaney asked. I was glad she didn't call me out on the gnome incarceration idea. But I wasn't sure where this was headed.

"With?"

"You. This." She waved her finger at me, sort of taking in my slouch, my messy desk, my pile of tiny ripped up pieces of paper standing like a mountain, a snowstorm, an avalanche between my Snape and Dr. Orpheus dolls.

"Nothing's going on." She'd buy that, right? Because it wasn't like I was feeling the dread, the horrible something-is-going-wrong-really-soon thing.

As a matter of fact, it was sort of the lack of that feeling that was making me itchy.

Hogan and I had been dating for months. *Months*. I couldn't remember the time I'd dated a boy for more than a few weeks. By Halloween, Hogan and I would have been dating for half a year. That was not like me. I was the fun one, the young one, the sister who wasn't looking for a full-time mister.

And yet Hogan had shown up in my life (okay, I'd totally hit on him until he sent me fancy donuts to get me off his back) and he just hadn't...left.

That's not how things worked for me. All my past boyfriends, and yeah, that one girl I'd messed around with in middle school, had left as soon as the fun ran out, as soon as the laughs ran out.

I did not blame them. Who wanted to date a doomsayer?

No one.

No one wanted to *be* a doomsayer either. But I didn't get a choice in that.

Delaney snapped her fingers in my face. "Testing, testing. Do you copy, Rubber Duck?"

"Annoying." I pushed her hand away, but smiled. She was funny. Sometimes.

"Talk." Delaney rolled a chair over and sat. I watched to see if any of her injuries were bothering her today. She wasn't favoring her side at all, which was good. It still made me furious that she'd been shot.

This was a small town. We didn't solve our problems with guns, no matter what the big city folk would like to believe.

Okay. We didn't do it very often.

"I don't want to be on gnome duty."

"Liar. Next."

"There is no next."

"Jean."

"Delaney."

She just stared at me with those big sister eyes.

I blew out a breath. "Fine. It's almost been six months since I've been seeing Hogan."

"And?" she asked when I didn't say anything else.

"Six months is a long time."

She sighed. "I thought that's what you wanted? A long-term relationship? Something more than just friends? Or are you getting bored with him?"

My phone chimed with a message from Hogan.

SexyMuffin: All out of frosting. Rolled through a metric ton of pumpkin-spice cinnamon buns in a half hour flat. Who's a baking god? Worship at the altar, baby.

I grinned, then texted back quick.

*Hotcop: No! You didn't save one for me? *crack goes my heart* You're a terrible god.*

SexyMuffin: If only I'd saved some frosting, I'd patch that heart right up for you.

Hotcop: Ha! Gonna take more than frosting to fix this, buddy.

SexyMuffin: Name it. Anything. (Except frosting, natch)

Hotcop: How are those mint brownies holding up?

SexyMuffin: Six left.

Hotcop: What? What kind of god can't sell a plate of brownies?

*SexyMuffin: Who said they're for sale? Boxed 'em up for you, baby. *god mode: winning**

Hotcop: God-smod. I don't see them in my mouth.

SexyMuffin: Three…two…

I tipped my head, wondering what he was up to.

"…one."

I knew that voice, and couldn't stop the squeal of delight that shot out of my mouth. "SexyMuffin!"

"Hey there, Hotcop."

Delaney groaned like she had just had enough of us already.

"How's your morning going, Officer Reed?" Hogan strolled into the station like he owned the air, the ground, and every single one of my heartbeats that inexplicably synched up to the rhythm of his steps.

He was built lean, with wide muscular shoulders, tight, flat stomach, and a bubble ass I couldn't keep my eyes off of. His skin was darker than mine, inherited from his Jamaican mother, his hair long black braids that he kept tied at the base of his neck.

That face I couldn't get enough of was angled, but softened around all the edges so it always seemed like he was about to break into a smile, his eyes a startling blue he'd gotten from the dad he never talked about.

The man was summer and sunshine and happiness. And love. Anyone could see that from a mile away. Anyone would be amazed to be around him, to be with him.

Just like I was amazed. Happy. Giddy, even.

Except...except when I thought about how long we'd been together. And that if he and I revealed all our secrets of who we really were to each other, maybe we'd both give up on this.

"Hey," he said, stopping on the lobby side of the counter like everyone in Ordinary should. Like he should, even though I hadn't thought of him as just another person who lived in town for months now. "Did someone here say they couldn't wait to get my brownies in their mouth?"

Delaney snorted, but didn't move away from my desk. She was watching Hogan, probably using her cop eyes to take in his body language: relaxed, his voice: sexy, his eyes: happy. Happy to see me. Not a mask, not a flicker of fear or lies.

I held back a sigh.

I sucked at this relationship thing. Which was weird, right? Because I could tell Delaney what she needed to do to make her relationship with Ryder work. I could tell Myra to stop not-flirting (totally flirting) with Bathin. Because, c'mon: demon.

I could poke at Hatter when he used those cheesy pick-up lines in the bar that worked for him, but only because he laid on the fake Southern accent so thick and followed it up with those puppy dog eyes.

I could even give out advice in all my gaming groups, both online and in person.

I was good at this. Good at helping people be their best selves, their honest selves so they could be with someone else. Build a best togetherness.

Like, if cupid was a job and not an actual person (who currently wasn't living in Ordinary) I'd so be shooting heart arrows at anyone who so much as made eye contact with me.

But when it came to my heart, my own honest self, I wanted to duck and cover big time.

Delaney slid her gaze to me. I wasn't sure what she saw, but yeah, Hogan wasn't the problem in this relationship. That was all on me.

She raised one eyebrow. I didn't know if it was the what-the-hell-is-wrong-with-you eyebrow or the aren't-you-going-to-answer-that-flirty-man eyebrow.

Maybe both. I squinted at her and resisted sticking out my tongue. Then I swiveled my chair toward Hogan.

"How about I come over there and you give your brownies to me for free, baby?" I asked.

Delaney shook her head. She got up and took her coffee and judgey-Mcjudgement back over to her own desk where she could mind her own business.

I swanked on over to my man.

My man. I'd been thinking about him that way for a while. For weeks, if I were honest. At first it was just for fun, a silly way to tease him but now...now it felt solid. Real. Right.

What did that even mean? Was this temporary thing becoming more than that? And if it was, did Hogan feel the same?

And if this was just a casual temporary thing for Hogan, how did that make me feel?

My chest tightened and my stomach clenched. It made me feel not good. Not good at all.

"Whoa. What's going through your head, Jeans?" Hogan asked gently, reaching out with one hand while he placed the pink box of what I assumed were six mint chocolate brownies he'd held aside just for me on the counter.

I so didn't want to answer his question. "Thought you couldn't leave the shop." I leaned on the counter and he leaned too, his wide, long-fingered hands reaching across to me. Warm, strong fingers wove between my colder thinner ones. He pressed until our palms were flat together, until his warmth seeped down into me.

"Billy's got it covered."

"On her own?" Billy rocked and I knew that. She'd run the local motorcycle gang years ago. She was in her nineties now, with traffic cone orange hair and a smoking habit she couldn't quit, even though she never lit the ever-present cigarette in her mouth when she worked the bakery coffee counter.

"Don't think there's anything Billy can't handle on her own."

"Sure, yeah. She's something. That Billy. So this is nice." I peeled back the little puffin sticker that held the lid of the box shut. I couldn't meet his eyes. Why was it so hard to look at that smile?

"It's breakfast, baby, not an obligation." He squeezed our fingers tighter together. "I should have sent Billy over instead, yeah?"

"What are you even talking about? I'm super happy you're here." My voice didn't sound super happy. It sounded super confused.

"Super liar," he said. Like he could read my mind or something.

I looked up into the sunshine of him. "Just have a lot of things on my mind."

"Like?"

"Gnomes."

It was out before I could think better of it. He nodded like that made perfect sense. "Sure. They're a thing."

"They're a thing in October. And this year I have to deal with them."

"How's that going?"

"Not great." I popped the lid on the box and peered inside. "Aw...you brought me a cinnamon roll too!"

"Think I'd leave you hanging with a crack in your heart? Please."

And how sweet was he?

Maybe I was reading too much into this. Worrying about what we might be instead of enjoying what we were.

"Never doubted you for a moment, baking god," I said.

He laughed, a deep warm chuckle that rolled over me like a caress. A sexy caress.

I lifted up on my toes and leaned across the counter, which put me on just the right level to kiss him.

"What do I owe you for the goodies?"

"I think you can start with a kiss." His gaze was full of something that made me want to make him as happy as he made me.

So I kissed him and made a wish that we could do this, find a way to stay happy together no matter how long 'together' might be.

CHAPTER SIX

BERTIE, OUR town's one and only Valkyrie, gave me a hard look followed by a fake smile that showed how white and sharp her teeth were, even though she appeared to be at least in her eighties and should, by all rights, be wearing dentures.

"You called?" I asked.

"I did. Have a seat, Jean."

Bertie pretty much ran the community center of Ordinary from this pleasant refurbished brick school building which also offered space for local artists. She single-handedly managed to pull off all of Ordinary's festivals, including the Rhubarb Rally, the Cake and Skate, something that involved knitters smothering Main Street in weird socks and ugly tree sweaters, and currently, the Haunted Harbor and Harvest Festival.

Basically, the streets along the bay were transformed into all-Halloween, all-the-time. Decorations ranged from homemade and quaint, to the level of Hollywood set designers, including an entire block that was nothing but haunted houses, each with a specific theme.

It was a huge thing for a little town to pull off, and it ran for the last two weeks of October. We were almost at the end of the month and so far, so good. Which wasn't a surprise. If anyone could not only make this festival go, but also make it grow, it was Bertie.

Because no one said no to Bertie.

"It has come to my attention that you are the contact for our autumn animated."

I blinked. "Is that a new film festival?"

She tapped her painted gold nails on the top of her desk. She had gone all out with her holiday decorations and I totally approved. There was a vulture in each corner of the ceiling, all peering down so that their hard gazes came to rest right where I was sitting.

Her desk was draped in a beautiful orange shawl of some kind. Intricate and obviously handmade lacework teased out knots of spiders, swirls of tentacles, and the detailed spread of owl feathers over the curl of ocean waves and crescent moons.

"Gorgeous," I said, pointing my Tootsie Pop toward her desk. I'd pretty much been eating a steady diet of Halloween candy for the last three weeks. Halloween was officially only two days away.

No, I hadn't figured out how to get the gnomes to elect a new leader, even with Myra's help.

Also no, they hadn't remembered they were leader-less long enough for it to be much of a problem. Like I said, short attention spans sometimes worked to our advantage.

"Thank you. It was a gift."

Was that a blush? Did Bertie have someone who was sweet on her? I grinned. "What a nice gift. Why it must have taken days and days to make. Someone must like you an awful lot, Bertie, to give you something so pretty."

She pressed her lips into a line and her eyebrows arched. "We are not here to discuss my...friendships."

Yes, I'd caught that slight hesitation. "You're blushing."

She pulled herself up straighter, which still didn't make her taller than me, and blinked rapidly like a startled bird.

I just grinned. The last time I'd seen Bertie flustered was...never. Like, seriously, she was the calmest, coolest cucumber in the whole crisper drawer. This was so great, I wanted to pull out my phone and take a picture for posterity.

But I didn't. Because I'm a professional, thank you.

Professional or not, I couldn't keep my gleeful chuckle inside. "You don't have to look so shocked," I said. "It's okay if you have a friend that likes-you likes-you."

She sniffed and just like that her blush disappeared. Flustered Bertie was replaced by the all-business, no-messing-around, community coordinator and battlefield soul-plucker I knew and loved.

"This is what I called you for." She placed a square brown box big enough to hold a coffee mug between us, closer to me than to her. It had a shipping label, but there was no return address. Bertie's office address was written by hand, large and clumsily, as if the author were writing with a blindfold on.

The address trailed off the front of the box, wrapped around the side, and appeared to come up the other side as well. I didn't think the post office would deliver a package addressed like that.

Maybe it hadn't gone through the post office.

A bad feeling crawled down my spine and curled up in my stomach. My gift kind of bad feeling. It wasn't a big one, wasn't a full-out doom twinge, but the sense of dread was big enough to make me take this box very seriously.

"I'm not opening that until you tell me what's in it."

Bertie must have sensed the shift in my mood. She couldn't read my mind, but if she could, she'd know I was wondering if I needed to call in back up. Or a bomb squad.

Not that Ordinary had a bomb squad. We'd have to pull in someone from Salem.

"It's not dangerous," Bertie said. "But it is a problem I do not have time to solve."

"Uh-huh. You know what's in there?"

"I opened it. Of course I know what's in there."

"So?"

"So?"

"So tell me what's in it."

"A gnome."

Oh. Well, that wasn't as bad as I'd expected. Since it was only eleven o'clock in the morning, I knew it had to be a statue at the moment.

"Aw...it's got to be a tiny wee one to fit in there." I pulled open the lid of the box and peeked in. "Holy shit!"

"Language, Officer Reed."

"That's not a gnome!"

Bertie dragged the box toward her with one sharpened fingernail. Tipped the box so she could see the contents.

"Red hat, bushy beard, round face, statue. Looks like a gnome to me." She let the box fall back and dusted her fingertips across her thumb.

"It's a head. It's just a head."

"If you must be technical, yes. But it's still a gnome."

I glared at her. Was that a small curve at the corners of her mouth? Was she enjoying this? Had the jump scare been her idea of fun?

I grinned. "Okay, that was pretty good." I looked in the box again. Now that I wasn't so spooked by my bad feeling, and surprised by the faded, chipped, one-eye-missing and nose-be-gone gnome decapitation in a box, I noted what I should have from the beginning.

"It's headless Abner's head, isn't it?"

"Yes," Bertie agreed. "It is."

"When did you find it?"

"It was...delivered to me this morning."

"By whom?"

"Let's say friends."

"Let's say the friends' names."

"That is wholly beside the point. The *point* is that Abner has been missing. I know that because I pay attention to what is going on around me, and not because I have a gnome spy."

"You have a gnome spy don't you?"

She took a drink out of a delicate pink tea cup with gold scrollwork and tiny black flowers. There was also an etching of a human skull nestled in all that pink and the words, BLOOD, SWEAT, AND TEA scrawled across the bottom.

"The gnomes are your responsibility this year, am I correct?"

"Nice pivot. You should get into politics." I stuck the lollypop back in my mouth and crunched on it a bit. I'd almost broken through to the chocolate middle. "What do you want me to do with the head? Have you any idea where the body is?"

"No. Although there was this note inside the box."

I made an exasperated sound while she pulled a dirty scrap of paper out from her desk drawer.

"You couldn't have led with this?"

She was enjoying herself. Really. Like the drama over the Halloween Harbor Festival wasn't enough to keep her busy?

I tipped the paper until I could make out the writing.

The penguin is next.

"Huh," I said. "Not what I expected."

"Do you understand the consequences?" Bertie asked.

"I'm guessing who ever shipped or delivered headless Abner's noggin to you just threatened Mrs. Yate's penguin."

"I knew there was a reason you went into law enforcement, Jean. Such a bright mind."

I rolled my eyes. "Do you know anything else about this?"

"Such as?"

"Such as why someone would deliver this threat to you?"

"I can't imagine what you're implying."

"Why does this," I held up the scrap of paper pinched between my fingertips, "threat come to you? Don't you think this should have been aimed at Mrs. Yates?"

"That," she said with a flash of her sharp, white teeth, "is certainly a mystery. I'm sure we'll never know the answer."

"Are you telling me not to look into it?"

"Me?" Bertie took another sip of her tea. "I'd be disappointed if you didn't."

CHAPTER SEVEN

I DROVE by to check on the penguin in Mrs. Yates's yard. The thing had become a sort of celebrity in our town ever since someone, or multiple someones, had started stealing it, then leaving it to be found in ridiculous situations.

It'd been tied to the top of a church steeple, stuffed in a cannon, dressed up and dangled over a busy intersection. It had been left floating on a buoy, hidden in the dinosaur bone museum, and once, duct-taped face-first to the camera the TV station in Portland used to check the weather along the coast.

Its blog, *The Ordinary Penguin,* had over a million subscribers.

If anything happened to the penguin–say, like a beheading–the entire town would go into mourning. There might even be a vigil. Or a manhunt. Could go either way.

So the little penguin was one more problem we had to keep an eye on.

Mrs. Yates's yard was looking beautiful in the misty cool October evening. The Japanese lantern plants lining her path had gone from drops of bright lantern-shaped orange flowers to skeletal-lace teardrops on spiny sticks with a single red berry inside each lantern. Hearty bushes were trimmed into neat round shapes, and a lovely ornamental maple's trunk and limbs twisted and curled like smoke frozen in place.

She had decorated for the season: corn stalks behind bright fat pumpkins stacked along her porch, more out amongst her wide flower beds, and what appeared to be a handmade scarecrow propped up in one corner.

Her yard was pretty enough to be displayed on the cover of a magazine. And right there in the center, where the eye of the average passer-by naturally paused, stood the penguin wearing a witch's hat.

The penguin very much still had a head. So that was one worry off my plate for now, at least.

I drove the neighborhood, noting the position and number of gnomes. They all seemed to be where they should be. None of them seemed equipped to pull off a beheading.

But I'd learned the hard way to never underestimate gnomes.

I passed one of our beach accesses and noticed a man sitting on the top of the fence. Since the fence was rickety enough, and the rocks and sand below were far enough, I decided he might need to be told to get off the fence before he fell.

I pulled the truck all the way to the end of the access, which was empty of vehicles since it was nearly the end of October. It was wet and the winds were picking up. A few tourists still visited, but usually only on weekends and mostly they stuck to the hotels and shops.

There was something familiar about the man. Even from the back. Something that made me pause before stepping out of the truck. Something that made me put a call in to Delaney to tell her where I was and what I was doing.

"I'll be right there," she said. "Do not approach him until I get there."

"If he moves, I move."

"If he moves, you wait."

I didn't answer and Delaney bulled on. "That's an order, Officer Reed."

"Yes, Chief," I grunted.

She was really getting overprotective since that car had hit me.

Yeah, I guess that made sense. I was worried about her a lot more lately too, since she'd been shot. So I could understand where she was coming from.

But then the man turned his shoulders and looked back at me.

I'd know that hard-angled face and piercing gaze anywhere.

Death.

As in the god of. Thanatos, himself. Last I'd seen him, he was kicking some ass and forfeiting his vacation time for a year so that he could deliver death to an undead vampire.

I'd missed him. On the outside, he was sort of stilted and stuffy. But on the inside, when he wasn't carrying the power of death, Thanatos was kind of like a little kid who hadn't gotten nearly enough time on the playground.

He *liked* being mortal. Liked experiencing mundane things like flying kites and peeling sunburns. But he did it all with a droll sort of detachment that didn't for a single second hide how much he loved being in Ordinary.

Being around Delaney and us other Reeds too.

I'd been sad when he'd had to leave town to pick up his power again and had hoped he'd show back up when the required one year absence had been paid.

Yet here he was, back in town, ten months early.

A chill washed over me as I realized why that might be. He was death, after all.

I sighed and got out of the truck. If death were here for me, I was pretty sure I'd know it, but since he wasn't, I might as well find out who was so special that he'd come all this way to collect them personally.

The wind was cold and pushy as I strolled over to him. Death watched me, still as a stone, that icy gaze unwavering.

"Afternoon," I called out all cheery and police officer-like. "Did you read the sign? No sitting on the fence."

And then a truly weird thing happened.

Death almost smiled.

Okay, it wasn't like he actually curved his lips. But there was a change in him, a charged sort of vibe he gave off, like he wanted to burst out laughing at a joke that hadn't yet been told.

"Am I breaking a law, Daughter of Reed, being here, on this fence, on the edge of your town?"

His voice was how I remembered it, cool and suave and deep enough to give me chills even while all of me went sweaty. But there was more behind it now. There was power. A power of endings. The power of a great cold empty.

This was the god, Death. This was not the vacationing deity who had opened a kite shop in our town.

"Do you see something on the sign that says 'Stay off the fence, except for you, Death'?" I asked him.

"Perhaps I am not here for the fence."

"I'd guess you're not." Despite my heart which was racing with fear, because, hello: Death, I moved closer to him.

He shifted so that his long legs swung over to the side where I was standing, his black shiny shoes touching down into the rocks and tough old sea grass that went instantly brown from his touch.

He wore a hooded cloak, but the hood was pushed back, his dark hair slicked and perfect, his eyes absolutely riveting. Beneath it, he appeared to be wearing an old-fashioned tuxedo, black on black on black.

The only color on him at all was his skin. White. Pale. Bloodless as a shadow.

The wind stirred his cloak. It was bitter and biting, but not to him. To him, it appeared to caress, to surround, to worship.

"Are you looking for Delaney?" I asked.

"You would assume so."

"I would and do. She's the only Reed who can bridge you to your mortal self. The only Reed who can help you put down your power so you can stay here. Vacation here."

"Perhaps I am not here to vacation, Daughter of Reed."

"All right. Then perhaps you want to tell me what you are here for."

Those eyes, which had seemed cool and distant ticked down to meet my gaze. It was everything I could do not to look away.

"I wish to be invited to the Halloween event."

Okay, that got me. I laughed. "Seriously?"

He arched one eyebrow.

Right. Seriously.

"We...the party that the gods usually throw? That's not happening this year."

"There is an event. It is planned near the harbor."

A chill washed over me again and it had nothing to do with the wind. "There are going to be kids there. A lot of little kids."

"Yes," he said. "I am aware."

"You can't..." I stopped because yes, yes he could. He could come to the celebration. He could take the life of anyone there. Because he was death. The big "D" death. And it was his job, his power, to end life.

"Ah," he said almost gently, though still too cold. So cold. "You see that I can, indeed."

And while it was making me a little panicky, along with angry and frustrated and horrified to know he only wanted to come to the festival to kill someone, I wasn't getting that sickening end-of-the-world feeling that told me we were in for a truly awful thing.

The sound of a Jeep arriving in the parking area and pulling up right next to my truck gave me hope.

"Delaney's here," I said.

"It would appear so."

"She won't let you kill someone. She'll tell you you can't."

"And why so ever would I listen to her?"

I flashed him a big grin. "Because she's your favorite and you like her."

He blinked, both eyebrow slipped up. Yeah, he could act surprised, but I knew how he looked at her. She'd even told me he'd all but admitted he liked her. Liked being here. Liked being mortal.

But this was not the powerless, mortal Than leaning against the fence on the edge of the world. This was Death.

A door shut. Boots crunched on gravel and then sand. "Thanatos," Delaney said. "You can't be here for ten more months."

Delaney stopped right next to me, shoulder-to-shoulder, facing off against the god of death.

I could see the slight shift in him. The relaxing of his shoulders, the sharpening of his eyes. He was happy to see her. Perhaps even delighted.

Something in my chest unwound a little. This would work out. This would all work out.

"You can not tell me where I walk, Reed Daughter."

And Delaney did that thing. It was the same thing Dad used to do. She went from looking like a police chief who had everything under control to something *more.*

She took a single step forward and somehow looked taller, stronger, a lighting-struck figure cracking with a power that pulsed up from deep within the ground beneath her feet, as if all of Ordinary, all the world, stood at her back, facing him. Facing the storm.

This was her power. Her ability to stand in front of any god and tell them to take a hike.

It was now, just like it had always been, pretty amazing to see.

It made me so proud of our family. It made me so proud of her.

"You are not going to walk this town, my town, as a mortal, Thanatos." Her voice was even and hard as hammer on steel. "And if you're here as a god, then I need to know why. You've never shown up like this before. There must be a reason."

"You know what my power is, Reed Daughter. I am here for just that. My business is my own."

"No," I breathed, and I could see Delaney's shoulder hitch a little from my reaction. "You don't get to stroll in here and kill someone," I went on, ignoring the fact that he could do exactly that because that was the one thing he actually did. "You're not going to take some little kid. You're not going to take someone I love. You're not going to take one of my friends."

Death's gaze slipped from the challenge in Delaney to the worry in me. He exhaled, once. It was as much of a gesture of yielding as I'd ever seen from him.

"Bring me the head."

"The...head?" Delaney asked.

"You aren't going to kill him are you?"

"Who?" Delaney turned toward me, the first time she'd looked straight at me since she'd arrived. Her eyes were blue, but sparked with that aqua and gold of the Reed power that rolled through her.

"Headless Abner."

"The gnome? You found him?"

"Someone found him. Or released him. A part of him. What do you want with the gnome?" I asked Death.

He raised one eyebrow. "Bring him, and I will show you."

When neither of us moved, he pursed his lips, and then said, "I will not harm him. Yet."

Another second, two, five clicked by. Finally, Delaney nodded. "Where is he?"

"In the truck. Hold on."

I wasn't worried about leaving Delaney with Death. If he'd wanted to hurt her, he'd have done it the moment she'd arrived.

Plus, a part of me wondered if he'd come back now, so soon after having to leave, because he'd missed her. Missed our little town that he'd only spent a couple of months getting to know.

The box was in the front seat. I picked it up and was standing beside my sister in a few seconds.

She glanced at my hands. "Let me see."

I opened the box.

Her eyebrows notched together and the wind whipped the stray strands of her long brown hair out of her face. "Abner."

"Abner," I agreed.

"Where'd you find him?"

"Bertie had him."

"Did she do this to him?"

"No. He was brought to her this way."

Delaney's gaze met mine. Yeah, there was something weird about the town Valkyrie ending up with a long-lost gnome head. Especially since she hadn't wanted to reveal her delivery source to me. Delaney's gaze told me I'd need to do some follow up.

My gaze told her I'd do it but only if she bought me extra candy.

She told me to stop acting like a kid.

I told her to stop acting like my mother.

"Daughter of Reed. The gnome head."

I handed him the box.

He reached inside and withdrew the head, holding it propped on just the tips of his long, boney fingers.

"Wake, gnome. And speak."

I felt the frigid push of his power. Delaney shivered, and I knew whatever I'd felt, she'd felt magnified by a hundred.

"Gnobody puts Abner in a box!" Abner's voice was creaky and sharp. His face, while still full of cracks and divots, was fully life-like. He was down to one eye, half a nose, and a lopsided beard, but he didn't seem to notice nor was he bothered by the remodel.

"This," Death said with grave patience. "Is a very dangerous creature."

Delaney and I waited. I bit my lip to keep from laughing in his face. One tiny giggle got away from me.

She elbowed me, and I coughed to try to cover it up.

Death sighed.

That did it. I laughed. "It's a gnome," I said. "All the gnomes in Ordinary come to life in October."

This," Death jiggled the head, and Abner gave a little yodel, "is not alive, nor is it dead. It is a zombie. I am here on business. To kill it..."

"Gnoooo!" Abner squalled.

"...but it has already infected others," Death finished.

"What?" Delaney asked. "How?"

We all stared at the head.

"It's gnot what you're thinking," Abner insisted. "I was just an innocent head. Out for a midnight roll. And who did I find myself clunking into but my buddy Johan? And then, well, one thing led to another and..."

"And?" I demanded after he'd been quiet for too long.

"I bit him."

"What?" Delaney said.

"Just a gnibble."

"You ate your buddy?" I asked.

"He just...smelled so good. His foot was right there. Right there in front of my face. Then his foot was in my mouth, and it was candy. Sweet rock candy."

Delaney groaned. "Zombie gnomes? Of course we have zombie gnomes. How do we deal with them?"

"There are options," Death said.

"I've been out checking on the gnomes every night," I said. "Making sure they're all where they belong. They seem the same to me."

"They are not."

Was he lying? He had done it before, as it was the only way to take down an asshole vampire that nearly killed my sister. So while I'm generally against lying, I was fine with his duplicity in that one case.

But why would he lie about this? About gnomes?

"How did Abner go zombie in the first place? Another curse?" Delaney asked.

"A beheading, a burying, a bite." Death listed it off like a boring oatmeal recipe everyone knew how to make. "But unless the power that originally created this false life—"

"—false!" Abner squawked.

"—is found, they will rise on Halloween night undead. Permanently undead. Zombies for all time, day and night, shambling through these streets for as long as the earth circles the sun."

Which meant we'd be on gnome duty for life. "That sounds—"

"Gneat!" Abner cheered.

"I was going to go with annoying," I said. Pulling gnome duty for a month of nights was bad enough. If we didn't stop this zombie threat in its tracks, we'd be chasing down these little buggers forever.

So. Not. Happening on my watch.

"We have to find whoever, whatever made them," Delaney clarified. "And make them break the curse? Is that the only way to opt out of the dawn-day-and-dusk of the dead?"

"There is one other way to end this." Death's dark eyes glittered.

This was what he really wanted. This was what he had come to Ordinary for. I braced for it.

"You shall invite me to the Halloween celebration. If the power that brought the gnomes to life has not been found by then, I will bring the unliving to a peaceful end."

"You'll turn them back into statues?" Delaney asked.

"We're statues?" Abner demanded.

"I would indeed," Death said.

"And you can't do that right now because?" I asked.

"The veil between worlds is the thinnest on Halloween. On that day, the power that grants them life will be within my reach to affect."

"Also you want an invitation to the party," Delaney said.

"Only as a matter of business, of course."

Out of all the deaths in all the worlds, this zombie gnome situation was the one that needed Thanatos's personal attention.

"*Bullshit*," I coughed.

Death gave me a look. He couldn't fool me. He wanted to party here in Ordinary on the spookiest day of the year, 'cause he was sort of adorable like that.

I winked at him. His expression turned droll.

"You know it's a costume party," I wheedled.

"Oh?" So much feigned disinterest.

"You'll have to come in costume."

"If I must." He sniffed.

Yep. He wanted to come to the party and had found a way to work around Ordinary's rules. Clever.

"You have to give your word that you are not the one who turned the gnomes into zombies and started this mess in the first place."

Delaney gave me the side-eye. That's right. I knew how to cop.

"I assure you," Death said, and I felt the weight of truth in his words. The wind stopped blowing, the air got heavier, and it was hard to breathe. "I have nothing to do with the unliving state of these Ordinary gnomes."

Okay then.

"Who you callin' ordinary?" Abner squeaked.

"You know who did this, don't you?" Delaney asked.

"Did what, Reed Daughter?"

"You know who put the curse or whatever this is on the gnomes."

I didn't think Death was going to answer. But she crossed her arms over her chest and there was that presence around her. As if every Reed in history were standing with her, behind her, lending their strength. As if all of Ordinary from the mountains to the sea were standing with her staring him down.

"Perhaps."

"Who?" she demanded. "Who gave these gnomes life?"

"A jinni. A very powerful one. Many, many years ago."

"And does this jinni live in Ordinary?"

"Currently? No."

"Does this jinni have a name?"

"Many."

"No name," she said, "no party invitation."

"Are you blackmailing me, Reed Daughter?"

"Not yet. What was the jinni's name?"

"Faris."

"Okay," Delaney said. "That's something we can work with. Thank you." She held her hand out. Death extended his arm and dropped Abner's head into her palm.

Abner went instantly still. He was a statue once again until sunset when he'd rise and try to accidentally eat some other friend's foot.

"Consider yourself invited to the Haunted Harbor and Harvest Festival. We'll see you in a couple days?" Delaney asked.

"Yes," Death said. "You will."

Just like that, he was gone.

The air temperature rose several degrees all at once and I shivered. I hadn't realized how cold it had gotten.

"Not my fault," I started.

"I know. We need to track down anything we can get on this Faris. I'll have Myra look through the books."

Delaney turned, handed me the head, which was cold, heavy, and rough as if it were nothing more than inert concrete.

Poor Abner. He'd certainly had better days.

"And what do you want me to do, boss?"

"I need you to keep Abner out of trouble. Do another patrol on the gnomes. Make sure none of them have their toes bitten off."

"What about Death?"

She stuck her hands in her coat pockets as she started back to the Jeep. "We'll deal with him when he shows back up."

"So you're going to let him into town?"

She shrugged. "The gods can come into town if they want. They just can't put down their powers and stay unless I say so." She opened the Jeep door. "Stop worrying, Jean. We're good. We've got this."

CHAPTER EIGHT

WE DID not got this.

I found three gnomes with missing toes that night. Abner, who I'd propped on the dash of my truck so he could confirm his previous nights' munchie victims, went through the five stages of zombie grief: denial, acceptance, hunger, more hunger, and knock-knock jokes.

Seriously.

"Gnock-gnock."

"Nope."

"Gnock-gnock."

"Shut up, Abner.

"Gnock-gnock."

The three other zombie gnomes I'd had to tag and bag were stowed on the passenger side floor of the truck. They chanted, "Gnock-gnock, gnock-gnock! Gnock-gnock!"

"No."

"Gnock-gnock," Abner asked again.

Fine. "Who's there?"

"Police."

Why did this feel like a trap?

"Police who?"

"Police let me bite somebody again."

Oh, the peanut gallery squirming in the duffle on the floorboards thought that was hilarious.

"Okay, that's it. You're getting the box."

I picked him up, careful to keep my fingers away from his mouth, stuffed him in the box, then set him down on the floor with the others.

Silence. Finally. I still had a few more houses with yard decorations to zombie proof before I went back to the station. So far it didn't seem like the zombie gnomes had spread the bite-and-switch very quickly or very far.

Lack of knees really slowed down total zombie domination.

Maybe we'd caught the zombie situation in time before it became something too annoying for words.

"Gnock-gnock," four voices called out at once.

Or maybe not. I swallowed a groan and turned the radio up louder.

CHAPTER NINE

I FILED reports, made Hatter give me back Abner, who he'd kept on the corner of his desk while he handled his own paperwork.

Hatter, the traitor, actually liked knock-knock jokes.

I hated him a little.

Dawn came late in October, so Abner was still animated by the time my shift was over.

"Want me to keep him?" Hatter asked.

"No. He's my problem and basically patient zero. I'm keeping an eye on him."

"We could lock him up in evidence with the duffle-bag gnomes. There's a safe back there."

"You're not supposed to know about the safe."

"Wouldn't be much of a police officer if I'd missed a big obvious locked safe."

"Hidden in the wall where no one should be looking."

"Even more reason to find it." He frowned a little. "What's really bothering you, Jee-Jee?"

"Zombie gnomes aren't enough?"

He waited.

Here's the thing. Hatter was pretty new to town. He knew about the monsters and gods and all the other craziness of the place. But I didn't know if I should tell him that Death was coming to town tomorrow night.

Because no matter how Death tried to charm Delaney, I had a sinking feeling he was here for more than just haunted houses and apple bobbing. I had a sinking feeling he was here to do his job. To actually collect someone who was about to die.

I searched my sense-of-wrongness. Didn't get a hard ping like I should. But then, most of my doom twinges only happened right before the terrible possibility was about to become a terrible reality.

So I could be right about death, or totally wrong.

It was stupid, this power of mine.

It was quiet in the station, most of the town still asleep. Only the crunch of Hatter feeding Abner baby carrots filled the room. Not that Abner was swallowing the carrots, but the crunchy vegetables kept him occupied, and better yet, had ended the constant knock-knock jokes.

Hatter cleared his throat. "Tell me. The more transparent these things are, the better we can all make good decisions if things go to crap."

I blew out a breath. "Death was here today."

"I read the report."

"He's coming back."

"For the Halloween celebration, and to deal with our little zombie problem, right?"

"Yes. That's what he says."

"You don't believe him?"

"I just...I'm worried that there's more to it. Things seem to go sideways when he gets involved. That whole thing with the vampire and Delaney...getting hurt."

"Well, we'll all be there. We'll keep an eye on him. Make sure he follows the rules," Hatter said. "I'm sure Ryder would be happy to dog him. If Death steps out of line, Ryder and that god of rules who owns him will zap him right back into place."

"I'm not sure it works that way," I mumbled.

"Then let's find out. Before the party, eh?"

"I'll talk to Ryder." I yawned, loudly. I glanced at the pile of candy wrappers on my desk, patted them, hoping I'd left something behind, but no. I swept the wrappers into the wastebasket by my desk and stood to stretch.

"Your shift was up three hours ago, Jean. Go home."

"Fine. Hand me the head."

He picked Abner up, then set him back in the box, which was looking a little worse for wear.

"Get some sleep." Hatter swiveled in his chair and held the box out for me as I passed his desk. "Cat?" He asked.

He'd been trying to guess what costume I was going to wear for the last three weeks.

"Nope. Cowboy?" I was trying to guess his costume too.

"Yep." Hatter had said 'yes' to everything I'd guessed.

"If you're really going to be a sexy maid alien banana dinosaur cheese sandwich pirate traffic cone cowboy, you're going to give off some pretty mixed signals."

"What can I say? I'm a complicated man."

I chuckled and gave him a wave. "Later."

"Take it easy, hear?"

"No problem."

I shrugged into my coat and got all the way to the door before I heard: "Gnock-gnock."

"If there's a zombie gnome head knocking at this door, he better stay quiet, or we'll find out how long a zombie gnome head can hold his breath when held under water."

There was a startled *meep*, and then nothing.

Silence. Blessed silence. I got in my truck, turned on the engine and eased out into the dark morning. Home wasn't far away. I could hear my bed calling from here.

CHAPTER TEN

I STAYED up until dawn. Not because I wanted to see the sunlight, but because I didn't want to take my eyes off Abner. While there wasn't any way to actually force the leader of the gnomes to shut up, I found a double layer of duct tape did wonders for muffling him.

Once the sun had finally crested over the edge of the hills, I flopped back in my messy bed and rubbed my eyes. Abner shouldn't be reanimated until tonight.

Of course, it was going to be Halloween tonight.

Death was coming.

Myra had had zero luck tracking down the jinni who had cursed the gnomes. Or maybe he'd granted a wish, not issued a curse. I didn't know the details, because it had happened a long time ago, and no one knew the details.

I rolled over onto my stomach, smushed the pillow into my face where I liked it, and wished Hogan were here in my bed, his long, warm body curled up around mine.

I jerked awake as something heavy pressed down on the foot of the bed.

"If you're here to kill me, please do it quietly, I'm trying to sleep."

"Mmm," Hogan murmured, snugging up behind me big-spoon style. "And what if I'm not here to murder you?"

"Then I like you a lot."

"And what if I brought you a real, hot meal, since I know your last three meals were various forms of sugar?"

My stomach growled at the thought, and Hogan chuckled, his breath a puff of warmth against the back of my neck.

"Then I like you even more."

"And what if I did this?" He placed a kiss, soft and damp against my skin. A second, a third.

I wriggled around until I was facing him, nose to nose, our ankles tangled, his head propped on his bent arm. He was wearing a red-violet slouchy beanie, his dark braids sticking out from where they were tied back behind his neck.

"I might do more than like you for that. Nice beanie."

"Billy made it for me. She's a K.I.N.K.."

"Yeah, I can see her being part of the knitting club."

He smiled and tipped my chin down with his thumb so he could kiss my forehead. He smelled of sugar and flour, of pumpkin and soft lemon, with a spicy note that was all him. I inhaled extra deep just to fill my body with the unique scent of him.

"What's wrong?" he asked, his lips moving to my temple, my cheek.

"Who said anything was wrong?"

He pulled back and gave me a solid stare. "It is Halloween, I'm home early, and you're moping in bed."

"Sleeping, thank you."

"Still in your jeans." He tugged on my belt loop.

He was right. And I hadn't even noticed, I'd been so distracted by the gnome. Speaking of which….

I turned and glanced at Abner. He was a statue now that it was daylight, and a pretty rough looking one with all his chipped up missing bits and duct tape wrapped all the way around his head.

"So, that's weird." Hogan rubbed his hand down my arm. "Are you headhunting old garden statues now?"

"No. It's a thing."

"Uh-huh."

"A case."

"Uh-huh."

"I can't really share the details with a civilian. You understand."

"Right. Because that gnome head is evidence and therefore needs to be kept on your night stand instead of the evidence locker."

Crap. He was starting to get the hang of the procedures I shouldn't be breaking.

He raised an eyebrow. "Yes?"

"It's not—"

My phone rang from under my pillow and I pulled it out, answering without even glancing at the screen. "Officer Jean Reed."

"There's been a kidnapping," Bertie said far too calmly for someone reporting a kidnapping.

"Who? Have you called the station? Myra's on duty. Does she know? Does Delaney know?"

"They don't know because I don't care to involve them in this situation."

I scowled at the ceiling while Hogan's hand rubbed a slow circle on my stomach. "Bertie, everyone in town follows the law. Report it to the officer on duty. Now. This is someone's life you're putting at risk."

"Not someone. Something. Or rather, some fowl."

"I'm hanging up. Call the station. I'll be there soon."

"It's the penguin."

I waited while my brain zagged from emergency mode to annoyed. "What?"

"Mrs. Yates's penguin has been kidnapped."

I sighed and dropped my hand over my eyes. "Still something you should call the station about."

"No, I don't think it is. This isn't a…normal hijacking."

"That penguin gets stolen at least twice a month. It's pretty normal."

"Not this time."

I didn't want to ask, because I really was off duty, and there really were other police officers who could track down our famous roaming penguin. "Why is it different this time?"

There was a hushing sound, almost as if Bertie had cupped her hand over her phone. "If I tell you this, it must be off the record. I will deny saying any word of it."

Okay, this just got interesting. "All right. Noted. Off the record. We're just a couple citizens of Ordinary, shooting the breeze. But be careful, Bertie. If this is serious, if this puts someone's life in danger, then all bets are off."

"I understand. It is possible I have some knowledge of previous penguin kidnappings."

I moved my hand away from my eyes and stared at Hogan who was frowning at me. I mouthed *oh, my, god.*

He mouthed, *what?*

"Are you telling me you have something to do with all those penguin thefts, Bertie?"

Hogan's smile was wide and his eyes sparkled. Yeah, it was amazing to think that the rule-following, event ball-busting Bertie was involved in what we'd suspected was just high school shenanigans.

"The penguin is wonderful advertisement for Ordinary. Someone needed to contact the…person or persons involved in creatively relocating the statue. To assure that the penguin, which is private property, not be damaged or degraded."

"Bertie, you little minx! You're running a penguin kidnapping ring."

"I refuse to implicate myself in those accusations."

Basically: yes. "If you know who is involved in, what did you call it? 'creatively relocating' the penguin, why don't you just contact them and tell them to bring it back?"

"Because this kidnapping was not done through approved channels."

"So you have some competition? One of your little minions gone rogue?"

She sighed and I heard the tapping of her sharp nails on the edge of her desk. "This wasn't any of the usual suspects. The penguin has been truly kidnapped. It may have been taken out of town, or it may be that the gnomes are behind it."

"Do you have any proof of any of that?"

"The note that was included with Abner's head was written by a gnome."

"Do you know that for sure?"

"No. But I believe it is true."

Well, hell.

"I'll look into it."

I ended the call and groaned, both my hands over my face to muffle the noise.

"What's wrong, pumpkin pie? Bad news?"

"Don't."

He pulled my hands away from my face. Frowned at my expression. "Okay," he agreed. "Something's really wrong. What's happening?"

There were things in this town I hadn't told him about. I mean, yes, he knew there were creatures who lived here, mortals with powers, and gods who vacationed, but other than shrugging and saying, yeah, that made sense to him, we didn't really talk about it.

He was happy to just be a baker, I was happy to just be a cop, and we were happy to just be together.

So this…this impending doom of gnomes, along with everything else, wasn't anything I wanted to burden him with.

It was a part of my life that he couldn't really be involved in. A part of me he would never know.

He sat up, and swung his legs over the side of the bed. He was still facing me, but the line of his shoulders, the set of his jaw, the narrowing of his eyes all told me he was angry.

"It's work stuff," I said.

"You're off duty."

"I'm never off duty." I pushed up and pressed my back against the headboard. "You know there are things I can't talk to you about."

"Crimes?"

"Yes."

"Was this a crime?"

"Technically? Yes."

"Someone kidnapped the penguin that gets kidnapped almost daily, the penguin that has its own blog fueled only by pictures of it being kidnapped, the penguin that tourists come to this town to see if they can take a picture with and then post those pictures all over the world–that's a crime you have to keep a secret from me?"

Okay, he was frustrated. But so was I. He couldn't expect me to tell him everything about my job. Everything about this town. Everything about me. We hadn't been together that long. This, whatever this was between us, might be a temporary thing. Fleeting.

As soon as he got a real look at me, at the town, at this crazy thing that was my life, he'd go back to his bakery, and that would be that.

"You don't understand," I said.

"About what?"

We had a missing penguin, tonight was Halloween, zombie gnomes were on the rise, and death was coming to visit. This town was going a little crazy right now.

I chose the easiest answer. "This town."

His eyes narrowed, but he didn't move. "What about the town?"

"Just. Halloween is crazy, okay?" I got out of bed, intending to take a shower. I'd only gotten a couple hours of sleep, but I knew I needed to go back to work. Help track down the penguin. Find out if Myra had dug up anything that would help us find that jinni, Faris.

"No," Hogan said, quietly.

I was glaring at Abner's stupid head. "No what?"

"Blaming this on Halloween. This isn't a problem with Halloween. This is a problem with you not wanting to tell me things."

"I—"

"Don't," he said. "Don't tell me that's not true, Jean. I'm not blind. I see things. I see you."

I turned and rested my hip on the dresser. I crossed my arms over my chest, not out of anger, but out of feeling suddenly vulnerable. "Halloween is a problem. We...there's a guy we need to track down. He's implicated in some…stuff we need to put an end to. Fast."

"What kind of stuff?"

I shook my head.

"Does he have a name? I see things. I hear things. A lot of people go through my bakery."

"I can't tell you. You wouldn't…you just can't be a part of this, Hogan."

"Part of this?" He waved a finger between us.

My stomach fell to my knees. He was thinking about ending this? Ending us. How could it have happened so quickly? I wasn't ready for him to leave. For him to be even less a part of my life.

Panic set my heartbeat pounding at my temples.

"No," I swallowed, trying to get moisture back in my mouth. "This town. Part of the stuff that happens in this town."

"I know about the creatures, Jean. And the gods. You were the one who told me about them, remember?"

"There are things about this town I can't tell you."

"What?" He shifted so he was facing me, legs crossed. "Bertie is a Valkyrie. Chris Lagon is a gillman. That kid who gives lighthouse tours is half kelpie. The blonde at the popcorn shop is a siren. We have three Furies on the roller derby team. And Crow, who I haven't seen in months, is a trickster god."

I was utterly, utterly stunned. I had no idea he knew those things.

"Who told you all that?"

"No one. I know it."

"How?"

"I told you. I see things. Those kinds of things. The things that make people what and who they are."

"Since…when?" My voice was a little thready.

"Always."

"And me?"

"I've always seen you, Jean."

"As...what?"

"A woman. My world. My home."

I exhaled hard, those words landing a direct hit to my heart. "Okay," I said trying to get my emotional footing. I couldn't address that. What he'd just said. I couldn't take it straight on. It was too much. It meant too much. It meant we were more than six months and I wanted that so much, I didn't want to ruin it, jinx it.

So I addressed the easier stuff.

"Um. Okay. We're looking for a man. Not a man exactly. We're looking for a jinni. His name is Faris."

Hogan scrambled off the bed and stood so fast, I thought his foot was going to get tangled in the blankets. He pressed his back against the door to the hall.

"Why are you looking for him? What did he do?"

Hogan's eyes were too wide, his breathing too shallow.

"Hey, hey," I said. "It's okay. Do you know him? Know who he is?"

Hogan swallowed hard and nodded. "He's my dad."

CHAPTER ELEVEN

SO FINDING out my boyfriend was half Jinn was a surprise. So was the little tidbit of info about how he could see what everyone in Ordinary really was beneath their masks of humanity.

He didn't know if he'd gotten the vision from his dad, the jinni, or from his mom who had some mild magical talent of her own, but he said he'd learned to be quiet about it since he was a kid. People who wore masks got twitchy when someone pointed out who they really were beneath them.

He'd adopted a live-and-let-live attitude about the people in Ordinary, and had never brought it up.

"You have no other powers?" Delaney asked. She and Myra had come over when I'd called, and we were all sitting in my living room. Hogan and I were curled into each other on the love seat.

I hadn't known what to do other than to call in my sisters. I was too close to this situation, my heart too close to Hogan, to make any kind of call that dealt with his absentee father, of all people.

"Not that I know of," he said. "Baking, which I think is talent more than power. The ability to know what someone really is. That's about it."

"Have you ever tried to make a wish come true?" Myra asked.

"I've made a lot of wishes. Most of them haven't come true."

"Someone else's wish, though?" she asked.

"Back when I was a kid, I used to wish my dad would stay away forever. For my mom. She…she didn't handle him leaving very well."

"Have you seen him since?" Myra asked.

"No."

"Have you tried to make any other of your mom's wishes come true?"

"Honestly, no. I never really thought about it. I was a pretty happy kid. We were happy."

Delaney put her coffee cup down on the side table, then leaned back and stared at the ceiling, thinking.

"Okay," she said. "Let me see if we're all on the same page here. We don't have the jinni who originally animated the gnomes, but we have his son, who is half Jinn, but hasn't tested or tried to invoke his powers, if he has said powers.

"We also have a rise of the zombies tonight, that if not stopped will land us with a permanent zombie gnome population.

"On top of that, the penguin has been stolen, possibly by the zombie gnomes who possibly want to destroy it. We have a couple thousand people wandering the streets—most of them children small enough to be bitten by zombie gnomes. Everyone in town will be wearing disguises, costumes and masks, and Death himself is prowling through our harbor for what he says is a benevolent visit. Do I have it covered?"

"You people know how to keep it fun," Hogan said.

Myra speared me with a sharp look. "You still aren't willing to tell us who alerted you to the penguin being missing?"

Okay, so maybe I wasn't playing exactly by the rules here. There wasn't a hard-and-fast reason why I was keeping Bertie's involvement with the penguin kidnappings on the down-low. But the truth was…she was right. That penguin had netted us a lot of good press. It drew people to the town who were generally looking for a bit of quirky, family-friendly fun.

The kidnapped penguin was good for the town. Good for Mrs. Yates, too, who loved showing off her quasi-famous yard. Good for the kids–or whoever–in town to put their own spin on decorating the little concrete statue, and set it up in funny situations that were blog-worthy once it was found.

Knowing that Bertie had stepped in like some sort of well-organized mob boss to coordinate the penguin's liberations insured that the little statue wouldn't be damaged.

I had a feeling anyone who wanted to steal the penguin had to run the kidnapping, photoshoot, and outcome past Bertie first. Probably had to fill out forms in triplicate.

By pushing her way into the whole penguin thing, Bertie had effectively taken one responsibility off us. We no longer had to worry about the penguin being in danger, or being handled in a way that would put others in danger.

I kind of dug the secret underground Fight Club aspect of the whole thing. Might even volunteer to be one of the people involved in the penguin snatching.

If Myra and Delaney were really worried about it, they'd push a lot harder to get a name out of me.

"Still not willing to rat the source out," I finally answered. "But trust me, my source knows exactly what's been going on with the penguin and by whom. My source wouldn't panic if there wasn't a reason for it."

Delaney picked up her coffee cup, tipped it before realizing it was empty, then frowned at it.

"So how are we going to handle this, boss?" I asked her.

"We're going to prioritize," she said. When she made up her mind, there was never any hint of doubt in her. I liked that about her.

"First, we find out if Hogan has any power over the gnomes. Are you okay with that, Hogan?"

"Totally cool. What do you want me to try to do?"

And yeah, there was a flare of pride in my heart for my man. He had never talked about his father, had never tried to tap into his family heritage. But when it mattered, when a scourge of zombie gnomes could be filling our streets, the man stepped right up.

"Can you break the…wish or curse or spell on them?"

He glanced at the duct taped head sitting on the coffee table, then unwound his arm from behind me. "I'm not sure I can really see what makes them what you say they are."

"Zombies?" Delaney asked.

"Animated. To me, right now, that just looks like a head carved out of rock."

"Do you think you'll see it differently once it animates?" Myra asked.

"Maybe?"

"Okay," Delaney said. "Then we'll wait. I'll go make us all some more coffee."

Timing was going to be a bit of a problem. Trick-or-treaters would be out in force before the sunset, and the Haunted Harbor would be open as soon as it got dark.

Myra stood and stretched. She checked her phone, swiped her thumb across it, and walked to my front door. "Be right back." She stepped outside to take the call, but not before I heard her say, "How did you get my number, Bathin?"

"That demon still bothering her?" Hogan asked.

"That demon still bothers us all." Delaney dropped back onto the couch. "Myra's looking for ways to get my soul back." She shrugged like it was no big deal. But I knew she didn't like it. Didn't like that so far, we hadn't found a way to get rid of the guy.

Sure, Bathin was good looking, but I didn't trust him as far as I could throw him. And since he weighed approximately as much as the Cascade Mountain Range, I couldn't throw him an inch.

"I think he's interesting," Hogan said.

Delaney and I both gave him the same look.

"Interesting how?" I asked.

He rocked his head side-to-side. "I don't know. Interesting."

"What do you see when you look at him?" I suddenly wanted to know how Hogan saw the world. How he saw everyone, including the demon.

"I see Bathin. How do you see him?" he asked.

"Not helping."

His smile spread like slow honey. The reddish-violet of the beanie he still wore set off a rosy tone in his dark skin. I liked him in a hat. Of course, I liked him in everything he wore.

Liked him even better when he wore nothing at all.

"I don't really have a lot to compare to how I see people. To me, he's Bathin. A demon, but…" he shrugged. "Not evil, I guess."

"Demons are kind of the embodiment of evil." I was baiting him. Because I knew better than to pigeonhole people, whether they were mortal, monster, or god.

"A lot of history says Jinn are evil spirits." Hogan scratched at the stubble on the side of his jaw. "I try to keep an open mind. Let people show me who they are before I make judgments."

"He took my sister's soul."

"I traded it," Delaney said. "You know that, Jean. And if I had to do it again, I would." At my look, she held up one hand. "Yes, I would have done some things differently, like tell you and Myra about the trade before I did it, though I don't know how I would have. But Bathin did save Ben. That's worth a lot to me. And he hasn't damaged my soul. I'll get it back."

Here she grinned. "That demon doesn't have a chance against us Reeds."

I rolled my eyes, but smiled too. If anyone could figure out how to get Delaney's soul back, it was Myra. And I knew she'd been working on that problem non-stop.

"Mmm-mmm-hmmph!"

Ah, the head was awake.

"Wow," Hogan sat forward, his long arms propped on his knees. "Look at the little guy."

Abner mumbled a reply. It was hard to tell through the duct tape, but he looked really excited.

"Go ahead and take the tape off," Delaney suggested.

"You so don't want me to do that," I said.

"Jean."

"Fine." I pulled off the tape and Abner smacked his mouth.

"Why do I feel so funny?" he asked. "Wait...I'm a zombie, aren't I? Gno!"

"Denial," I said. "First stage of zombie gnome grief."

"Well, it could be worse. Zombies are such popular critters right now."

"Acceptance."

"Boy, I could use a bite to eat."

"Hunger."

"Like, a lot to eat. I could chew my way through a concrete truck."

"More hunger."

"Got anything to eat?" he asked no one in particular.

"No," I said. "And the last stage...."

"Gnock-gnock."

Hogan laughed.

Delaney shook her head. "I thought you made up the knock-knock part of this."

"Nope. So what do you think?" I asked Hogan.

"He's...hey, your name's Abner, right?" Hogan asked.

My front door opened and Myra walked in. "Do you have candy? There are kids on the block and they're headed this way, fast."

"In the kitchen in the worm bowl."

Her gaze flicked to Abner, then Delaney and Hogan, then she walked off to the kitchen.

"I am Abner Doboodoo, the head of all Ordinary gnomes."

"Nice," Hogan said. "I'm Hogan. I bake things. Can you remember the jinni who brought you to life?"

"There was a jinni?"

I sat forward and patted Hogan's thigh. "Gnomes have really short memories. He won't remember how this all happened to him."

"Did you take the penguin?" Delaney asked.

"There was a penguin!" Abner blinked his good eye and looked completely confused. "Anyone got someone I could eat? A statue, a relief, maybe some sweet yard art? Abner sure could use some candy."

Hogan laughed. "Dude. You are so metal."

"Can you tell what's making him animate?" Delaney asked.

"Can you tell what's making him a zombie?" I asked.

Hogan tipped his head a little and scratched under his hat. "A beheading, a burial, a bite."

I shivered. It was exactly what Death had said. "That is so cool."

My doorbell rang with a buzz followed by a scream because it was Halloween, and I didn't do anything by halves.

"I'll get it," Myra said.

"It looks, kind of...colorful?" Hogan asked, like he was talking to himself. "Yeah, colorful. Like fire and smoke. It's kind of orangey."

"What is?" I asked.

"The wish that was granted. It was something for a…child, I think. A gift. That's…well, that's not what I expected."

I could imagine he hadn't expected his absent father to have done anything as nice or maybe mundane, if one considered that he was a jinni, as granting a kid's wish for a statue to come to life.

"Trick or treat!" a chorus of kid voices called out.

"Wow, you look so scary," Myra said from the door. "Are you a vampire or a shark?"

"Both!" a little kid crowed.

Aw…I was missing out on the kid costumes. That was one of my favorite parts of Halloween.

"Abner's old." Hogan waved his hand. "But I think…I think he belonged to a kid once. A long, long time ago. A little girl?"

"Poppy," Abner said with a wistful note. "Sweet, bright Poppy."

"You remember her?" I asked.

Abner's already clouded eyes got cloudier. "We used to play tea party. Every gnight in October. She'd open her bedroom window and bring me inside. We ate candy corn."

"What happened to Poppy?" Delaney asked.

"It was the strangest thing," Abner reminisced. "She kept getting bigger. Until she wasn't little. Until she was like you. And then she drove away."

"She didn't take you?" Hogan asked.

"I fell out of her hands when she was packing me in the trailer. Head broke right off. She leaked water out of her face and buried my head. Left my body standing above it."

So *that's* how Abner lost his head. I couldn't imagine how many years ago that had happened. Fifty? A hundred?

And all this time we'd been dealing with his body as the leader of the gnomes, not knowing his head was buried beneath it. I wondered if someone had decided it was time to bury the body too. Or throw it away in the land fill.

That, then—both parts of Abner being buried, and him also being beheaded—must have triggered the zombie plague.

I felt sorry for the old guy.

"Gnock-gnock."

Scratch that. I didn't feel sorry for him at all.

"Who's there?" Abner answered himself.

"Oh, gods, no," I said. "You do not get to do both parts of this joke."

"Banana," Abner said.

"Do not say banana who," I ordered.

"Banana who?" Abner said. Then: "Gnock-gnock."

I groaned. "Make him stop. Hogan, whatever you do, make him stop."

"Who's there?" Abner asked. "Banana!"

"I don't think," Hogan frowned. "There's…I don't see any way to stop this. Not…it's not like the wish comes with instructions."

"Banana who?" Abner shouted. "Gnock-gnock!"

"Do something," I said. "Anything at this point would be good. A yip. A yop. Anything."

Hogan puffed out a laugh. "A *yop*? What does that even mean?"

"It means stop laughing at your girlfriend and do some jinni stuff to fix the gnome."

"Who's there?" Abner stage whispered, his eyes going shiftily back and forth.

The doorbell rang. The scream screamed.

"Trick or treat!" Maybe it was my imagination, but that was a very low voice.

"And what are you supposed to be?" Myra asked in a tone that sounded like she was trying to hold back a laugh.

"You must give me the candy, or I shall trick you."

My gaze snapped up and met Delaney's. That was Death. A breeze much chillier than the temperature outside pushed in through the door and dropped the air in the living room by several degrees.

"He's here to kill Abner," Delaney said.

"Banana," Abner whispered loudly.

I suddenly wondered why we were fighting this. Maybe letting Abner go to the great—wherever gnomes went when they were dead, revived, then dead again—was his destiny. His fate.

I could probably even ask Fate about that.

"Maybe we're thinking about this the wrong way," I said.

"That's not how trick or treat works," Myra said. "First, I get to guess your costume. Then maybe you get candy. Let's see, are you a butterfly?"

"No."

I couldn't tell if he was delighted or disgusted with this game.

"Are you an angel?"

"Well, yes. Of death. But no. That is not my costume."

"Something with wings. Let me think." Myra was stalling. Or maybe she was just really into having Death on the doorstep begging for a three-dollar candy bar.

Like I said. I did not do Halloween by halves.

"All the gnomes have been living in Ordinary for years," Delaney said, reminding me that we had a problem right here in the living room. "Maybe they're only alive for one month a year, but they are citizens here. We don't discriminate against our citizens. We protect them, uphold their rights, make sure that their needs are met, no matter if they have been here for a day, or if they've been mostly dead all of their weird little lives."

"Fine," I said. "We'll try to keep Abner alive. So, Hogan, can you break the zombie spell?"

He shifted a bit. "I'm not sure. Hey, Abner."

The gnome glanced at him, then away.

Hogan said, "Knock knock."

Abner focused on Hogan like there was nothing else in the world. If he'd had lungs, if he'd had a breath that he could wait with bated, he'd be doing that too. "Who's there?"

"Head gnome."

Abner's smile got wider and wider. Frankly, it was a little creepy. But Hogan grinned right back at him. "Head gnome who?"

"Head gnome me."

I admit it, I gasped a little. For one thing, it was a dumb joke. Like, it wasn't even funny. But for another, everything in the room sort of shifted.

I wouldn't say that the orangey-ness of it changed, but really? The orangey-ness of it changed.

"Oh. Seriously," Hogan said. "Wow. So, I'm the gnew leader gnow."

And just like that, Abner looked a lot more alive. Both his eyes were now bright and blinking, his beard a nice white triangle beneath his chin, his ears evenly curled under his bright red pointed hat.

"Our leader," Abner said. "You are here."

"What?" I asked.

"Hold on," Delaney said. "Hogan, what did you just do?"

"You are abhorrent at guessing a simple disguise," Death said from the front door. "I would have expected more from a police detective."

Myra made a *tsk*ing sound. "Someone's sassing their way out of the jumbo Snickers bar."

"What did you do?" I asked Hogan. Since he wasn't paying any attention to me, I grabbed his shoulders and shook him a little. "What did you just do?"

"It's cool. Like. Good. Real good. I'm like, the leader of these little dudes now, and I make the rules. Hey, Abner," he said. "You aren't a zombie anymore."

"I'm gnot?"

"You're gnot." There was that feeling again. The slight shift in a color I hadn't even sensed in the room until it changed. "And that means gnone of the other gnomes are zombies anymore."

"They're gnot?"

Another slight shift.

"They are gnot. You still hungry?"

Abner frowned, his hat shifting forward as his eyebrows knit together. "Candy corn?"

"You got it." Hogan reached over to the jar next to the love seat, shook out a handful of candy corn, then poured them next to the head.

Abner smiled and bit into a candy corn with a lot more finesse than I'd have expected out of a bodiless gnome.

My boyfriend was the head of the garden gnomes. What did that even mean?

"What does this even mean?" I asked him.

He dropped his arm back around me. "It's not a big deal. I'm gonna look after them. They'll listen to me. I'll have a bunch of little buddies every October. It's going to be fun."

"You can do that?"

"I can now."

"A duck," Myra guessed.

"Would that be frightening?" Death asked.

"On you? Probably."

"Perhaps you will invite me in." Death wasn't a vampire. He didn't need an invitation to enter a place. So I wasn't surprised to hear their footsteps coming our way.

"Are we good?" I asked Delaney.

She stood, putting herself between Death and the gnome head.

I stood too. So did Hogan. Now that Abner was alive and done with the zombie thing and the knock-knock jokes, there was no reason for Death to kill him.

Two cops, a baker, and the head of a gnome stared down Death.

"I see that my services are no longer needed," he said.

"Hogan took care of the zombie gnomes," Delaney said. "Unless you have some other business here you should tell me about?"

"Death is a shadow, Reed Daughter. Death does not share his To-Do list."

I snorted a laugh.

"Well, you can't stay here on vacation," Delaney said. "But this *is* the night when the veil is the thinnest. There is precedence to all manner of gods and monsters having some fun in the mortal world. If you decide to stay, I won't tell you to leave."

"I don't believe I was here to ask for your permission, Reed Daughter."

"Moth?" I asked. Because I couldn't figure out what he was supposed to be either.

He wore a black suit that appeared to be stiff and dusted with ashes. Tattered gray wings drooped on his back, and he was holding a huge ceramic mug of coffee in one hand that was very clearly illustrated by a hand holding up a defiant middle finger.

Death sighed. "It is my understanding that Halloween is intended to be frightening."

"Yes?" I asked.

"Therefore I chose a frightening costume."

"But what are you supposed to be?" I asked.

"Monday."

Hogan started laughing first. We were all right behind him. I kept a close eye on Death's face. He didn't smile, but there was a twinkle in his eye and one eyebrow raised.

"I also understand that some mortals laugh when they are terrified," he said. "Therefore, I will not punish you for your reactions."

Wow, that was almost a joke.

"That's good," Delaney said. "And as long as you follow Ordinary's rules during this very small window of time while you are here, I hope you enjoy the event."

"Are you not attending?"

He took a moment to glance at each of us. Probably noticed for the first time that none of us were wearing costumes, which was a crying shame. I mean, even Myra usually put on a pair of kitty ears.

"We have a kidnapped penguin to find," Delaney said. "And some gnomes to check in on."

"Ah," Death said. "Perhaps this will help." One minute he was just standing there. The next he was standing there with a very familiar penguin statue at his side.

"*You* kidnapped the penguin?" I asked.

"I merely assured it would come to no harm."

"And the little red devil horns it's wearing?" Delaney asked.

"In following the rules of Ordinary, I understand one can not kidnap the penguin unless one is willing to decorate it in such a manner as is blog-worthy."

I grinned and reached for my phone. "Yeah, we have got to get a picture of this."

And we did. The aloof, ashen angel of Monday, and the sweet little penguin with devil horns.

I could already tell it was going to be my new favorite picture on the blog.

"Shall we?" Death asked.

"Shall we what?" Delaney asked.

"Shall we attend the celebration?"

"We don't even have costumes," I said.

Delaney and Myra both reached into their pockets and pulled out head bands. Myra's gave her kitty ears. Delaney's gave her a unicorn horn.

Delaney unzipped her coat to reveal the "Sparkle Hard, Baby" T-shirt she wore. Myra did her one better by having not only a leopard-print shirt, but by also having a kitty nose and whiskers to wear, and a cute little pink bell on a choker.

"For real?" Because my sisters outdoing me on Halloween would simply not do.

"At least you're not in costume," I said to Hogan.

"Got it right here." He pulled a white beard out of his pocket, attached it over his ears, then picked up Abner's head. "I'm the gnome-whisperer. Want to see my amazing talking head?"

Oh gods.

"Say something, head," Hogan said.

"Something head," Abner mimicked.

Hogan laughed, and I rolled my eyes. I'd almost rather they went back to the knock-knock jokes.

"Fine," I said. "Give me a second. I'll out-costume you all."

Because there was no way Jean Reed was going to do Halloween by half.

CHAPTER TWELVE

WE WERE officially on duty for the night. Halloween meant we had to keep track of petty mischief, but Ordinary didn't have a lot of serious crime on this night. I chalked it up to half the town being full of monsters or people with powers who could put a stop to mailboxes being knocked over and trees being T.P.'d pretty quick.

So while we each had to patrol some part of town, we each had at least part of the night off to do something fun too.

And I wanted to do the Haunted Harbor.

Lucky for me, Hogan wanted to do it too. I agreed to meet him at eleven so we could cruise through all the haunted houses before midnight.

He was waiting for me in front of the first haunted house, a red rose in one hand and a gnome head in the other. Even the bushy white beard couldn't hide how fine that man was. Couldn't hide the look in his eyes when he saw me coming.

"Hey there, beautiful," he said as I made my way around a gaggle of ten-year-olds hyped up on so much sugar, I could practically taste it in the air around them.

"Hey, yourself." I stopped in front of him and smiled. "How's your night going, Gnome Daddy?"

He snorted. "We're gonna have to come up with a sexier name than that."

"I'm not calling you master."

"Not in that costume, you're not."

"Like it?" I held my arms out to the side and did a little pose.

"You're wearing a laundry basket."

"And wadded up socks. And some underwear." I flicked at the clothing stuffed around me, and the hat I'd made out of a box of detergent. "Like Death said, Halloween is about being something people dread."

"You're dirty laundry?"

"Oh, yeah, baby. I'm all kinds of dirty."

He laughed and slipped the rose behind my ear. "Do you know what day it is?" He took my hand, pulled me close until my soft plastic basket buckled between us.

"Halloween?"

"Yes. Also, it's our six-month anniversary."

"Oh," I said. "It is." I knew that. I'd been thinking about it for weeks. Was this a milestone for him? For us? And if it was a milestone, was it an important one, or just a little one?

Maybe this was the point where we reassessed what we were doing, who we were together, what we wanted.

Maybe this was the point where we said good-bye.

"You know what I want to do to celebrate our first six months together?" He smiled, and shifted his hand so that it cupped my face, his thumb running gently across the curve of my bottom lip.

"What?" I asked, lost in his eyes.

"To do it again. And again. And again."

"That's a lot of six months, Hogan."

"It is, isn't it? I'm liking the sound of that. How about you?"

A year with him? Two years? Three?

"Yeah," I said, a little too softly to be heard over the shrieks of fright around us. "Yes," I said a little louder. "I'd like that too."

I searched his eyes. And I thought I saw words unsaid in their warm blue depth. I thought I saw love.

I hoped he saw it in my eyes too. Because that's what was in my heart. Solid as a rock, sweet as candy.

"Can I tell you something?" I asked.

"Go."

"I wished for something."

"Oh?"

"Just now."

"And what was it?"

"Everyone knows that if you tell someone what you wish for it won't ever come true."

"So I have to guess?"

"Or use your jinni powers to figure it out."

He didn't hesitate. "I already know what it is."

"Do you?"

"It's written right here." He brushed his thumb across my bottom lip again. He tipped his head down and gently nudged my face to the angle he wanted.

Then he kissed me, with all his warmth, his heart, his joy. And I kissed him right back. No secrets between us.

Yeah. Yes. This was exactly what I had wished for, exactly what my heart hoped for. Him. Us. Together. A promise. A wish. And all the time in the world to discover just how many ways we could make our dreams come true.

PAPER STARS

One magical holiday. Some assembly required...

POLICE CHIEF Delaney Reed loves the holidays in Ordinary, Oregon, the beach town where gods vacation and monsters reside. But this year, she has a lot on her plate. It isn=t just the creature who follows her home, or the terrible storm barreling toward town. It isn't that Mrs. Yates's penguin has been stolen. Again.

It's that her boyfriend, Ryder Bailey, has been gone for two months and is growing more distant. She's beginning to think she knows why.

But when a demon, a dragon, and a god bearing unusual gifts get thrown on top of her to-do list, Delaney decides to roll up her sleeves and make this holiday unforgettable. One disaster at a time.

CHAPTER ONE

"SNOW QUEEN, Jack Frost, Old Man Winter," Jean said as we clomped our way through wet sand toward the cave. Rain sliced sideways, stinging hard despite the all-weather police jackets we wore. "Uh...the Abominable Snowman. There. That's four people besides my boyfriend who could grant my wish, Delaney."

"We are literally at sea level." I waved toward the Pacific Ocean roaring and churning behind us like some kind of monster with a toothache. "We're not going to get snow here on Christmas."

"Not with that attitude we won't." My sister Jean Reed. Eternally optimistic. And just a little obsessed with Christmas.

"Don't ask Hogan to grant you a snow wish, Jean."

"Just because he's half-Jinn doesn't mean he'll grant wishes willy-nilly. Also, his schedule at the bakery is crazy right now."

She snapped her fingers. "You know who could ask someone to make it happen?"

"Give it up."

She ignored me.

"Why *you* could ask, Delaney. I bet Jack Frost or Old Man Winter would listen to the

amazing Delaney Reed, Ordinary, Oregon's chief of Police."

I grinned even though she couldn't see me. I had never known someone more into Christmas than Jean. "As if. You know how Jack gets this time of year."

Sassy was one description. Mob-boss-ish was another. You wouldn't think being in charge of frosty spangles on car windows would make someone such a militant, sulky diva.

"Besides, Jack doesn't live here. And if he did, I'm sure he'd rather not have his town buried in a snow storm."

"But it's almost Christmas," she whined. "Three days, Delaney. You could send an email. Make an official request.

Ooh, make a wish."

I snorted. "One: What are you, a three-year-old? Two: Do you know how many *actual* three-year-olds are wishing for snow for *their* Christmas? Who do you think Jack or Old Man Winter are going to listen to? A twenty-something police officer who should know the reality of weather patterns on the Oregon coast, or little kids who have their hearts set on magic and snow?"

"We're all little kids at heart. Plus, I like magic and snow."

"Like it somewhere else. We aren't prepared for snow. Ordinary doesn't even own a snow plow."

"You sound like Myra."

"Good. Myra acts her age, and like me, saves her wishes for more important things. Unlike our youngest Reed sister."

We stopped at the mouth of the cave, Jean muttering the whole time.

"What?"

"Where's your Christmas spirit? I don't remember you being this grumpy last year."

"I'm just waiting for Christmas, like a normal person, instead of going all Jingle-bell crazy before the Thanksgiving dishes have even dried like one abnormal person I know."

"Hey, I waited a whole week before Thanksgiving to play my holiday tunes in public. That's a late start for Christmas music. It's no fun to wait all the way until December."

"It's not about fun, Jean." I picked my way over the huge rocks that jutted out of the sand. "It's about being a police officer who doesn't wear a Santa hat for six weeks straight."

"What's wrong with wearing a Santa hat?"

"Along with a gun? It confuses people."

"Don't hate on my hats just because Ryder's been gone for two months."

Ryder, my long-time-crush and recent boyfriend, had been on a job building a new care center over in Bend.

Our daily texts and long after-dinner phone calls had dwindled down to him sending me an occasional text every other day complaining about the weather, and how slow the project was going, and why no one could follow simple directions and do what they were contracted to do on the job site.

I missed him. I hadn't heard him say he missed me, which was making me worry that he'd been gone long enough to re-think our relationship. Re-think the spark that had drawn us together in the first place. Had we been drawn together because of a natural attraction or was he just interested in the supernatural things that surrounded me and filled this town?

I'd like to think it was natural attraction that brought us together. But Ordinary was full of unusual people, powers, and things, including vacationing gods and supernatural creatures. I was in charge of looking after everyone who lived here. Those duties meant Ryder's and my relationship had already been tested by some heavy stuff. This year alone, I'd been shot twice in the line of duty. I'd bargained away my soul.

Ryder had tied his life to a god of contracts who really didn't like me or my sisters being the law here in Ordinary.

I'd died.

My heart stuttered and my stomach clenched. Every time I thought about that, it hit me hard. I licked my lips, tasting salt and pushing away those memories.

Ryder had been there for all of that. Had been there for me. So why was I worried?

He hadn't made it home for Thanksgiving and wasn't coming home for Christmas. That's why I was worried.

Looking at our lives through the high-stakes we had experienced could make the holiday less interesting. Less important. Would it matter if we missed our first Christmas together? Our relationship was strong enough to miss one holiday. We'd been there for each other when it really counted. Many times.

When things were dangerous.

But what about when things were happy? Safe?

Worse, what about when things were boring?

Just because we weren't talking, never saw each other, and he hadn't been brave enough to say he loved me (except for that one time when he was yelling it at a vampire) didn't mean our relationship was sinking before it had even left the shore, right?

I sighed. Maybe I was kidding myself. Maybe we were boring now. Maybe there was a big ol' iceberg out there ready to sink this ship and it was time to deploy the floating door.

"Has he said it to you yet?" Jean asked.

Jean didn't have mind reading abilities. Her family gift was that she knew when something bad was going to happen. Actual mind reading didn't run in our family. Or at least I hoped it didn't.

"Not talking about it."

"You don't have to be afraid of the 'L' word, Delaney."

"Lifeboat?"

She gave me a weird look. "What is going on in your head?"

Yep. No mind reading.

"Not that 'L' word," she said. "Love. As in: *'I love you, Ryder Bailey with your dreamy green eyes and your hunky strong shoulders and your superpower patience when I'm being stupid like getting myself shot. Or when I'm being too stubborn to just* call *you and tell you I miss you. Or when I'm too moody to admit I want you to come home before Christmas.'* Love-love. I checked the rule book and women are allowed to say it first."

"Good. You should say it to Hogan."

"You think I haven't?"

"Have you?" I wouldn't be surprised. Out of all of us sisters, she was the freest with her affection. But she and Hogan hadn't been dating for very long. She had spent most of that time worrying about letting him in on all the supernatural secrets of the town. I'd just assumed she would be cautious with the secrets of her heart too.

On the other hand, this was Jean. Fearless and full of surprises.

She grunted as she hopped from rock to rock. "Not yet. I'm waiting for the right time to spring it on him. When it's totally inappropriate and he least expects it."

I laughed and wiped rain off my face. We ducked under the cave's overhang. "Why is it so easy for you to believe that romance always works out?"

Jean's cheeks were red from the wind. Her hair, bright green today, escaped her hood to frame her face. "Wait. I have an answer for this one. Romance, my dear Delaney, is also known as *love.* Love is one of the best things about life. A magic thing. A magical romantic thing. Magical romantic things always work out, otherwise they wouldn't be magical." Her blue eyes sparkled. "You know what else is magical and romantic?"

"Don't say snow."

"Snow! Especially Christmas snow. Add in a handsome guy, a nice warm fire, and ooh la la, is it hot in here or what?"

"Stop it," I said.

"What?" All innocence.

"Stop trying to make Christmas romantic."

"Why shouldn't Christmas be romantic?"

I opened my mouth to tell her it couldn't be romantic because my boyfriend wasn't going to be around, but before I could say anything, movement deeper in the cave caught my eye. I flicked on my flashlight and Jean did the same with hers. Twin beams cut into the restless shadows.

"It's the police," I shouted loud enough to be heard over the waves grinding behind us and the damp dripping inside the cave. "We need to talk with you. Please come out into the light."

My heart beat a little faster, a little harder. I wasn't sure what we were dealing with here.

An over-excited rockhound who shouldn't have been exploring the hidden cave at this time of year, had come into the station this morning. He had insisted some kind of huge, dangerous creature was snarling around in the shadows.

He said it was a gigantic crocodile. Or a massive snake. Or a dinosaur.

He hadn't gone so far as to suggest it was a sea monster.

I wouldn't have believed him anyway. At this time of year most of our sea monsters liked staying out at sea. That didn't mean some other kind of monster hadn't decided to stake claim to the cozy cave though.

Jean and I had hot-footed it out here while Myra and Officer Shoe took the rockhound's statement. We wanted to get this under control before the papers picked up the story.

I could feel the tension radiating off of Jean as the cave's blackness remained black.

It was rare that a creature of Ordinary became violent, but it had happened before.

"There." She angled the beam onto the shape coming toward us.

I held my breath. Reached for my gun.

The shadows slid around, at first huge, then wide, then long and then…

A creature paused in the light, right there on the inside of the cave overhang.

"Is that…?" Jean breathed.

I exhaled all in one rush. "Yep." I put away my flashlight. "It's a dragon."

"Piggy!" Jean crowed. "Look at all that pink. That little nubby nose, chubby cheeks and pointy ears. And that tail. So curly! That's a pig, Delaney. A wee little piggy-pig-pig."

The dragon oinked, its curly tail wagging a mile a minute.

"Jean, I'm not kidding. It's a dragon."

She tipped her head, considering it. "Are you sure?"

I studied the little monster. It looked like a baby pig, all pink and sweet-faced and adorably sandy from its chubby little legs up to its squishy round belly. It opened its mouth in what could only be described as a darling little smile. But there was a sort of wobbly haze around it, as if looking straight at it caused a slight warping of reality behind it.

Dragons could appear as anything they wanted, any size they wanted. This one, apparently, wanted to be a tiny pig.

"It's a dragon," I said again.

"Aw," Jean cooed. "Who's a cute dragon? Is it you, little piggy? Cutey-pootie dragy-wagy?" She knelt. "C'mere, baby. C'mon, piggy-poo, cuddle boo-boo."

It oinked, absolutely delighted with her. I raised one eyebrow, absolutely suspicious of it.

Then it ran at us. Well, not at Jean who had her arms wide open ready for some pig-on-police mutual admiration. No, it ran at me.

Not good. Not good at all.

"Hold it right there, dragon," I said in my cop voice. "You know the rules. No violence within the boundary of Ordinary, Oregon. If you want to remain inside Ordinary, you will follow the rules."

The pig slowed to a cute little trot, then stopped at my feet, tipping its face up at me.

Okay, so far, so good. I had its attention.

"We've had a complaint," I explained. "A man looking for rocks saw you in what I assume is your more natural form? You frightened him."

The little tail wagged faster. The dragon liked getting a scare out of the guy. I tried not to smile.

"We've talked him out of coming back here to get a picture of you because we do not need news of a dragon spreading on the internet. Citizens of Ordinary expect to live here without their supernatural nature being discovered by the world at large. You've endangered that. What I need from you today, is a guarantee that you will take the form of a creature belonging to the natural world if anyone else stumbles upon your cave."

"Oink."

"D'aw..." Jean cooed again. "Look at its little face. You can't be mad at that little face, Delaney."

"I'm not mad. But I am serious," I said to the pig. "We're going to tell the man that he probably saw a sea lion or a lost cow. If you'd rather stay in piglet form if he comes by again, that's fine too."

The dragon just stood there, wagging its little loopy tail, face tipped up to me like I'd uncovered the sun.

"Do you understand?"

The dragon trotted a little circle, and oinked once.

Jean snorted.

"Good. Okay."

The dragon didn't say anything even though I knew dragons were capable of human speech. So I guessed that was pretty much that. Job done.

"All right then. Hope you have a nice day."

"And Merry Christmas," Jean added.

"Yes. Merry Christmas." Did dragons celebrate Christmas? Who knew? Probably Myra.

I turned back into the rain that was still pelting down at an angle. At least now it was at our backs.

We didn't try to shout over the racket of the wind, rain, and ocean as we picked our way over stones, soft wet sand, clumps of driftwood, more rocks, a tangle of kelp, and finally trudged toward the land's edge.

We hiked up the gravel access road, the sound of storm and

ocean dampened by the rise of the land on either side of us. It was several degrees warmer without the wind, and I rubbed at my face to slick off the rain.

Jean hummed *Jingle Bells* as she walked around to the passenger side of the Jeep. She'd been humming *Jingle Bells* for three weeks straight. It was epically annoying but I knew if I told her to stop, she'd only sing it louder.

Sisters.

She studied the phone in her hand, thumb swiping across the screen.

I found my keys, got the doors of the Jeep open, and was debating pulling off my soaking jacket when I heard a sound at my feet.

"Oink. "

"Jean."

"Yes?"

"The dragon is following me."

"Dragon pig, dragon pig, fol-low-ing us home," she sang to the tune of *Jingle Bells*. "I told you this is the best Christmas song. You can put any words to it!"

"Not helping."

Jean just laughed.

"Do you need something?" I asked the dragon. "Are you all right? Are you hurt? Lost?"

It trotted in a circle again, jumped up into my Jeep then hopped into the back seat, making itself comfortable with a snuffle and grunt.

"You want a ride?" I continued the apparently useless twenty questions. "Somewhere down the beach? Into town? By the lake?"

The pig snuffled again, then closed its eyes, cute as an internet meme. It started snoring.

Jean chuckled. "Oh, my gods. So cute." She held up her phone and snapped away, then typed something.

"It can't stay there," I said, trying to feel grumpy about the situation and failing. The cute was powerful with this one.

"Looks like it can." She pressed one last button. I had a feeling that pig was going to show up on all of her social media. "See how happy it is?"

Yes, I could admit it made a adorable picture. I was just trying to get my head around the fact that I had an actual dragon curled up in my vehicle.

"This is my Jeep. I need it for work. I can't drive around with a dragon sleeping in the back seat."

"I don't think it's listening to you. And unless you want to do battle with a dragon…." She paused, a little too much hope in her expression.

I scoffed at her.

"Spoilsport. Fine. Then I'd suggest you stop worrying so much and let the dragon situation work itself out naturally."

"Naturally?"

"Naturally. Like how nature intended."

"Nature didn't plant a dragon-pig in my backseat, Jean. The dragon-pig did. And this is…"

"…our job?"

I sighed to cover a groan. She was right. This was our job.

"Fine." I got in the Jeep and glanced at the dragon in the rearview mirror. "You let me know if you want off anywhere, okay? One grunt for yes, two grunts for no."

It grunted once.

Jean chuckled. "Progress! Actual dragon-pig, human communication. See how great things work out when you stop worrying and just go with the flow?"

The hazy warp still surrounded the piggy, but it wasn't as noticeable. The dragon was getting better at controlling how it was perceived. If someone saw it in the back seat, they'd probably think it was a normal pig. So at least it knew how to hide in plain sight. That was a good trait for surviving in Ordinary. Maybe it wouldn't be any trouble.

I put the Jeep in gear.

"Hold on." Jean pulled off the Santa hat she'd been wearing under her hood and dropped it gently on the pig's head.

It sat up and oinked. It turned its head side to side as it tried to bite the edge of the hat. Jean snapped more pictures. "Adorbs to the millionth power! Hey, dragon, can you make it snow?"

"Jean."

The pig oinked twice.

I laughed. "That's a "no" sister."

She shrugged. "It was worth a shot. You know what else is worth a shot? Calling Ryder and telling him to come home."

"He's busy."

"He's lonely and so are you." She shifted in her seat and stared at my profile as I drove.

"What?"

"I know you keep wondering when you and Ryder are going to stop being a thing, but two months apart isn't going to change what you are to each other. "

She was right. I knew it. But a small part of me still worried.

She patted my knee. "Believe in a little magic, Delaney."

"Dragon in the back seat looks like a pig. I believe in magic."

"Then it should be easy to believe in love." She smiled and fiddled with the radio. Christmas music rolled out loud and strong, ordering us to "let it snow, let it snow, let it snow."

Jean sang along. Loudly and off-key just to bother me. It must have bothered the dragon too because it ate her Santa hat. Sucked it down like a noodle until the little white pompom popped in its mouth. Then it chewed and swallowed.

Jean thought it was hilarious. She recorded it on her phone.

CHAPTER TWO

"YOU GONNA get that?" Bathin, tall, dark and demon-y, blew over the top of his quad shot espresso with the Blue Owl's logo on the side. The diner had been playing Christmas music non-stop since December first. The current tune sounded a little warped as it yodeled about halls that needed decking.

The Blue Owl was warm, customers were smiling, and that happy, fluttery mix of holiday good will and hopeful expectation was thick in the apple pie-scented air.

Outside, the rain and wind came down hard and cold. We wouldn't get snow, but we were in for a heck of a storm.

My phone rang again.

Bathin nodded toward it, like I hadn't noticed the noise. "Gonna?"

"No."

He grinned. "Oh, please. I can hear your heart beating love notes from over here. Don't ignore your boyfriend on my account."

I picked up my coffee and went back to the reports I was scanning. Ignored Bathin. Ignored the phone.

Bathin twitched one eyebrow. He liked a good game of chicken. "Maybe Ryder's hurt." He widened his eyes and gasped, going for the theatrics. "Maybe he's dead."

I scowled and took another drink. Ryder didn't usually call me before dinner. Half—asleep-after-eleven-o'clock calls had become the default lately.

"Why, he hasn't even told you if he loves you or not." He chuckled at my scowl. "You think I don't know your innermost secrets? You think I don't know what you feel?" He leaned forward on his elbows, eyes kindled, mouth tipped in a smirk. "Answer him. Talk to him. Tell him you love him. You know you want to," he sing-songed.

"Remind me again why you're sitting here?" I slurped coffee. I'd found it was best to ignore his drama. Since I dealt with gods on a daily basis, tricksters and attention hounds were old hat.

"Three days before Christmas, I haven't been invited to the Reed's famous Christmas Eve shindig—an oversight, I'm sure. I'm just a lonely demon looking for a little company and fun." He stuck his lip out in a pout.

Yeah, that wouldn't work on me either. I started reading the reports again.

"Fine," he huffed. "I want an invite. Please invite me to your family Christmas party. Besides, where else would I be? I am sort of attached to you."

Since he could read my mind, I envisioned some places I'd rather he be. I had a vivid imagination.

That got one short, surprised laugh out of him, and I had to work not to give him a smile in return.

He was charming when he laughed. Handsome when he smiled. Enough so that it was deceptively easy to forget he was a demon in possession of my soul. And sometimes, like whenever he thought my sister Myra couldn't see him watching her, I could even see a kind of confused warmth in his eyes that didn't appear to be fueled by the fires of hell.

The rest of the time, he was an annoying pain in my neck.

"You should call Ryder back."

"No."

The phone rang again. Bathin watched me. "Do you want him to start worrying about you? Selfish. It really could be an emergency. There are creatures out in the world beyond Ordinary, you know. Gods, demons, monsters...."

I made a frustrated sound and grabbed my phone. "Delaney," I barked.

There was a pause on the other end of the line.

"Did I catch you at a bad time?"

And just like that, the warmth and rumble of Ryder's voice, low and warm and sexy, made everything around me less annoying. The crackly sound system filtered Nat King Cole crooning about chestnuts and roasting fires. Rain rattled down the windows. Street lamps set each raindrop ablaze: sparkling like melted stars caught in dark glass.

I was surrounded by people, heat, noise, life. Christmas was in the air.

All I heard, all I felt, was Ryder.

"Not a bad time," I said, my own voice dropping, all the hard edges and frustration sliding away.

I missed him. His laugh. The way he tried to trick me into telling him which supernaturals lived in town. The way he rolled out of bed in the morning and walked to the bathroom with his eyes closed, groping at the light switch and shower and not opening his eyes until he was under the warm spray for at least five minute. The way he always offered me the last French fry on his plate.

I wanted to see him, touch him, know he was solid and real in my life. That we were solid and real in this life together.

"You're good," I said. "This is good. Is everything okay?"

"Yes?" He inhaled, held it. "Why?"

"You're calling early."

That pause again. "I…things are winding down here. With the build. With the holiday coming up, I thought, maybe I should…."

I waited. He didn't finish the thought. "Should what?" Did he want to stay there? The long drive home with holiday traffic would be a hassle, especially since he'd just have to turn around and go back to tie off the project's loose ends the day after Christmas.

My stomach knotted. I pressed my lips together so that I wouldn't make any disappointed noise when he told me he was going to stay there.

"Should come home," he said.

I exhaled hard, the rush of my heartbeat making my breath a little hitchy. Bathin raised his eyebrows at me then shook his head. *Told you so* he mouthed.

"I'll try to be there by early afternoon tomorrow. If that works for you?"

"That sounds good. Really great." I cleared my throat. "But the passes are pretty bad after the last freeze. Are you sure?"

"I'm sure."

"Okay. Promise you'll drive carefully and chain up."

"I will."

Another long pause where I listened to the inhale and

exhale of his breathing. I strained to hear more of him, of what was around him. I could just make out the radio over the rumble of his truck engine. Another Christmas song, this one about peace on Earth, carried by the smooth chocolatly baritone of Bing Crosby mixed with Bowie's caramel-sweet tenor.

I wondered if he could hear my breathing too, wondered if he strained for more of me like I strained for more of him. Wondered if he could hear the diner around me as Nat King Cole's buttered-rum vocals wished us all a Merry Christmas.

"Delaney?" Ryder said.

"Yes?"

"There's something important I've been meaning to tell you."

"Yes?"

"Oooh," Bathin said. "Here it comes. He loves you. Or he's breaking up with you. Fifty-fifty chance here, no wrong answer."

I flipped him off. He grinned.

"Something I should have said a long time ago," Ryder said.

"He's finally gonna say it. Love? Hate?" Bathin pressed his palms together in prayer position and looked to the heavens. "Hold me, Jesus."

I glared at him. To Ryder I said, "Okay."

"I don't know why it's taken me so long." Ryder paused. "But..."

I held my breath. Waited. Everything in me tingled with a rush of excitement. The boy I'd had a crush on all my life, the man I'd fallen in love with, was finally going to say the three words I'd been waiting to hear.

Maybe Jean was right. Christmas was romantic.

"...tell Spud I miss him, okay?"

Reality slammed back into place with the smell of grease, ketchup, and wet coats mixed with the overly-loud dinner crowd. A Christmas song I despised, sung by rodents who should not have gotten their own movie, much less a sequel, added to the noise.

The demon across the table from me grinned like a fool and sighed happily, enjoying my emotional whiplash.

"Spud," I said in the most blasé tone I owned.

"Spud." Was that a hint of laughter in his voice? Was Ryder

teasing me?

"Your dog."

"Last I knew."

"Tell your dog, you miss him. Your *dog*."

"Yes. Because I do. Oh, and there's one more thing." Pause. Maybe for dramatic effect, maybe for navigating a tricky spot in whatever road he was driving. "Tell Spud that I love him."

Really? I pulled the phone away from my ear and stared at it. Was he pranking me? Had Jean called him behind my back and told him about our conversation?

I knew Ryder loved me, because he'd proved it over and over again with his actions.

But Jean had gotten that stupid "L" word stuck in my head and then Bathin had been all over it, and now I wanted to hear it, dammit. I wanted my Christmas romance.

Bathin snorted.

I scowled at him. "Stop reading my mind."

"Stop being so entertaining."

I imagined throwing him in a dungeon with a thousand hungry rats.

"Promises, promises. And now I'm suddenly famished. I need pie." He wandered off to sweet talk the waitress out of a free slice, something at which he was surprisingly adept.

"Delaney?" Ryder's voice brought me back to the conversation.

There was no need for me to get upset about him teasing me. There was no reason for me to be annoyed that he was more emotionally open with his dog than with me.

I could be calm. I could be happy that he was coming home in time for the holidays.

Who needed the "L" word? Nobody. Who needed Christmas romance? Not me.

Take that, Jean.

Also? Two could play this game.

"You'll be glad to know I've already told Spud I love him more than you do. And guess who he believes? Me. I didn't want to break it to you over the phone, but ever since I've been taking Spud on walks, feeding him bacon, bringing him a dragon to wrestle with, he's made it pretty clear he loves me best now."

"A...did you say dragon?"

"By the way, you'll need new curtains. The dragon likes fabric. And there's a strong possibility Spud won't even recognize you by the time you get back. Why, just the other day he was staring at your picture and growling."

"Delaney." He coughed to smother a laugh. "Are you okay?"

"I'm just fine. I'm just *great*."

"Mmmm-hmm. You sound great." His voice dropped into that sexy burr that made my mouth water. I bit the corner of my lip and waited for my stupid heart to stop fluttering for him. Waited for the butterflies in my stomach to get the message that there would be no takeoffs today. All flights were grounded.

"Don't," I whispered.

"Don't what?" Sexy voice. Sexy man. I closed my eyes and could almost feel his arms wrapping around me, his body hard and heated against mine. I could almost feel his breath ghosting across my cheek to my lips, where he would pause, thumbs framing my mouth before he pressed a kiss exactly where he wanted it.

How could I miss him so much when he'd only been gone for a couple months?

Hearts were confusing.

I might have made a little sound.

"Don't think I'm not missing you," he rumbled. "I can't sleep at night. You're all I think about. And every time I hear your voice...I just want to turn the project over to some other company, pack it all up, and come home."

"Yeah?"

"Yeah."

Who knew one word could make everything seem better?

I opened my eyes and stared at my cup while the Hula Hoop-obsessed rodents sang me back to the here and now.

It was almost Christmas. Songs were playing, people were laughing. That lift of kindness and hope and nostalgia filled the air, thicker than the scents of cinnamon and peppermint. Bright lights blinked along the edges of windows and silvery snowflakes hung brightly from the ceiling.

"I'll be there," he said. "Soon." Promising me. Promising himself. "We'll talk. Okay, Delaney? We'll really talk. Because I have things to say to you. Important things I need you to know. About us. Things I've been thinking a lot about."

"Okay." Even I heard how soft my voice had gone.

He made a frustrated sound. "I need to say them when I can see your eyes. When I can feel your heartbeat."

"Okay." He was coming home. That was good. That was enough. "I miss you like I miss the stars in the sky."

"Aw," Bathin whispered as he settled down with half an apple pie. "Stars. How poetic. Most people only aim for the moon."

I reached across the table with my spoon and scooped all of the whipped cream off his pie.

"Hey."

I stuffed the entire pile in my mouth and gave him a what-you-gonna-do-about-it look.

"Baby." Was all Ryder seemed able to get out. But it was enough.

That word was love.

"Hey." I swallowed the sweet cream then took a quick sip of coffee. "There is a storm headed inland. It's going to dump a lot of snow in the passes. Do you think you should wait until it blows through?"

"No. I want to be home. I'll be careful. I promise."

"Just…don't push it if it looks too bad."

"I won't."

"Call me before you leave. And make sure you have a full tank of gas."

"And cold weather gear, chains, water, granola bars and jerky. I'm only three hours away, Delaney, not trekking across Siberia."

"A hundred and ninety-one miles, Ryder. There are two mountain ranges between us."

"You think a couple mountain ranges could keep me from spending Christmas with you?"

"If they're going to throw a blizzard at your head? Maybe."

"Let them try. I'm still coming home. Blizzard or no blizzard."

"Okay."

"Delaney." Soft, intimate. "I'll be home for Christmas."

"Don't you start quoting songs at me."

He chuckled, and just like that, things felt better again. Things felt right. "Jean's right," he said. "You have no Christmas spirit."

"Excuse me? You're taking my sister's side on this?"

He laughed. "It's okay. Not everyone gets into the season like Jean gets into well, everything."

"Right?" I said feeling vindicated. "It's been *Jingle Bells* 24/7 since before Thanksgiving. *Before* Thanksgiving, Ryder."

"Totally rude of her."

"You know what I want for Christmas?" I asked. "Ear plugs. And therapy."

"Maybe if you're a good girl, Santa will bring you both. Or you could just ask him. Are you sure Santa isn't…around?"

"Santa doesn't live in Ordinary, Ryder," I told him for the hundredth time. "I'm sure we are not the North Pole."

"It's Mr. Kristofferson, isn't it?"

His guesses were getting better, and by better I meant total bull's-eye. Man had good instincts. But I wasn't going to let him off that easily.

"If Santa lived here, don't you think I'd tell you?"

Bathin *tsked* at my lie.

"I think you'd wait until Mr. Kristofferson saw me doing something naughty so he wouldn't bring me any presents."

"You've put a lot of thought into this, haven't you?"

"I've had time to do a lot of thinking lately."

"Oh?"

"About a lot of things."

"Naughty things?"

"Always."

This was not the time or place for dirty talk. There was a family of six plowing through a full turkey dinner just one booth down, and everyone else in the diner had to be over ninety years old.

Still, I tucked my head toward the window, cupped my phone, and pressed my face close to it trying to keep this on the down-low. "Tell me," I breathed.

"Did you just put on a ski mask?"

"No." I moved my hand. "What naughty things are you thinking?"

An old man one table over grinned at me. He did that two-finger point-at-eye thing then point-at-me thing.

I raised one eyebrow like I didn't know what he was insinuating.

He made a circle with his pointer finger and thumb then thrust his other index finger into the hole several times.

Nope. No. I was not going to sit here and watch some old guy make dirty sex signals at me.

"Like I bet you haven't even gotten a Christmas tree yet," Ryder rumbled. "Or decorated it. Or put up any Christmas lights. Shame, shame, Delaney."

This was naughty talk? A Christmas tree?

"Lights are up and twinkling, Mr. Judgy McJudgerson." I had put them up yesterday. Just a single string across the mantle above the fireplace. But still. That counted.

"And the tree?"

"Chopped, dropped, and propped in the living room. Covered in bows, bulbs, and balls." That, was a complete lie.

"Well." He sounded impressed. "I stand corrected."

"Yes, you do. I have Christmas spirit oozing from the top of my nog to the bottom of my mistletoes."

"Tree and everything," he said with a chuckle again. I liked the sound of it. "You know one of my favorite Christmas memories?"

"No."

"When I was a kid, I would lie under the Christmas tree and stare up at the lights in the boughs."

"Okay?"

The old guy shifted at his table so he was in my line of vision again. He jabbed his finger in and out of his ear.

I did not want to know what kind of sex move he thought that was.

"This year, I'm going to make a new memory," Ryder said. "I'm going to lie you down under that tree, Delaney Reed."

The old man made even faster finger-in-ear motions. He looked alarmed.

"And then I'm going to do to you, what I do with all the gifts I've been waiting too long for."

I didn't make a sound, my heart pounding too hard to do anything but listen to his words.

"I'm going to unwrap you slowly…"

"Officer Reed!" the old guy shouted. "Turn off the button." He shoved his finger through the "ok" sign he was making. I suddenly realized what all those dirty signals really meant.

"…and when I have you there, shivering and bare beneath me…"

"Speaker!" The old guy thrust his finger frantically in and out of his ear.

"…I'm going to put my mouth…"

"Wait!" I yelped and dropped the phone like it was made of bees. It clattered across the table and landed on the floor. Every person in the diner looked at me.

Inexplicably, the one person who hadn't heard my outburst—Ryder—was still talking. But by whatever luck was left to me, the speaker had clicked off while I was fumbling with the phone.

There was a pause, just a second or two. Bathin was shaking with laughter. All eyes were on me, waiting to see how I was going to play this. I opened my mouth, closed it. Yeah, I had nothing. I waved, though it kind of looked like frantic jazz hands.

Bathin bent in half to try to catch his breath.

Jerk.

The old guy nodded. "All right then. Let's all get back to our nice quiet meals, folks." He buckled down to his mashed potatoes and stuffing. That seemed to be the signal everyone was waiting for. They all turned back to their own meals too.

Someone turned up the Christmas music. Extra loud.

Bathin wiped the tears running down his stupid handsome demon face, but kept right on shaking with silent laughter. I hoped he silently asphyxiated.

"Delaney?" Ryder asked from somewhere by my feet. I retrieved my phone.

"Sorry. That's, uh, great. Interesting stuff. We'll have to

follow up on it later. In private."

"What just happened?"

I turned down the volume for good measure.

"Nothing. Technical difficulties. It's fine. All fine. Real fine. Just come home safe." I said that with all my heart in my voice.

"I will, baby," he said just as thickly. "I promise. We're going to break in that tree."

He ended the call. I stared at my phone. That was...well, that was slightly embarrassing, but also made me feel a lot better. The call had been more than I'd expected. A warm flush washed over my cheeks.

Ryder Bailey was lonely and headed home. To me. Even though there was a storm in the way.

I liked the sound of that.

A little boy at the table of six was singing *Jingle Bells* and rhyming it with "my sister smells." His sister punched him in the arm. He just laughed until ketchup dribbled down the side of his mouth.

"*Jingle Bells* suck," she shouted.

Yes, yes they do, kid.

But maybe not everything about Christmas sucked. Maybe Christmas and romance could go hand-in-hand like magic and life. Like twinkle lights and evergreen trees.

I stood and grabbed my jacket from the back of my chair.

"'Away to the window, she flew like a flash,'" Bathin quoted, leaving most of the apple pie on the table. He had a habit of following me around now that he was in possession of my soul. I didn't like it, but I wasn't going to let it slow me down.

"Where are you going?" he asked.

"To find a Christmas tree."

CHAPTER THREE

THE SAFEWAY parking lot was the last place in town still selling Christmas trees. Once I got there, I found out why.

"Delaney my darling. So good to see you!"

I crossed my arms and glared at the man who was standing between the discount trees.

He was my height, darker skinned, brilliant-eyed, and his smile could light a coal mine. His spiky black hair was hidden beneath a hat knit with little Christmas trees and a deer armed with a gun, stalking a hunter.

It had been a while since I'd seen my not-uncle, Crow, who was at the moment also the trickster god, Raven.

"Raven," I said.

"Now, now," he chided. "It hasn't been that long. You can still call me Crow. Give Uncle Crow-Crow a hug, Del-Del." He held his arms wide open and made *come here* motions with his hands.

I sighed. What I should do is tell him to get out of Ordinary. Recently, he'd cheated with both holding and not holding his power, which broke the rules of Ordinary. That had gotten him kicked out of town for a year. His little rule breaking trick had also set into motion the events that resulted in Ryder pledging himself to the god of contracts, which I kind of hated.

But he was my not-uncle, had known me my entire life, had been a friend of my father's. I missed him. So I walked over and gave him a hug. He smelled of pitch and warm pine needles and the spicy scent that was all him.

"You can't be here," I mumbled against his sweater. "You're a god and have to stay a god until a year has gone by. No putting down your power and vacationing. It's only been a few months since you left."

"Which is why I'm still a god. Raven. Trickster. Busy, busy time of year for a trickster god. So many New Year's resolutions to see to. So many new leaves to not turn over. I just dropped by to see if you liked my gift."

"Gift?"

"That's not something you see every day," Bathin said from behind me.

Crow stilled and I could feel his power moving through him, surrounding him, surrounding me. It was familiar. Protective.

But I didn't need protecting from the demon. The demon was old news. I stepped back.

"No fighting," I told them both.

"Wouldn't dream of it," Crow said. "You know I'm a lover not a fighter." That was true of the Crow on vacation without his god power. But Raven the god? Yeah, there were stories written about just how vicious a fighter he was.

"Black Feather," Bathin said. "It's been some time."

"Not long enough, Black Heart," Crow replied. "How did you manage to slime up onto this shore?"

"I was invited."

Crow looked at me. Really *looked*. I braced myself for a scolding. I knew he could see that Bathin had stolen my soul. I knew he wouldn't like it.

Surprisingly, he just winked.

"Negotiation is not the same as invitation, Black Heart," Crow said. "You of all people should know that. Have you gotten my gift, Pumpkin?" he asked me.

"No?"

"Pink, cute as a baby pig. Looks like a baby pig? It's a baby pig."

"The dragon?" I asked. "You sent me a dragon?"

"Dragon?" Bathin sounded truly startled. Enough that both Crow and I turned to look at him.

"Yes, demon," Crow said with so much smug-and-swagger, I rolled my eyes. "Delaney now has a pet dragon. Your move."

Bathin opened his mouth. Closed it. Scowled at Crow. Scowled at me. Then stuck his hands in the pockets of his slacks feigning indifference. "I don't see how a dragon makes any difference in anything."

"Don't you?" Crow was grinning now, and it was a lot more

god-Raven than Uncle-Crow.

It made me happy he was on my side. Usually.

"A dragon is of no concern to me."

"Of course it's not," Crow agreed. "It would only be a concern to you if you were trying to hide. You're not trying to hide from anyone or anything are you, Prince?"

Bathin went hard, all stone and blackness shot by silver light. His demon nature shone through the illusion he presented the world, and burned, burned, burned. He was angry.

He might even be afraid.

Of Crow? Or of the thing he was hiding from?

"No," Bathin said, the word ground out between teeth locked tight. "There is nothing I hide from."

"Isn't that wonderful?" Crow said. "Delaney, isn't that wonderful? Bathin here has nothing to fear. Not even your dragon."

"Do either of you want to tell me what you're really talking about?" I asked.

"No," they both said at the same time. Typical. The one thing a god and demon could agree upon was keeping me in the dark.

"Fine. Then move aside so I can buy a Christmas tree."

Bathin stepped back toward my Jeep, but Crow just grinned. "What kind of tree are you looking for today?"

"You aren't selling these."

"Actually, I am. Oh, and unrelated: you might hear about a tarantula infestation, but we both know that would be impossible. These trees were grown in the Northwest."

"Spiders? You sold people trees full of spiders?"

He glanced at the sky. "Maybe?"

"Maybe?"

"It might have been scorpions. Scorpions are much more available round these parts."

I slugged him in the arm. "Tell me you didn't sell trees infested with *anything*."

"Or what? You'll throw me out of town? No, wait. You already did that."

"Or I'll return my gift."

"Dragons are non-returnable."

"Nope. I am serious. I will find a way to kick the dragon out of town. You know I can."

He chuckled. "Fine. The worst anyone will find in the trees are some dead needles. Cross my heart." He swished his finger over his chest.

"That's your stomach."

"Or is it?" He waggled his eyes at me and I shook my head.

"Sell me a tree, Crow."

"Call me Uncle Crow and I'll make you a deal."

"Sell me a discount, uninfested tree, Uncle Crow."

"Now you're talking. Let me show you to my noblest of firs."

He wrapped his arm over my shoulder and I walked with him through a stand of dried out lopsided trees, and just for a few minutes, everything felt magical and good.

CHAPTER FOUR

"YOU'RE SURE it's a dragon?" Myra sorted the box of ornaments on the coffee table making sure each one had a good hook attached. "Crow is a trickster."

They were brand new red, gold, silver, green, and blue bulbs. They came with hooks. I didn't know why she was double-checking them.

"Pretty sure, yes." I stepped back from the six-foot tree that Myra and I had wrestled into the house a couple hours ago. It was not a prime example of its species.

It had missing branches down one side. Clumps of brown needles ringed the bottom third of the thing and shed at the slightest touch, like a porcupine had had an unfortunate run-in with a bottle of Nair.

The whole tree leaned precariously to the left. I'd tried to counter-weight it by adding an extra string of lights on the right, but that made the tree's deficiencies stand out, like a neon sign with too many blown letters.

"Think that's enough lights?"

Myra glanced up. Her black-lined eyes, page-boy bob, and bright lipstick gave her that sweet-but-tough rockabilly look. "If you put any more lights on that poor tree you're going to blow a fuse."

"The house has breakers, not fuses." At least I thought it did. Ryder and his dad had pretty much built this house on the lake just east of the main road that ran through town. Since Ryder was an architect, I didn't think he'd live in a house that was still using fuses.

"And the tree isn't poor. It's…well, I'm not going to lie, it's way past its sell date. Maybe I'll just add one more string."

"Step away from the twinkle lights, crazy woman," Myra said without looking at me. "It's perfect. A couple dozen ornaments, some tinsel, and he'll never know you installed it all at the last minute."

I lifted my hair off the back of my neck, thought about binding it back in a ponytail, then decided it didn't matter. "Okay, ornament me." I held out my hand like a TV show doctor demanding a scalpel.

"You put a star on top," Myra noted.

A shiny red five-pointed star crowned the tree. I shrugged.

"I didn't think you liked stars on trees," she said.

"Seemed like the right thing to do. A tradition."

"Why did you even get a tree, Delaney?" Myra walked over with the ornaments and nursed a fragile glass orb into my hand. "You haven't gotten a tree for years."

"It always seemed like a lot of work." I placed the first bulb. I smiled. The glass orb glittered so prettily, it made me happy. Then it hit me. This would be the first Christmas I'd ever spent with Ryder. This was the first ornament I'd ever hung on our tree.

Our tree. A warm hum thrilled beneath my skin. I had the sudden urge to put on a Santa hat. To make hot cocoa and stir it with a candy cane.

It was almost like I was starting to catch the Christmas spirit. I blamed Jean.

"Delaney?"

"What?"

"Why the Christmas cactus?"

"You mean the tree?"

"That's not much of a tree."

"Mean." I turned toward the tree. "Don't listen to her. You're beautiful."

"Ugly-cute at best."

"Just because you and Jean always pick such perfect trees doesn't mean this one

should go to waste. At least it doesn't have tarantulas."

Myra frowned. "Crow?"

"Crow."

"And he's not in Ordinary any more?"

"He said he had just stopped in to see me. He left town as soon as he sold me the tree."

She shook her head and handed me another ornament. "So why now? Why do you want a tree this year?"

I didn't say anything as I hung three more bulbs. That was a good question. I had a good answer, but I wasn't sure I was ready to share it.

"It's Ryder," she supplied. "You're doing this because of him, aren't you?"

I could argue, but she'd know I was lying. I nodded. "He told me that when he was little, he loved the lights on the Christmas tree. That it's one of his favorite parts of the holidays. I didn't want him to come home to a dark living room. And even if it's only for a couple days, we—*he*—should have a tree. That's not too ridiculous, is it?"

"No. That's…" Her voice went soft. "That's sweet. That's good. That's…love."

Neither of us said anything, but the dragon by the fireplace snuffled loudly, then squeaked at Spud.

Spud had been crouched in front of the dragon, ears up, tail wagging. He now crept forward, belly-crawling toward the pig with a small stuffed frog in his mouth.

The dragon seemed to enjoy watching the ever-cheerful dog cautiously approach. They'd been going at this since I'd driven the dragon around yesterday and it had finally just trotted into the house and straight to the fireplace, as if it were perfectly happy to live here.

At first Spud had barked. Then, after one deep rumble from the pig, which, yes, it is sort of startling to hear a pig roar, Spud had wagged his tail like it was going to propel him to the moon.

All of Spud's running around and barking at the amused but unmoved dragon yesterday had turned into Spud sneakily offering to share his stuffed toy hoard with the pig today.

This, it appeared, might be a winning tactic. The pig had already been gifted with a stuffed hamburger, a flounder, and a one-legged cow. It looked very, very pleased with its growing stash.

Myra nodded. "He'll love it. When is Ryder supposed to be here?"

I tried not to let my worry show. "A couple hours ago."

"That's not too bad."

"More like five hours ago."

"Weather?"

"That's what I'm guessing."

As if to punctuate the point, the wind and rain battered the west facing windows hard enough I could feel the sturdy little cabin take the hit.

The near-freezing rain had flung onto shore last night with seventy-mile-an-hour gusts. The storm had already galloped east over the Coast Range and dumped five inches of snow there, iced up the valley, and according to weather reports, was in the process of slapping blizzard warnings across the Cascade Range.

Children from the Coast Range eastward were vibrating in joy over the white Christmas they'd be getting. Travelers were advised to stay home and stay away from the passes. All the stores were out of milk and bread.

I wondered if Ryder had decided not to chance the trip. He might have turned back or sheltered somewhere along the way. That would have been the smart move. The forecast called for more ice to follow the snow, enough to shut down the passes and much of I-5.

"Have you called him?" Myra asked.

"It goes to voice mail."

She didn't say anything while I hung the rest of the ornaments. Whatever Christmas spirit I'd been feeling was getting railroaded by worry.

"He'll be okay." Myra pressed a mug of coffee into my hand, and I realized I'd been standing there for a while, staring at the tree, my mind a million miles away. Or exactly one hundred and ninety-one miles away.

"I know," I said. "He's lived in Oregon and Chicago. He knows how to handle snow. He won't do anything stupid."

But my heart was heavy and my pulse was rapping. Why hadn't he answered his phone? Maybe he'd been stranded, ran out of battery on his phone. Maybe he was stuck in traffic, moving slowly along.

Maybe he was just outside of town and almost home.

"Are you sure it's a dragon?" She pointed her coffee at the fireplace.

The dragon-pig had acquired several more stuffed things and had stacked them into a pile. Spud must have offered enough of his toy hoard to have gained the dragon's favor. The dog was curled up on top of the toys. Dragon was right there with him, sprawled on his mountain of treasure, little piggy head propped on a blissed-out Spud's back. That dog and that pig could not look more content.

It was cute. They were cute.

"I'm sure it's a dragon," I said.

"Isn't it too small and soft? I know they can be anything, but I've never heard of one that turned itself into something so…adorable. Plus, this is Crow we're talking about. *Crow.*"

"You know what?" I said in a loud conversational tone, "you're right. I should take some of those toys back to Spud's box. They don't need that many."

The pig opened one eye. It glittered with fire, and a little puff of smoke drifted out its snout. The pig drew the toy hoard in closer, making it clear I touched it at my own peril.

I raised an eyebrow at Myra.

"Okay," she said. "I see it. It's a dragon. I thought he was joking."

"Nope."

"Any idea why Crow wants you to have it?"

"Something to do with it bothers Bathin. He can't hide from it? They weren't very clear."

We both drank our coffee and stared at the mythical farmyard conundrum.

"Crow called him Black Heart," I said.

"The pig?"

"The demon."

"Huh."

"He also called him Prince."

Myra sipped her coffee. I knew she was turning those little hints over in her big, beautiful brain, seeing which pieces of her research into all things demon fit with that information.

"Want me to try and figure the dragon out?" she finally offered.

"Gods, yes," I said on an exhale. "I was hoping you'd volunteer. I've asked it a hundred yes/no questions but it just ignores me."

"I'll check the books. See if we've ever had this dragon out of its cave before and if so, what happened then. See what kind of history it has with demons. And trickster gods."

"Perfect. I owe you one."

She handed me her empty coffee cup. "You owe me so many more than one. I'm going to check in at the station before I head home. I'll call if there are any emergencies. Otherwise, try not to worry too much about Ryder."

"I won't." Lies.

"He's okay and he'll be home soon."

"I know."

She narrowed her eyes. "And don't sell your soul while I'm gone."

"That joke's getting old."

"Not a joke. You promised us you'd make no stupid decision without consulting with at least one of us."

"I promise I will make no deal, do no stupid deed without either you or Jean consulted and on board between now and when I see you next."

"Good."

I followed her to the door so I could lock it behind her.

"He's going to love that ugly tree." She waved one finger up and down at me and smiled. "I like this look on you, Delaney."

"What look?"

"Love."

I tried to act annoyed, but couldn't hold it for very long. She flipped up her coat hood and forged out into the wind and rain.

I stayed there inside the doorway, needing to see her walk down to the cruiser, needing to see her get in it, start it, and drive away safely.

Then I went inside and tried to keep my promises.

CHAPTER FIVE

I'D LEFT the porch light on, and the fireplace still warmed the living room. Myra had left hours ago and I was curled up in a blanket on the couch with the stuffed eyeball Spud had offered me for comfort. It was almost midnight and I couldn't sleep. Tomorrow was Christmas eve.

The storm wasn't letting up.

My phone in my hand was fully charged and utterly, exhaustingly silent. So silent I'd turned on Ryder's sound system and queued up a Christmas music playlist to take my mind off my worry.

It wasn't working.

The song switched to Karen Carpenter's soulful alto soothing her way through *Have Yourself A Merry Little Christmas.* As soon as she reached the troubles being out of sight lyrics, I couldn't stay still.

My troubles were right here in front of me. Or, really, that was the trouble. Ryder wasn't here in front of me.

I got up and paced. The glittering, twinkling lights of the tree filled the room with a sense of promise, of miracles, of magic.

Before I could overthink it, I lay on my back and scooted under the tree. I spit a few dead needles off my mouth and wiped my face in case of spiders, then looked up through the branches.

Bundles of tiny lights spangled the tree in a fairy field of reds, blues, green, yellows, and purples. White twinklers winked like galaxies stirred by a winter wind. Fir needles prickled against the light, shadows coyly curled around curved-mirror ornaments that hung joyful and fat.

It was beautiful. I could see how this would enchant little Ryder. It felt private, hushed, magical. Here under the tree was a secret moment where all the hopes and wishes of Christmas hung waiting on silvery hooks.

I'd told Jean I wasn't going to wish for snow. I'd told her

I'd use my wishes for more important things.

I'll Be Home For Christmas started, and Ryder's promise to be here, with me, echoed through me with every note.

So I made a wish.

Please let him be all right. Please let him be safe. Please let him call me so we can laugh about this. I need to hear his voice. I need to know he's okay.

I repeated those words, over and over until the song ended.

And then my phone rang.

I scuttled out from under that tree so fast, I nearly tipped it over.

"Are you okay?" The words were out of my mouth almost before I'd swiped the screen to accept the call.

"Hey, beautiful." Ryder's words were a little slow, like he'd had one too many drinks. "Merry Christmas."

"Where are you? Are you okay? Are you drinking? *Drinking?* You better not be driving."

I couldn't hear any noise in the background, which was a little weird.

"So, change in plans." He cleared his throat, which turned into a hard rattling cough. "There's been. Change."

"Where are you?" I jogged over to my laptop, pinging Jean, who was on duty tonight.

Her face appeared in a little box on my screen. "What's wrong?"

"Ryder's on the line."

"Your phone?"

I nodded. "His speech is slurred."

She was already busy typing. "Keep him talking."

"In my truck?" Ryder finally answered. "The…I must have blacked out for a minute." He coughed again and it didn't sound good.

"Are you hurt? Honey. Are you hurt?"

I could hear his breathing, wanted him to answer, needed him to answer.

"Delaney?" he said it clearly, like he was trying to get a grip. "Right. I'm outside Sisters. Was…last I…before I blacked out."

"The GPS on your phone is active." I had resorted to cop-voice because any other voice would be trembling. "Jean's getting a lock on you. Are you on the road? Are you driving?"

"No? No. I got out. A woman and kids. Oh, hell. I need to check. They were stuck and I was pushing, pushed. The ditch." He grunted and I heard the creak of what I could only assume was his truck door opening.

"Ryder Bailey, do not exit your vehicle," I ordered. Images of him on a precarious cliff or stalled in the middle of the highway, or stuck in a snow bank filled my mind.

"They were babies, Laney, just babies."

"Who? The woman and kids you pushed out of a ditch?"

"Yeah." He panted, each inhale hitched as if hooking on something sharp. "They were here…"

"Are you on the road? Do you see any markers?"

When he didn't answer, I shot Jean a look.

"I don't think he's outside Sisters," she said. "Heavy snowfall took out a couple towers. Give me a second."

"Ryder," I said. "you need to get back in the truck where it's warm."

I heard wind, I heard his breath, then all I heard was a very soft, "Oh," before his phone cut out.

The Christmas music in the background was sweeping through *Carol of the Bells*. For some reason, I noticed it, like that one detail was important. The rest of my brain refused to work, to move past the silence, that final: "Oh."

I stared down, down, down at my phone as if my hand belonged to someone else. As if I were floating somewhere near the ceiling, operating my body from a distance. "Answer your phone." I whispered as I dialed him back. It went to voice mail. I dialed again.

And again.

And again.

"What?" Ryder's voice. Rough. Faint.

I blew out my breath, anger, fear, panic. Inhaled slowly.

Keep it together, Delaney.

"Ryder, tell me exactly where you are right now."

He grunted. I could tell he was moving around. "On my back? In snow. You woke me up?" He moved. "Blood. Someone's bleeding?"

"Is someone with you?"

"No."

"Are you bleeding?"

He paused, finally: "Yes."

"Where?"

"Head. I'm seeing double too. Hell." He sucked a breath and sort of exhaled a shaky laugh. "I think I got run off the road. I don't remember getting hit…"

"Where is your truck?"

"Uh. Over there."

"Get in your truck. Now, Ryder. Right now."

"So bossy."

I bit my lip to keep from screaming at him. "I *am* your boss, Reserve Officer. Now move it."

He groaned. "My GPS?"

"Yes. We're narrowing it down."

There was nothing but short, huffed breaths, and then more groaning, a few curse words, and finally the sound of a door shutting again.

"Try the engine," I told him.

I could hear the battery clicking and knew that engine wasn't going to turn over.

"Well, that sucks." He swallowed thickly. "I'm down a ravine."

"Can you see anything else?"

"Snow."

"He's in a ravine in his truck," I told Jean.

"Keep that cell on," she said.

"Do you have emergency supplies?" I asked him.

He shifted a bit. "I think I gave them to the mom." He exhaled slowly. "Freezing to death was not in my holiday plans."

"You're not dying. I won't let you die."

"Was joke," he slurred.

"You stay awake," I ordered. "Bundle up with everything you have and stay awake."

More movement. His voice was a little muffled when he spoke. "Talk to me, Delaney. Keep me awake."

"I put up a Christmas tree."

"You told me that already."

Right. Oops.

"I laid down under it and stared at the lights."

Pause.

"Ryder?"

"Here. Still here. Was it nice?"

"Beautiful. You need to stay awake. Are your eyes open?"

"Mmm."

"Liar. Open your eyes."

A sigh. Then, "Tell me something. A thing you liked about Christmas."

"When I was little?"

"Yeah."

"Presents."

"If you want me to stay awake, better tell me a longer story."

"All right, hang on." I wracked my brain and glanced at Jean again.

"Somewhere off of Highway 20 near Three Fingered Jack." Jean's fingers were flying. "Emergency services are stretched thin. There's no way a vehicle can get through that. Highway 20 is closed under snow and ice. I'll see if I can contact Santiam Ski Patrol. But that's a lot of terrain to cover."

"Hey," Ryder's voice was rough and whispery. "Thought I got a story?"

"Right. Hold on, I'm thinking."

Jean speared me with a look. "We need to call on something other than emergency services if we want to find him quickly."

That was one advantage to being a small town full of supernatural beings and vacationing gods. We could call on people with unusual abilities when things got bad.

Of course, most supernatural beings wanted to be compensated for their effort and time. And some of them, I thought as my soul-losing deal with Bathin sprang to mind, set a pretty high price.

"Get someone," I told her. "Now."

I turned all my attention back to Ryder. "Okay, you have to answer every time I say your name. Got that, Ryder?"

"Affirmative. Roger that."

I started pacing again, envying the dragon and dog who

were curled up and comfy in front of the fire as the storm raged outside.

The tree lights caught my eye, and I gazed up at the star. I knew what memory I should share.

"When I was little, my mom read me a book about a Christmas star. It was supposed to be a sweet story about the little star that fell to earth and got lost. Finally, with some help from forest creatures, a snowman, and a couple children, the star was set upon a Christmas tree to shine brightly and bring joy to all. Are you listening, Ryder?"

"Star. Tree. Snowmen. Riveting."

I couldn't help but smile. "Hey, you wanted me to share. I could just read you the phone book."

"You don't own a phone book. Get back to the star. What happened?"

"First, you need to know I *hated* that story."

"This is supposed to be a happy memory, Delaney."

"Shut up. I'm getting there. I hated the story because it always made me sad."

He grunted. "Why?"

"Dad asked me that one night when he found me staring at the Christmas tree and crying. I tried to lie. I was never very good at lying to him."

"No," he agreed, "you weren't."

I liked that Ryder knew that about me. That he had been there in my life, known me that long.

"I told him the story made me sad. I was sorry for the star because when it fell, it had to leave behind all its family and friends. Even though it got to shine bright as a Christmas star for a few days, after that it would be all alone, stuck down on earth and looking up at the friends and the place it would never be a part of again.

"Still with me, Ryder?"

"I'm here. Little lonely star far away from home and friends. You know, you could have come up with a less depressing story to take my mind off my situation."

"There's more to it. Dad told me distance couldn't keep us from the ones we love. He said we are all made of stardust, all a part of each other. Even though the little star was stuck here on earth, it carried its friends and family in its heart because it held the memory of the things they had shared, the laughter, the sorrow, the joy. He said we can't lose those we love, because the sky, the earth, and everything between—including us—is part of the same thing: love."

A pause ticked by.

"I miss him," Ryder said. Still a little slurred, still a little slow. "Your dad."

"I do too. But when he told me that, it didn't make me feel better. I was still sad for the little star."

"Such a softy. How did you end up a cop?"

I laughed. "A lot of hard work. Dad knew I was still sad. I could never hide that from him, either. So you know what happened?"

"Mmmm?"

"I woke up on Christmas morning and the living room was filled with stars. Paper stars hung from the ceiling, from the windows, from the branches of the Christmas tree." I swallowed a smile remembering. "He'd cut a hundred paper stars out of gold, silver, white, and blue. Must have taken him hours to hang them all. Written on every single one of them was one word: love."

I was quiet while I tried to corral the emotions that came along with the memory. I hadn't thought about that Christmas morning in years. "He told me the stars had come down from the heavens to visit the Christmas tree star so it wouldn't be lonely. He told me it was a Christmas wish come true."

"Delaney," he said, as if just talking was taking every ounce of energy he had. Or maybe the story had touched him, a little bit of my remembered joy and sorrow now his. "I need to say something. I should have said it a long time ago. Thought I'd have time. Thought we'd have time…"

"Don't," I interrupted, afraid that if he said something, if he said he loved me, he'd really be saying good-bye. "Just save whatever you have to say for when you come home. Because you promised you'd come home, Ryder."

"Laney…I'm sorry."

CHAPTER SIX

"YOU PROMISED." I wiped at my stinging eyes and straightened my shoulders. I was not going to lose him before Christmas. I was not going to lose him at all.

"Delaney?" Jean said. "Myra should be there in a minute."

As if summoned by her voice, there was a knock at the door. Myra must have been close by. I jogged over, glanced through the peep hole, then let Myra and the demon who stood beside her into the house.

"Bathin is going to find him and bring him back," Myra said before I'd even shut the door.

"This is news to Bathin," he said. "We do remember Bathin is a demon and doesn't like to do helpful things?"

Myra's eyes went hard and glittery while her eyebrows lowered. "We know Bathin will do this because it's an order and requirement if he wants to remain in Ordinary."

"As if you would let me leave, Myra Reed. I own your pretty sister's very pretty soul."

Yeah, like I said, sometimes the supernaturals named a high price for a favor. I still hadn't found a way to get my soul back, though I was working on it, and so was Myra.

"Don't care," I cut in. "Ryder is injured, in his truck, somewhere near Three Fingered Jack. The highway's blocked, and Jean hasn't had any luck getting hold of search and rescue. Name a price, Bathin. Let's get this rolling."

Finding people and moving them was one of Bathin's powers. He'd already rescued a kidnapped vampire who'd been sunk beneath the ocean in a crate. Finding a truck in a snow storm shouldn't be nearly as difficult.

"What will you give me if I do this little favor?" he asked.

"No," Myra said.

"A favor in return," I offered.

"No," Myra said again.

The corner of Bathin's mouth slid up into a sexy grin.

"Choices, choices ladies. Yes or no?"

"One favor," I said again, "from me, to be collected within one year's time. It can be anything you want, as long as it doesn't break any of Ordinary's laws, nor go against my own moral code."

"Anything I want?" His grin turned a little predatory. I had to wonder how I always ended up bargaining away parts of myself for the good of others. I'd like to say it came with the job of being Chief of Police in this oddball little town, but I knew better. I would bargain away almost anything for Ryder.

"Don't." Ryder's voice was distant, but still clear. I pressed the phone harder against my ear.

"It's okay," I said. "Myra's here. She won't let me break the don't-do-anything-stupid rule."

"Bargaining with a demon is the reason we *made* the rule," he reminded me. The last few words faded a bit, as if he was having trouble getting enough breath in his lungs to speak. "It's stupid."

"I know. But it's going to be okay. You just stay awake and keep breathing. You're going to be home soon."

"I'll do it," Myra said. "For you."

Bathin straightened as if everything in him was suddenly awake and laser focused. Then he turned, all fire and heat and wide shoulders and muscular body crowding into her space. "You'll do what, exactly? For me." His voice was more rumble than words.

For a moment, Myra's eyes lost that edge and something else filled them. Desire? Lust? Surprise?

The look he was giving her should have had a combustible warning on it.

"For Delaney," Myra said all soft and breathy. "Not you."

He smiled, lifted one hand as if to touch her face, as if to stroke her skin.

And never got the chance. Myra took one strong step back, her cheeks flushing red, her eyes cool and hard again.

Her breathing was a little faster than a moment ago, but that could just be adrenaline from anger.

It wasn't adrenaline from anger.

"I'll offer the same terms as Delaney," she said. "One

favor, to be collected within the year. I'll do what you want as long as it doesn't break any of Ordinary's rules or laws, nor go against my moral code or free will."

"You added a few terms."

"I don't give anything away easily."

His eyebrow quirked. "I know."

Pretty sure he liked that about her. A lot.

"One favor, due to me, upon my request, in so much as it doesn't break Ordinary's rules or laws, nor go against your moral code or free will. Correct?"

"Wait," I said.

She nodded, the color still high on her cheeks as she stared up at him. "Yes." She squared her shoulders as if steeling herself against the pull of his charisma. "In exchange, you will find Ryder now, and bring him here, to us in this room, whole in body and mind, and in no way bound to you nor any other creature, person, or thing."

"Wait," I said again.

"Done." And then Bathin was gone.

"You did not just bargain with that demon," I nearly shouted.

She shrugged like it was nothing. It wasn't nothing. "One of us was going to."

"Not one of us, *me*."

"You already gave up your soul. It was my turn to do something. You aren't the only one looking after this town, you know. And all I traded was a small favor."

I glared at her for a minute, but it was like trying to stare down a brick wall.

"Ryder," I said while I scowled at my sister. "Bathin's coming to get you and bring you home."

I waited. There was no answer, not even the ragged breathing I'd gotten used to.

"Ryder?"

I heard the truck door open, and a small groan that was almost a whimper. Then the shushing static of the phone being moved. "I've found your nearly frozen Prince Charming," Bathin said.

"Is he breathing?"

A pause, then, "So far."

"Bring him to me."

"Oh, I will. Eventually."

The phone disconnected. "Eventually? What kind of crap is *eventually*?" I yelled.

Myra rubbed at her forehead. "I didn't narrow the time specifications. I should have thought of that."

"No, you shouldn't have promised him a favor, Myra. What were you thinking?"

"That you aren't supposed to make any more deals with demons."

"And *you* are?"

"This time? Yes. Ryder needs you. I didn't know if Bathin was going to demand an immediate favor just to take you away when Ryder needs you."

Oh. I hadn't thought of that. "We seriously need to find someone else in town who can teleport," I muttered. "Maybe for the price of donuts. Demons are too complicated."

"Who can we call?" she asked.

I pushed my fingers back through my hair, thinking. My gaze landed on the pig. Crow said Bathin couldn't hide from it. Did that mean the pig could find the demon?

"Dragon?" I really needed to find out if it had a name. "Do you know where the demon is?"

The pig lifted its head from where it was propped on Spud's back.

"Demon?" I repeated. "Bathin? He was just here. We told him to go find Ryder?"

"I don't think it understands you," Myra said.

"Dragons understand human speech." I said. "He's called Black Heart?" I tried.

The pig jumped to its feet and trotted over to me. It sat in front of me, head tipped up. And while it was still cute, there was fire in those piggy eyes, and smoke in that piggy snout. The space around it had gone wobbly like a fun house mirror.

"Find Black Heart and the man with him. The man is Ryder Bailey. Bring them here. Now."

The pig stood. For a moment, just the flash of a splintered second, there was a dragon in my living room. It was huge and black with wings of fire and claws of steel. And then it disappeared.

The scent of burned coal and sandalwood filled the air.

"Wow," Myra said. "You have a dragon."

I exhaled a shaky breath. "I really need to read up on the care and feeding."

Spud hadn't missed out on the commotion. He was on his feet and at my side, stiff-eared, stiff-tailed, staring into the space the dragon had just vacated. He growled, then barked.

The room went wobbly again, and I reached over for Myra at the same time she reached for me.

The pig appeared. It snorted out a satisfied plume of smoke that curled around its head and then drifted toward the ceiling.

Next to the pig, stood Bathin. Bathin did not look happy. As a matter of fact, he looked a little shaken.

I did not care. Because Bathin had his shoulder propped under Ryder's arm, his hand holding him firmly around the waist.

"You sent the dragon after me?" Bathin asked. "The *dragon*? Do you know how much noise it makes in the…you know what? Never mind. If you ever do that again, Delaney Reed, I will make you pay."

"I've already paid. Myra's paid too. Hold up your end of the bargain next time, Bathin." I wasn't listening to his threats anyway.

Ryder was unconscious. "Bring him to the bedroom." I rushed over and touched Ryder's face. Cold. Touched his neck, pressed for a pulse.

There. Strong and steady. Some of the fear in my stomach unclenched. I could breathe again, could think again. "Move it, Bathin. Now. That way."

Bathin rolled his eyes but didn't argue. In the distance I was aware of Myra talking to Jean, was aware of Spud barking like crazy and rubbing on the dragon while the dragon stared at the demon like he was something it would enjoy eating. In the distance I could hear someone singing about silver bells. But everything in me was tuned into Ryder, all my senses, all my focus.

He was alive. Unconscious. Blood, sticky and thick,

streaked from the hairline above his left eyebrow down his cheek. He was bundled in snow gear: heavy coat and gloves, layered shirts beneath, snow pants and heavy boots. His clothes were damp, either from when he'd been lying out in the snow when we were on the phone, or maybe before that, when he helped the mom and kids.

Bathin laid him on the bed, gently enough it surprised me.

"He's too cold," the demon said almost as if he were talking to himself. "Has a lump on the side of his head, but that wound's not serious. Get him warm and he'll be fine."

"You get a medical certificate from Hells R Us?" I pushed at his shoulder so I could move around him and get in the bed to take care of Ryder. It was like pushing a steel building. He was built like a concrete mixer.

He'd once told me he could take any form he wanted. It only made sense he'd chosen more muscles than a barbarian under that white button-down shirt.

"I've seen a lot of people on death's doorstep," he said. "I do my best wheeling and dealing in their time of desperation and need. When they have nothing left to lose." He stood back, crossed his arms over his chest. "He's not going to die."

I was listening, but working fast to get Ryder's boots unlaced, pulled off. His socks were dry–that was good. I took them off anyway, then his snow pants and the thermals he wore beneath them.

I rubbed my palms over his thighs, warm, muscular and strong with a long bruise spreading down his left hip. Then I stroked down his legs to his thick, firm calves, ankles, and checked his toes, cupping my hands over them briefly. No frostbite. No breaks. No wounds.

He started shivering, which was a good sign. I dragged all the blankets and the down comforter over him, then scrambled off the bed to dig out two more blankets from the top shelf of his closet.

Myra was suddenly next to the bed, a warm washcloth in her hand and a First Aid kit open on the bedside table. She gave me the cloth and I cleaned the blood off his face, felt for the bump Bathin had told me about. Left side, but the bleeding had stopped.

Taking off his coat and shirts revealed more of his skin, and it took everything I had not to just strip and curl up beside him. I wanted to be close to his heartbeat, drown in the scent of him, be captured in his heat.

I wanted to touch him, wrap around him, make him understand he was undeniably mine.

I settled for a single kiss on his non-bruised shoulder before I covered him back up. His left side had taken most of the impact of whatever had happened to send him off the road. His head, shoulder, ribs, and hip were all black and blue.

He stirred at my touch and made a small sound at the back of his throat like he was having a good dream.

"You're home," I told him. "You're safe. You made it before Christmas. You didn't break your promise."

His eyes fluttered, finally opened a slit. "Delaney?"

"I'm right here. You're home. You can sleep. You can sleep now."

He shivered a little harder.

"You should get into bed with him," Myra said.

I jumped. I had forgotten she was still in the room with us. "Do you think he needs a doctor?" I pulled the covers away and slipped beneath, immediately curling up on his right side. His arm drifted down to hold me close.

"No," Ryder whispered.

"You don't get a vote, baby." I leaned my face into his chest, wrapped my arm over him, then tangled our legs up together. He made another happy sound.

"I think he's okay," Myra said. "I'll stay here tonight and come in and check on you both a couple times, okay?"

I nodded. She must have seen it because she cleaned up a few things–probably the clothes I'd thrown on the floor–then left the room. I didn't know if Bathin stayed too, but I knew Myra would handle him with the same calm she handled everything else. Plus, we had a dragon on our side.

I pressed myself across as much of Ryder as I could reach.

I'd almost lost him.

He'd almost said good-bye.

What would I have done without him?

"I love you, Ryder," I whispered. "I think I always have. I

know I do now. And I'll say it every day, no matter what happens. I love you. I love you."

I felt the bed shake as Spud jumped up to join us. He crawled up to carefully nose at our faces, then, satisfied, settled down behind Ryder's legs. The bed took another dip.

"*Oink.*"

"He's hurt. You need to get off the bed."

"*Oink oink.*"

"Did you just tell me no?"

"*Oink.*"

I scowled, but the dragon-pig turned a quick circle then curled up on Ryder's bad side, rooting at the covers until half his head was hidden by the folds of the blankets.

Ryder shivered, then sighed. And I knew why. I could feel the heat radiating off the little dragon from here. It was like sitting next to a fire. Warm and relaxing.

Ryder's breathing evened out, deep and slow, and his muscles all softened and became heavy. I listened to his heart beat, listened to winter chewing away outside our cozy warm bedroom, listened to the dragon and the dog breathing, and fell asleep with them all.

CHAPTER SEVEN

MYRA WOKE me up before she left. It wasn't even light out yet. "I'll take your shift this morning. You stay with Ryder."

I blinked until my vision cleared. Ryder had shifted in the night and was now curled around both the dragon and the dog, his back to me. They were all snoring.

I smiled. I so needed a picture of that so I could blackmail him with it later.

"See you tonight." Myra started toward the bedroom door.

"Wait, Mymy." I slipped out of bed and stopped outside in the hall with her. "You go home. I'm going to take my shift."

"You need to stay here."

"He's sleeping. I'll call someone to keep an eye on him while I'm out. It's your day off."

I always worked Christmas Eve. Now that Ryder was home safe and the storm had blown through, I wanted to get eyes on the town. I needed to see if there was any damage, and make sure everyone had a warm place to celebrate the holiday.

"Just let me get dressed," I said.

"Prefer you didn't." That voice, low with a burr of sleepiness, had me turning quickly.

Ryder stood in the doorway to the bedroom. Well, leaned there. The comforter was wrapped around his shoulders, held closed at the front. His hair was sticking up at all angles. There was a crease down the side of his face from how hard he'd slept on one side, and his beard was thicker than he usually kept it.

But his smile made his eyes light with green fire, and set butterflies loose in my heart. He'd never looked more amazing.

"Hey," I said. "How are you feeling?"

"Better. A little foolish. Happy to be home. Happier to see you."

He'd moved while he spoke, and stopped right in front of me. "I thought I told you not to make deals with demons."

"You did. And I didn't. Myra made the deal."

"Thought you knew better, Myra." He pitched his voice so she could hear him, but didn't look away from me for one second.

"I missed you," he said.

"I missed you too."

He opened the comforter, welcoming me into his warmth. I went willingly, thankfully, wrapping my arms around his ribs, pressing my cheek against the healthy heat of his skin, inhaling the scents of love and trust and home and him.

"Maybe you should stay." He shifted so we were slotted together even closer.

I took one last deep breath and rubbed my hand down his back. I could feel him wince a little when my fingers ghosted over his bruises.

"I need to work. I'll be home in time to change for Christmas Eve over at Myra's house."

"Or you could stay in, if you want," Myra offered because she was a pretty awesome sister most of the time. Okay, all of the time.

"No." I stepped out of the comforter, every inch of distance between Ryder and me making me wish I'd let Myra take my shift so I could stay wrapped up in him all day.

"Delaney," Myra said.

I took one look at her bloodshot eyes, the tired lines across her forehead, and her wrinkled clothes. She'd stayed all night here on the couch, keeping an eye on us.

"You're officially off duty, Officer," I said.

She scowled. "Do not pull the boss card."

"Shuffled, cut, and dealt. Go home. Take a nap. Get the feast cooking. Ryder's gonna be fine here, and we'll be by around eight for drinks and dinner."

"Are you bringing the demon?" she asked.

I couldn't tell from the carefully blank look on her face if she wanted a yes or no answer. "He doesn't really listen to me," I said. "Frankly, I'm surprised he didn't stay here bothering us all night."

"I told him to leave us alone."

"And he listened to you."

She shrugged. "There was also the dragon issue."

"The dragon was sleeping with us. Mymy, Bathin doesn't listen to anyone…"

"Not this again," she muttered.

"...except you."

"Yeah, well, he knows I have all of Dad's old journals and can banish him from Ordinary if I want."

"Can you?" Last I heard she hadn't found a way to be permanently rid of the pest.

"Not yet." Then she gave me a dazzling smile. "Getting there though."

She waved and headed toward the door. "See you tonight. Don't worry if you're late. Ryder, call if you need anything." I heard the door open, then shut behind her.

There was a commotion of four-footed things running out of the bedroom behind us, the dragon in the lead, carrying a pillow in its mouth with Spud quick on his heels.

They disappeared into the living room and we were silent a moment.

"So we have a pig?" Ryder asked.

"Dragon."

Spud barked, the dragon oinked then growled, a very dragony-sound. Spud barked again as if excited he'd made the piggy do a dragon thing.

"Dragon. Okay. What does it eat?" Ryder asked.

"Whatever it wants." I smiled sweetly at his raised eyebrows. And yes, he looked excited to have a dragon in the house.

"Is there some way it communicates? Telepathy? Song? Riddle?" The man loved finding out what kind of creatures we had in town, and I loved his enthusiasm, even though he was trying to play it cool.

"One oink means yes, two means no."

His eyebrows dropped and he frowned. "That's no fun."

I laughed and pressed a kiss on his mouth. A quick kiss, a gentle kiss, a kiss that was not supposed to linger. But his hands shot out, caught both of my arms. He held me to him, stepping into me as he did so, angling his thigh between mine. I was walked backward until my back bumped into the wall.

We never stopped kissing, couldn't stop kissing. I swept my

tongue along his bottom lip and he opened, his tongue licking into my mouth as we tasted, hungered, devoured.

I never wanted it to stop.

Never wanted to know a day when his hands wouldn't be warm on my body, when his mouth wouldn't be pressing secret words into mine.

Finally, we came up for air and we hung there, heads tipped, both of us staring at the other's mouth.

I wanted to say it again. To ask him if he had heard me last night. To know if he understood that I loved him. Loved his laughter, his strength, his steady calm.

But I had already told him once, in the dark, in the relief that he was alive and with me. Maybe that would be enough.

Maybe that was all we were supposed to have. Maybe we didn't need the words. Maybe we just needed this. Us.

I shifted, sliding my leg down off from his hip where I had somehow put it, and settling all my weight on my feet. I pressed his chest, and he stepped back.

"Go to the doctor and make sure you don't have a concussion," I said.

"I don't have a concussion."

"Go anyway."

He sighed. "So you'll be home before eight?" His voice was sex, and it took everything I had not to just strip right there and drag him off to bed.

"I promise."

He searched my gaze for some other meaning behind those words, the same words he'd told me before he'd gotten stranded.

"Are you going to be okay alone?" I asked.

"Yeah. If I need anything, I'll call. Delaney? Thank you for being on the phone with me. For keeping me awake. For getting me home."

"Like I'd let you miss our first Christmas together."

I waited for the words. They were there, in his gaze, in the soft pause of breath when he studied my mouth, my face, my eyes.

"I–"

A muted thump in the living room was followed by a crash

then the sound of Spud running for his hiding corner.

Moment destroyed.

"I should check on the dragon?" he said.

"You should."

His hands fell away. "But tonight?"

"It's Christmas Eve, Ryder. It's going to be a good night." I smiled, then moved past him and into the bedroom to change into my uniform.

CHAPTER EIGHT

ONE GOOD thing about living on the coast of Oregon: we knew how to weather the storms. Things didn't usually get sketchy in our sturdy little town until the winds reached somewhere above an hundred-mile-an-hour.

But there were always little damages from high wind gusts. A fence, a store sign, garbage cans in the wrong yard.

Mrs. Yate's penguin getting stolen.

Not that the wind had taken it, but apparently a storm was the perfect cover for the pranksters who liked to abscond with her concrete yard penguin.

"It's Christmas for goodness sakes," Mrs. Yates said for the tenth time as I stood there on her twinkling light-draped porch taking her complaint. "I always decorate the yard."

"It looks nice."

"And the house."

"That looks nice too."

"And the penguin. Really, he's the star of the whole thing."

"I understand."

"He has a blog, you know."

I did know. The penguin's frequent kidnappings, creative hiding places, and hostage photos had taken a small corner of the internet by storm. That penguin was pretty much our most famous citizen. And Mrs. Yates ate up the stardom-by-proxy with a spoon.

I'd always suspected that most of the kidnappings had been orchestrated by the high school kids, but lately, the kidnappings and photos seemed more professional. Almost as if the kidnappers were a well-oiled, well-coordinated machine.

It wasn't just Mrs. Yates who liked the limelight. Most of the town was totally into our adorable concrete claim to fame.

"He deserves to be home for Christmas," she said. "We all need him home for Christmas, Delaney. It would mean so much to the town."

And that's when I knew I wasn't going to get out of penguin search and rescue duty. "I'll do what I can to find him before the night's over."

"Yes," she said, finally happy. "People drive by to take pictures of him in the yard, you know. Tourists too. Especially tourists. We wouldn't want to disappoint them." She fluffed her hair and stared past me at the road, looking for drive-by photo ops.

"No," I said. "I'm sure we wouldn't."

CHAPTER NINE

"WHERE?" JEAN asked.

I took another drink of the Tom and Jerry Myra had made from scratch from the family recipe. It had just a splash of bourbon in it to cut the thick, sweet warm milk and nutmeg, and it warmed me all the way down. The music was softly playing in the background, Ryder's arm was draped over my shoulder, the house was decorated in that cozy but classy way that only Myra seemed to be able to pull off. If I decorated like her, it would end up looking like I was living in a garage sale.

"Aaron's patio at the back of his nursery," I said.

Aaron was the owner of the garden shop. He was also the god of war, Ares, who up until a few months ago, was vacationing here. Since he was gone, we kept an eye on his property for him.

"Doesn't seem like much of a hiding place," Hogan, Jean's boyfriend, said.

The baker had had a drink or two, and he and Jean were cuddled up on the loveseat, both wearing hideous holiday sweaters. Hogan had accessorized with a pair of felt reindeer horns that flashed red and green. Jean wore a hat shaped like a Christmas tree, lights and all. Apparently, it also sang. Apparently, Myra had yanked the batteries out of the "obnoxious thing" after hearing *Oh, Christmas Tree* on repeat for an hour straight.

Apparently, Myra was "no fun" but since she "made a boss Tom and Jerry" the Christmas tree hat had remained silent.

"They weren't trying to hide it, not really." I shifted and Ryder tucked me in a little closer to his chest. He was quiet, relaxed, and looked right at home with his stockinged feet propped up on Myra's coffee table.

His bruises were just bruises, and the knock on the head was not a concussion. As accidents went, he had been very, very lucky.

"They wanted the pictures on the blog for Christmas?" Myra asked.

"I think that's what they were going for. This had to have taken some time and more than one person. They set up a whole holiday scene, using a bunch of the other statues on his lot complete with Christmas tree, a menorah, and a kinara and corn. Here." I leaned forward and Ryder sighed at the loss of contact, his fingers drifting down my back as I pulled my phone off the table.

I hadn't gone home to change, since the penguin hunt had taken so long. They'd waited on me for dinner, which was nice of them. Dinner was delicious and perfect because Myra had inherited almost all the cooking genes in our family.

I leaned back into Ryder. He grunted softly in contentment.

I scrolled through my photos to the pictures I'd taken of the concrete gathering, held it up for Ryder. He chuckled.

"They went all out," he agreed.

"Lemme see." Jean made grabby hands, and I relinquished my phone. She made big fake wide eyes in big fake surprise. "Look at that Hogan. All those statues doing all those holiday things. How cute is that? They even remembered Kwanza."

"Mmm-hmmm." He planted a kiss somewhere below the boughs of her hat and then grinned at her over her shoulder. "Kwanza doesn't get nearly enough representation here in Ordinary."

Okay, they were being totally suspicious.

"Here, Myra. Look at what those awful vandals did." Jean waggled my phone toward Myra who was giving Jean and Hogan a narrow-eyed glare.

"Was the lock broken?" Myra asked me even though she wasn't looking away from Jean.

I wasn't looking away from Jean either. "No. Whoever did it had a key to the gate." Jean had a key to the gate. We all kept keys to the businesses the no-longer-vacationing gods had left behind.

"Probably just some high school kids finding some other way into the place." Jean waved, then dropped back against Hogan. She threaded her fingers between his hands where they were clasped on her waist. I studied their fingers. Dark against creamy white. Their knuckles looked a little abraded. Like maybe they'd been moving heavy concrete statues around in the middle of the night.

"Oh, for real?" I groaned. "Jean, tell me you were not involved in theft, breaking and entering, and trespassing last night."

"I plead the Fifth."

"Why?" I moaned. "I spent hours looking for that penguin. In the rain. In the cold. On Christmas Eve!"

She shrugged. "They were already there doing their thing. And, no, I'm not going to rat them out. So we just helped them get it all set up."

"We, babe?" Hogan asked. "I guess it's the Fifth for me too, Reed ladies."

I shook my head in disappointment.

"They were supposed to take pictures and get the penguin home before dark," Jean said. "Probably the storm got in the way."

"I can not believe this. Haven't you had enough with yard statues? Remember the gnome debacle? Two month ago. Involving zombies?"

Jean wrinkled her nose at me. "Do not mention the gnome-zombie debacle. Hogan still has Abner's head on the dash of his car."

"Ew," Myra said.

Hogan ran his fingers through Jean's red and green hair. "He won't be alive again until next October. Why not let him see things around town until then?"

"Nice," Ryder said.

I opened my mouth to get us back on the subject of Jean and Hogan being any part of the penguin kidnapping, but Jean talked right over whatever I was about to say.

"You know Mrs. Yates loves that penguin being a star, no matter what she says. It makes her feel young and special. All that attention. All those tourists coming by to catch a glimpse of the famous penguin in her yard with the flower beds she likes to fuss over. If someone hadn't stolen it for a big Christmas photo-op, she would have been disappointed."

"Rule breaker," Ryder noted with a yawn.

"Settle down, Mr. Warden. I didn't break any actual contracts."

"Theft is illegal," Myra pointed out.

"One, I didn't steal it, I just found the people who did. Two, Are you going to arrest your sister on Christmas Eve for being a part of a community building exercise?"

From the look on Myra's face, she was thinking pretty seriously about it.

"You'll tell me who did it," I said. "All the people involved in this little 'community building exercise'."

Jean sighed noisily. "Fine. Yes, boss."

"We're going to talk to them and their parents, if necessary. Make them apologize to Mrs. Yates and pay any damages she asks for. We can't let something like this slide. That was private property, Jean."

She made a rude noise. "I was very stern with them as we were arranging the photo shoot. Told them I disapproved of their shenanigans, but that I'd let it pass this once, because it was Christmas and it was going to make an awesome picture. They really did promise to get the penguin home safely."

Ryder's fingers had shifted so that he could brush the side of my shoulder. I didn't know if he realized he was petting me, but it felt so good, I didn't tell him to stop.

"Please tell me you're not going to make me call them on Christmas Eve," Jean said. "Can't we just put it off a bit?"

"I think we can address it after the holidays," I said.

Jean lit up like a string of lights.

"Is the picture on the blog yet?" Ryder asked.

I nudged him. My sister did not need any encouragement.

Jean grinned. "Wanna see?" She bounded out of Hogan's arms to find her tablet before any of us could answer.

"I thought you'd be a better influence on her," I groused at Hogan.

He just spread his hands wide and smiled. "Come now, Delaney. I thought you knew me better."

The twinkle of wicked mischief in his eyes was irresistible. I chuckled. "At least try to rein in her worst tendencies."

"I do," he said with mock seriousness. "You should have seen the hat she wanted to buy you."

Ryder snorted at that, then Jean showed up with the pictures and excitedly read us the blog post.

I had to admit it, that little penguin wearing a baggy Santa hat that drooped over one eye, surrounded by concrete Buddha, frogs, fairies, elephants, Bigfoot, and an octopus doing yoga, looked pretty darn cute.

They'd strung the whole scene with Christmas lights and candles, greenery stuffed in just the right places to somehow make the gathering feel both whimsical and sweet. Like we were looking in on a little moment when the yard statues all got together in the cold and storm of winter to remind each other of friendship, happiness, and love.

Okay, maybe I was reading too much into the scene, but at the very least, it was cute, fun, and festive.

"Has the blog gotten any comments yet?" Hogan asked. Yeah, I could see how hard he was working not to encourage her.

Jean scrolled for a minute. "About a hundred. Oh, here's a good one: 'Darling photo, but remember, even little penguins like to stay safe at home during the winter windstorms. Merry Christmas, Mrs. Y.'"

Mrs. Yates.

"That doesn't sound angry," Ryder said with another huge yawn.

Jean made a sound. "I told you, she loves this stuff."

"Mmmm." He leaned forward, his arm wrapping around my waist, his head tipping down to rest against my shoulder.

He had to be exhausted. "Did you sleep today?" I asked.

"Some."

"Some?"

I could feel him smile against my shoulder. "I did some Christmas stuff."

"Like what? We already have a tree. And a dragon. Merry Christmas."

"Your gift was in the truck. And that dragon is not my responsibility. It ate my welcome mat."

"You went shopping? You drove?"

"Gnawed on a corner or swallowed the whole mat?" Hogan wanted to know.

"The entire mat in one gulp. It was startling."

"Testify," Hogan agreed.

"Tell me you didn't drive," I said.

"I didn't drive. Jean helped me."

Jean grinned and flicked us a thumbs-up.

My cheeks went a little warm. "Ryder, you didn't have to go out and buy me a gift when you're injured."

"It's Christmas, Delaney," he mumbled, only half-awake. "Worth it."

He was getting heavy against my back. I shifted us so that he was resting against the couch. He pulled me close, wrapping around me like he was afraid I'd walk out when he wasn't looking.

We really had been apart for too long.

The rest of the evening was spent talking with my sisters and Hogan. As was our tradition, our promise to each other, we drank and nibbled on cookies, fudge, and toffee Hogan had made, and gazed at the Christmas tree covered in softly pulsing lights. Myra had an angel atop her tree.

It was peaceful. The music soft and soothing, the company my favorite in the whole world.

And then, when it was midnight, we followed through with our other tradition. It was a family thing passed down from our great-great grandparents. And as long as at least two Reeds were in the same room together at midnight on Christmas Eve, we'd always done it.

We joined hands, held our breath, and made a wish that could last for exactly however long we held our breath.

I wish joy, peace, health and love for all those within Ordinary, especially Ryder, who might or might not love me, but whom I love with all my breath, all my heart, all my soul.

We all exhaled, except for Jean who held up one finger and squeezed her eyes shut, nodding along with whatever list of wishes she was rapid-firing her way through.

She did that every year.

She finally let out a burst of air, and Hogan chuckled, then tipped toward her and kissed her lips. "Can't wait to find out what that was all about," he murmured against her mouth.

"Can't wait for you to," she said.

"No snow," I warned.

She made kitten eyes. "Would I wish for snow on Christmas?"

"Yes," we all said in tandem.

She laughed. "Well, I'm not telling because then *whatever* I wished for won't come true. And believe me, I really, really want it to come true."

From the look she was giving Hogan, and from the look he gave her back, I had a good feeling a few of those wishes were going to come true tonight. I guess it paid to have a half-Jinn as a boyfriend.

"Ready?" Ryder squeezed my hand. I realized I hadn't let go of his yet.

"I'll drive," I said.

We all wished each other a Merry Christmas, said our good-byes, and hugged as if we were seeing each other off to a new adventure in a faraway land.

And maybe we were. Because it was officially Christmas day, and that was a day when wishes came true, right?

A tall dark and dashing figure walked down the sidewalk then right up to Myra's porch, pausing on the stairs.

Bathin.

Myra crossed her arms over her chest. Bathin held up a bottle of wine and said something I couldn't hear.

She paused, then shrugged and stepped aside to let him in. I caught her eye, but she just waved me off. Well, well, well. Could there be something more going on between these two than Myra trying to find a way to get rid of him?

I hesitated. Maybe I should stay and make sure she was okay. No. I knew whatever the demon wanted, she could handle it.

"Merry Christmas, Delaney!" Jean called out.

"No snow," I said again as Jean slid into Hogan's car.

She just laughed. "Good-night, Scrooge."

CHAPTER TEN

I HAD expected Ryder to fall asleep on the drive back to his place. Well, our place, I guess. His cabin on the lake had been feeling less like home over the last couple months he'd been gone, and me more like a stranger drifting through it.

But not tonight. Tonight, it was the only place I wanted to be.

I didn't know how we went forward from here. Maybe we would drift like this, sometimes together, sometimes at a distance. Maybe our relationship would be caught in the pause between right now and forever and that was okay.

Maybe it didn't matter that he'd never told me he loved me, never said those three words. I knew what I saw in his eyes when he looked at me, I knew what I heard when he laughed with me, I knew what I felt when he touched me.

It was love.

I parked the Jeep, and we sat there in the dark for a moment, the porch light glowing warm and yellow, inviting, waiting.

"So, it's officially Christmas morning," Ryder said.

I glanced at the dash clock. Twenty minutes after midnight. "Yes."

"That means I can give you your present." He pushed open the door, grunting as he carefully slid out of the seat. It was probably time for him to take more painkillers.

I followed him to the porch. It was cold out, like the thermometer had suddenly dropped ten degrees. I shivered and my breath came out in clouds.

Ryder worked the lock, but turned around before opening the door, his body blocking the threshold. "Close your eyes."

"Didn't have time to buy wrapping paper?"

He grinned. "Close your eyes."

It was late, and we were both tired, but there was a feeling in the air, a kind of timelessness and peace that made warmth bloom inside me.

I didn't care what gift he had gotten me. Would be just as happy with nothing but his arms around me. He was what I wanted in my life. He was my gift.

I smiled and closed my eyes. "Don't run me into a wall."

I felt him step closer, then his arms wrapped around my waist, his mouth so close to mine, I could feel his breath on my cheek. "Promise." He kissed me gently, once on the center of my lips, then took hold of both of my hands in one of his.

I heard the door open, heard Spud and the dragon gallop toward us, felt them both nosing around like we'd hidden treats or welcome mats in our pockets.

Ryder drew me deeper into the house. I had pretty good spatial awareness, knew we were standing in the middle of the living room, facing the tree. He must have left my gift under the tree.

"Now?" I asked.

"Hold on." He let go of my hands. "Don't peek." He moved away, and I heard him reach for something with a slight grunt.

I shook my head. "If you didn't buy wrapping paper, you could have just thrown a blanket over whatever it is."

"Hush." A little more fiddling. "Okay." He stood in front of me again, and linked our hands together. "Open your eyes."

I opened my eyes.

Stars. Hundreds of paper stars hung from the ceiling, fluttering on thin strings of tinsel and winking lights. Silver and gold, blue and white, red and green, the stars were a constellation of wonder, a childhood memory, a wish come true.

Because across every star was written three words in Ryder's bold, sharp handwriting.

I love you.

He'd written it in the stars. Literally.

This. *This.* What we had right now, this connection, this need, this warmth, this love was enough. Would always be enough, words or no words.

Tears gathered behind my eyes, and I pressed my hand to my mouth on a small, incredulous laugh.

"You did this?" I asked.

"I did."

"For me?"

"For you."

"All of it?" My voice came out small and a little shaky.

"You don't like it?

I shook my head, because I couldn't find words under all of the emotions inside me. But then I caught the worry in his eyes. "No!" I said, "I mean yes. I do! It's...it's amazing. Perfect."

He cradled my face with his free hand. His eyes were the color of sunlight through deep green waters, his smile soft, his body strong and sheltering and familiar and inviting. "Delaney." My name fell from his mouth like a caress. "I love you."

My breath caught on another laugh and this time I couldn't stop the tears.

"I love you too." I sniffled.

He smiled, and drew me into him, stepped into me, pulling our bodies together as if we were two parts of one whole, complete on our own, but so much more together. His thumb brushed my lower lip, his eyes focused on my mouth as he bent, just slightly, and lowered his head.

I stretched up, just slightly, our breaths mingling, our lips finally touching, sliding into that soft rhythm of give and take, of taste and sensation and joy, and promise, and yes, love.

I savored him, the quiet catch of his breath, the shifting of his wide shoulders as he erased every millimeter of distance between us that he could.

Nothing had changed with those three little words.

Everything had changed with those three little words.

I was dizzy with bliss.

When we finally pulled apart, it was only an inch, as if neither of us could stand the thought of letting the other go.

We stood there, holding each other beneath the paper stars, as the light of the tree twinkled with memories and promises. And just beyond the window, it started to snow.

Jean.

I groaned, and he chuckled. "It is kind of romantic," he said.

"Say it again," I whispered.

"It's kind of romantic?"

"The other thing."

"I love you."

I sighed. "I love you too." I slipped my fingers between his and stared out the big window at the softly falling flakes and the lake beyond.

"Think it will stop snowing by morning?"

He lifted one shoulder. "Maybe. Or maybe we'll be snowed in. Together."

I leaned my head on his shoulder, an immense relaxation settling in me. As if I'd been holding the weight of something, waiting on tip-toe, stretched too thin, hoping for more than just those three words. Hoping for him.

Which I supposed was true. I'd been wishing for him every Christmas since I was a child. And he had, no, *we* had, finally come true.

"How about we enjoy tonight, together, alone, and worry about tomorrow tomorrow?" He pressed a kiss into my hair.

That sounded like a wonderful idea. We kissed again, and then made our way to the bedroom, slowly shedding our clothes.

"Merry Christmas, Ryder Bailey," I whispered against his lips as he pulled us both down onto his huge, soft bed, while the snow gently tapped the windows, and the dragon and dog curled up in front of the fire.

"Merry Christmas, Delaney Reed."

SCISSOR KISSES

This Valentine's Day there's more than hearts at risk…

Police officer Myra Reed prefers her life orderly, predictable, and logical. Unfortunately, she lives in the little beach town of Ordinary, Oregon where gods vacation and monsters cause all sorts of trouble.

Her most recent headache is a sexy demon named Bathin, who has tricked his way into both living in Ordinary, and owning her sister's soul. She wants him out of Ordinary. He wants…her.

Myra will get her sister's soul back no matter the price. But first she must deal with a stalker, a crossroads deal, and a dangerous spell that could fix everything, or reveal the one secret she's buried deep: she might be falling in love with a demon.

CHAPTER ONE

The valentine shoved under my screen door was written on a very thin page—page 1492, to be exact— torn out of a very large dictionary. Scrawled across the entries that spanned from LOVABLE to LOVERING was this little ditty:

Roses for the dead
Violets for the blue
It won't be long now
I'm coming for you

I loathed Valentine's Day.

The note was addressed to me: Myra Reed, Ordinary, Oregon. Since Ordinary was a town that all manners of gods, monsters, and creatures made a home, the note could have been left by anyone.

Or anything.

Kill me with a cow kick. I did not need to deal with a stalker right now. I was already stretched thin enough holding down my shifts at the station, and researching how to rid the town of one specifically annoying demon who owned my sister's soul.

"Nope," I said as I folded the letter neatly along its creases and placed it in the slot by my desk where I kept bills and unanswered correspondence. "No time for this. Not today."

I was already late.

I tucked a few things into my pockets: a couple of vials of rare oils, holy water, and a lighter. I also picked up a little packet of paper that had a pressed angelica flower inside.

I checked that I had my gun and my badge, then grabbed my coat and left my house.

Whatever came at me today, I'd be ready.

I WAS not ready.

"This is not in the plan," my younger sister, Jean Reed, said from where she was slouched in the passenger side of the cruiser. "Seriously, Myra. There is nothing remotely romantic out here."

I ignored her and turned the cruiser into the wayside park. It was one of the many viewpoint turnouts along Highway 101, the strip of highway that pierced the heart of Ordinary, Oregon like a compass arrow aiming north/south.

"The plan," Jean went on, as if we were having a conversation instead of me listening to her complain for the last five miles, "is to come up with some sort of romantic gift for Hogan. You said you'd help."

"I will help. After we check out the viewpoint."

She sighed. "It's my day off."

"I know."

"It's your day off too."

"Yep."

"You brought your gun and badge."

"So?"

She shrugged. "Do you know why you brought them?"

Jean was the youngest Reed sister, and her family gift was knowing when something bad was going to happen right before it happened. I was the middle sister and my gift was being in the right place at the right time.

I'd learned to go with my instincts when I felt I should be somewhere. I'd also learned to bring along whatever random items seem appropriate.

"I don't know why I wanted the gun and badge," I said. "But it seemed right."

She accepted that with a small grunt.

"Do you have any bad feelings about this?" I asked.

"Not a twinge. But they come on pretty quick, without warning." She pulled a candy out of her pocket, unwrapped it, and popped it in her mouth. The sweet scent of mint filled the car, along with the sound of the candy clicking against her teeth as she sucked on it.

"If you don't feel anything bad is going to happen," I said, "nothing bad is going to happen."

She crunched her candy. "Hopefully. So why don't we just

go shopping now? Valentine's Day is in two days."

"But romance is forever, right?"

She rolled her eyes.

"You are worrying too much about Hogan," I said. "You know he'll be happy if you gave him nothing more than a kiss."

"But Valentine's Day should be romantic. The most romantic."

"Romance isn't gifts. Hogan doesn't need a holiday invented to sell candy and cards to know how you feel about him."

"Aw," she said. "That's sweet, Myra. Look at you being all sweet."

"I am not being sweet. I'm being practical," I said. "And truthful."

"And boring," she said.

"You mean responsible?" I replied.

"Oh, yeah, that's totally what I meant." She flashed me a smile. Her teeth wore a blue candy film.

The outlook was a wide paved loop that ran along the edge of the cliff above the Pacific Ocean. If I'd parked along the grassy edge of the place, we'd be getting a postcard view of waves and rocks and beaches scalloping up the shore into the blustery February sky.

Instead, we were staring at a restroom. The concrete building sat in the center of the grassy medium that took up the middle of the loop.

The building was concrete, no windows, brown metal roof, separated into men's on one side and women's on the other.

"So?" Jean asked. "What now?"

I didn't really know why I was here. I'd never used this bathroom before, had never been called out on any kind of crime here—hadn't been called out on a crime today.

But that tingly-finger feeling dragged down my spine and set off the "go-now, move-now" heat in my chest. I needed to be here.

So here I was.

"I don't know," I said.

"God, monster, magic?" she asked.

Good question. In our town, gods put down their powers

to vacation here. We also were a safe haven for every kind of supernatural creature and being.

So there were a lot of options for what might be going on in that building.

"So…the restroom?" Jean shifted in the seat, leaning down to give the place a harder look. "Why?"

"Still don't know."

"Tick tock, sister. You promised me lunch. And dessert. And a plan for Valentine's Day."

"We can still do all that. After."

A patter of rain clicked across the roof, wind buffering hard enough to rock the cruiser. Sunlight licked through the clouds, the palest promise of summer warmth. February was cool and fickle along the Oregon coast. Picture-perfect moments bookended by rain, fog, wind, and stunning sunsets.

Jean rolled her head against her seat to look at me. Her hair was Lego-brick red and pulled up into a messy bun. Strands of it twirled down beside her face and made her look mischievous and cute.

She pulled off carelessly messy and still looked so pulled together. My own style of dark hair cut severe across my forehead and curved above my shoulders took a cut every two weeks, like clockwork, to keep it exactly the same.

"You know what?" Jean said. "I've never been in there. Is that strange?"

"We've lived here all our lives. Everything's strange. And of course you've been here."

"The viewpoint—sure. But I've never been in that bathroom."

"Huh," I said.

"What?"

"I've never been in it either," I said.

As kids we'd practically run wild over and under every inch of the town, bay, cliffs, and sands. But for the life of me, I couldn't remember ever setting foot in this particular bathroom.

"Spell?" Jean suggested. "A warding of some kind, maybe? Making us ignore the place? Making us avoid it?"

"I don't feel any magic," I said.

"Do you usually?"

"No. Are you picking up any twinges yet?"

She shook her head. "Think we should call Jules?"

"She's up to her elbows in pre-Valentine's Day love potions, gewgaws, and love readings for the tourists," I said. "And I'm not sure her tarot reading will tell us anything we couldn't find out by just walking in there."

"So. Walk in there."

"I'm planning on it."

"Okay, have fun."

I frowned at her. "You're coming with me."

"Nope. I am off duty. Off. I don't have to investigate a bathroom if I don't want to."

Technically, she was correct.

"And you're not my boss."

Technically, she was correct about that too. Crap.

"And if you try calling Delaney and telling her I have to do this, I will tell Shoe where you keep your fancy chocolate stash."

Shoe was one of the officers we'd lured away from the town of Tillamook up north. He and his partner Hatter had worked with Dad on some of the crazy stuff that happens in a town full of gods and monsters. When we realized we needed more people on the force, they had been the first people we asked.

Turned out Shoe had a habit of sniffing out every locked box, stashed envelope, and hidden goody or trinket in the station. It was so bad that I'd accused him of having some kind of supernatural talent for finding things.

He'd told me he was a cop, and finding things was actually what he was trained for. He'd been smiling when he said it, a slow-moving stretch of his usually surly scowl.

I was convinced he either saw me stash my good chocolates—the extra-dark truffles from Euphoria Chocolate Company in Eugene—or there was a snitch in the office.

And by snitch, I meant Jean.

My sister, Jean. Total snitch.

"Fine," I said. "I'll go into the bathroom alone. You stay here and pout because you have just discovered you don't have a romantic bone in your body because you've never taken a relationship seriously before."

"Ouch." She tapped the right side of her chest. "Wait…I mean…" She switched hands and tapped over her heart. "Hurtful. Right here."

I shook my head and opened the car door.

"At least I have a boyfriend," she yelled. "And, oh, yeah, I've been dating since high school. Unlike a sister I know who is too chicken to—"

Nope.

I slammed the door. I didn't need to hear her tell me that I was closed off, cold, too aloof to date. I didn't need her to tell me I should live a little. That I should loosen up and take chances.

I'd taken chances in my past and it had ended… Well, not in heartache. But he'd moved overseas, and I'd never heard from him again.

I just wasn't the kind of person that other people wanted to settle down with. Too demanding, too orderly, too…jaded? Maybe. Too responsible and levelheaded to really engage my heart into overdrive.

Most of my other short, failed relationships had crumbled beneath my desire for order and rules. Who could blame me for wanting at least one place in my life to be drama-free?

Maybe I'd settle down someday when I found a nice, reasonable, calm, organized person who found comfort and happiness in a nice, reasonable, calm, organized life.

Or maybe I'd remain happy and single. I didn't need a boyfriend to be happy.

Although, even I had to admit Delaney and Jean were pretty happy before they were dating. And now that they were dating, their happiness had compounded.

For a second, just a flash, the image of Bathin flickered through my head.

I scoffed, my breath coming out in a little cloud. Right. That demon was not boyfriend material. He was tall, dark, broody, and handsome as hell, but that was all an illusion. Beneath the smolder of all those good looks was a demon.

A demon who had trapped Dad's spirit, and then traded his freedom for Delaney's soul.

He was not only *not* boyfriend material, he was also my

current problem.

I wanted my sister's soul back. I also wanted to exile Bathin from Ordinary and close any loopholes that would allowed him—the only demon we'd had in Ordinary—to ever return.

He could take his handsome face, his wide shoulders and muscles. He could take that wicked smile and chuckle that hit notes from the bottom up, rash and full and dirty.

Yes. He could take all those things and leave my sisters, my town, and me alone.

The wind shoved a little harder at my back, reminding me that rain was coming.

I walked the perimeter of the building, my boots getting wet in the grass that hadn't been mowed since October. Nothing unusual caught my eye, so I knocked on the men's bathroom door and called out, "Ordinary Police. Coming in."

I pushed open the metal door.

A wall of urinals, a wall of sinks, a couple stalls with doors half-open. Nothing else.

It was empty and smelled of wet concrete, salt, and cold.

Okay, nothing going on here.

I walked out into the wind and around to the woman's restroom. Knocked and called out, "Ordinary Police. Coming in."

The metal door swung open easily. The room was identical to the men's room, except instead of urinals, the extra space was taken up by more stalls.

And a demon.

The demon, a woman with long black hair, gorgeous pale skin, and eyes the color of honey, tipped her head as I stopped short.

"A Reed sister?" Her voice was alto and sunlight. "Oh, now, isn't this interesting?"

Yes, it was interesting. Because one: there were no demons in Ordinary except for the very recent, very annoying Bathin. And two: why was she wearing a tailored gray business suit? Okay, and maybe one more thing: why was she tapping a pen against a clipboard?

"Who summoned you?"

Her smile was swift. "Oh, now, that would be spoiling the

fun. Don't you want to guess?"

"No, I want you to tell me."

"I'd heard the Reeds ran a tight ship in Ordinary. I'm surprised one of you didn't visit me years ago. I could have made so many things so much easier for you."

"Still waiting for my answer." I knew my banishment spells, knew my incantations and how to mix herbs. I'd even brought along a thing or two today, but first I wanted answers.

"Name," I said. "Reason you're here."

"I am Zjoon." The pen paused in the tapping. "And not that it's any of your business, but I don't know who called me today. Someone is longing. Lonely. Wishful."

My heart thumped a little louder with each statement, but I was good at ignoring my heart. She, however, was paying attention.

"Was it you, Reed? Is your heart confused? Is your mind cloudy? Are you searching for something you are afraid you'll never find?"

She didn't move, didn't take one step away from where she was positioned in the middle of the room. Something about that niggled at the back of my mind, and I did a quick scan of the room to see what bothered me about all this.

Why was she so still? Could she be a projection?

No, I could see the steam that rose off her body as she tapped the pen. She was a very solid demon, but not as good at hiding her nature as Bathin was at hiding his. She was hot under the illusion of skin she wore, steaming in the chilly February weather.

The scent of heated roses with just a hint of brimstone wafted off her skin.

"You're not allowed in Ordinary, Zjoon," I said. "No demon is allowed in Ordinary."

She blinked, her eyebrows drawn up. "Need I remind you that Ordinary already has a demon in it?"

She knew that? She wasn't supposed to know that. We were pretty sure Bathin was hiding out in Ordinary. Trying to fly under the notice of his own kind.

"Oh, the prince thinks he hides, but I can feel him. Can feel his power. He has been near you, hasn't he? What a pleasant turn of events."

She clicked the pen, then pointed it at me. "You feel him too, don't you, Reed? His presence, strong and burning. A fire you long to touch even as you fear the burn. He stirs you. Calls to your every heartbeat. Even as your mind tells you to run, run, run."

I unzipped my jacket. "Uh-huh. Are you done trying to lure me into a deal? Because you are terrible at it."

A scowl crossed her pretty face, clouds storming over the sunlight of her (fake) beauty.

For the first time since I walked into the room, she really studied me. Looked me up and down. I had a funny feeling she looked *into* me too, but that was probably just another illusion.

"One last chance," I said. "Exit Ordinary peacefully, or I'll compel you to do so."

Her gaze locked with mine, stilled and hot, like metal burning.

Yes, I could compel her. I'd done a lot of research into all things demon lately.

"You can't," she said.

"Want to try me?"

Some of the shine on her dimmed. She was still a stunning beauty, but that influence or charisma she'd been projecting was gone.

"I see what he sees in you, Myra Reed."

I didn't know what she was talking about, or, if I wanted to be honest with myself, I didn't *want* to know what she was talking about. But it was interesting that she knew my name now.

Or she had from the get-go and had only pulled it out to make me think she had dug around inside my head for it.

"Just in case you've forgotten," I said evenly, "I asked you who called you and I asked you to leave Ordinary."

She shook her head. "This isn't Ordinary."

I resisted the urge to glance around the bathroom. I wasn't sure what I'd think I'd see. A tornado carrying the restroom away like a one-way ticket to Oz? A galaxy of stars and time, Tardis-style? Trickling neon-green numbers Matrixing through the air?

Okay, I was a bit of a closet geek along with being a nerd.

But the room was still concrete and dark green metal, lit by the light seeping through pine-needle-covered skylights. I was in Ordinary. I could feel it in my soles. We Reeds had been chosen by the gods to protect their vacation town, and I felt a connection to this soil that I'd never felt anywhere else in the world.

When I was here, I knew it. Ordinary grounded me, held me strong. Ordinary knew me, and I knew it right back.

"This is Ordinary," I said. "And demons are not allowed."

"Oh? I've been here for years, Reed. Long before this town had this name."

Demons lied as naturally as breathing. She was lying.

"Why don't we take this outside?" I said.

The scowl again, briefer this time. "Are you afraid we'll be bothered here? Or maybe you're bothered? There are so many ways I could help you, Myra. So much knowledge I can obtain for you."

She still wasn't moving from that spot. "What do you mean, this isn't Ordinary?"

"What?"

"You just told me this isn't Ordinary."

"Did I?"

"Innocence doesn't suit you," I said.

"It could." She laughed. "Why, after all these years, are you here, Myra Reed? Why have you come to this one place, this one day, at this one hour?"

"You have nothing I want."

She shrugged. "A police officer, a *Reed* walks through the door with a gun at her side. There must be something you want. Maybe someone?"

I closed the distance between us, then paced a slow circle around her. She didn't move, just stood there waiting until I stopped in front of her again.

The ground beneath my feet felt solid. Magnet and metal solid. This was Ordinary.

I stretched one foot out six inches and placed the toe of my boot right in front of the demon's foot.

Her eyes narrowed.

It felt like the ground was pulled away from my foot. As if

my boot hovered there over an empty expanse, even though logically I could also feel the concrete of the floor I pressed against.

There was soil there. There was ground there. But there was no Ordinary there.

Interesting.

"This is a crossroads," I said.

The demon rolled her eyes. "Why couldn't one of the stupid sisters have come here instead?"

"You're a crossroads demon."

She tipped her head down just a bit. "At your service."

"Who puts a crossroads in the middle of a bathroom?"

"It wasn't always a bathroom. It was a crossroads first. The city planners didn't pay attention when they carved out this viewpoint. I tried to warn them." She nodded, very seriously. "So I offered them a deal or two. A couple of them saw things my way." She winked. "Wasn't that fun?"

I rocked back on my heel, taking weight off my foot, then crossed my arms over my chest. "You aren't allowed in Ordinary."

"We just went over this. Here, this space"—she waved at the square foot or so around her—"is not a part of Ordinary. You can't make me leave because, technically, I am not even inside Ordinary."

"You've been making deals with people in this bathroom."

"Maybe a few. A little pat on the back here, a little spurned-lover revenge there." She shrugged. "A girl's gotta make rent, you know?"

I did not know, since I never dealt in souls for currency.

But she was right about one thing: I needed information. I'd hit a wall in finding a way to banish Bathin and take my sister's soul away from him.

"Why aren't you in the records?"

"It's your family's job to keep track of who and what is wandering around this place. Not mine."

"What is the price for your deals?"

"Why, are you interested?"

I stared at her, and she clicked the pen on the board again. "Fine. Crossroads deals run the gamut. Sometimes it's a favor for a favor. Sometimes it's a life or a soul. And sometimes I've been known to extend a certain amount of…charity."

I snorted.

"It's true! Is there a secret desire you want, Myra Reed? A lover to hold you? A companion to walk with you through this life? Would you like to finally put down your burdens and lean on someone strong enough to hold you? Strong enough to love you? No matter what shameful faults you try to hide? Do you want someone who would live a nice, reasonable, calm, organized life?"

The shock of her words, so close to how I really felt, what I really wanted, lanced beneath my skin, zapping down to my feet and gluing me to the ground.

She couldn't actually know all that. This was just what a crossroads demon did—they dug for vulnerabilities. It was what all demons did. It was why they could never be trusted. Why they had never been allowed in Ordinary.

Supernaturals in Ordinary were sworn to live peacefully with each other. Sworn to do no harm to any other supernatural or person or god in town. Demons all refused to sign any contracts that would hold them to the town rules.

Bathin had gotten around that by trading my dad's spirit for my sister's soul, and he'd done the additional trick of saving someone's life once he was inside Ordinary.

"I don't make deals with crossroads demons," I said with no hint of weakness. "I do know how to get rid of them. I also know how to destroy the crossroads. Permanently. Because it's my family's job to keep track of that."

Her eyes flashed fire. Then she smiled. "They say the Reed sisters are born to the elements. Eldest earth, steady and strong. Youngest water, flexible and changing. But you…you're fire, aren't you, Myra Reed? Burning deep and hot. Hidden beneath layers and layers of normalcy you hope no one will dig deep enough through to uncover the real you. The anger. The hatred."

I raised my eyebrows. "Nope. Try again."

She frowned. "No, you're fire. I can see that. It radiates from you even though your exterior is"—she waved one manicured nail at me—"that."

"That?"

"Cold. Implacable. Calm."

I shrugged. It didn't matter how she saw me—fire, earth, or strawberry milkshake. She was changing the subject, shifting the conversation to try to trap me into making a deal.

Yeah, that wasn't going to happen.

"Well, this wasn't at all enjoyable," I said. "And since you're not willing to answer my questions, I'll just destroy your crossroads now."

I reached into my coat, where a few vials of crystals, salts, rare oils, and other focusing tools were stashed. They were sealed, but a demon as old as she had to be must sense them.

I didn't know why I'd put these particular things in my coat this morning, but they were just what I needed.

Thank you, family gift.

"Wait!" She held up her clipboard.

I paused, hand still inside my coat.

Her gaze was riveted on my hand. "Ask. I'll tell you what I can. I promise you."

"How can a soul contract be broken?"

Her eyes went wide. "I can't tell you that."

"All right." I pulled out three vials. She visibly paled.

"Every deal hinges on different rules," she said in a rush. "Every demon seals deals differently. The ways to break them are just as varied. No one true answer."

I knew that. I'd done my research. "I want to know how one specific demon seals his deals."

She pulled her shoulders back. "I don't know how every demon handles their deals. I don't know every demon."

"I think you might have heard of him. Bathin."

She stopped breathing. Just. Stopped.

Wind outside the building shook the trees. Pine needles shed in soft rain against the skylights.

"The prince?"

I'd run across that title attached to his name in a couple of the obscurer texts I'd been reading, but hadn't been able to confirm that it was an actual title and not some sort of self-aggrandizing description.

"Is there another demon by that name?"

She shook her head.

"Tell me how to break a soul deal Bathin made."

"I can't."

"Well, that's too bad." I flicked the top of one of the vials with my short thumbnail. The scent of pine sap and something deeper, smokier, filled the space.

Her gaze ticked over to the vial, and it wasn't fear that filled her face. It was anger.

"He'll kill me."

"Not my problem."

"It's not just a simple answer." She was trying to buy time. Probably trying to distract me until she could come up with some way to get out of this situation.

"Uh-huh." I poured a drop of the scented oil on the ground to one side of her, then took a couple steps so that I was behind her and tipped out another drop. She tracked me. And yes, I was hitting the compass points correctly. North, east, next would be south, and when I was in front of her again, west.

No action with a demon, especially a demon limited in their location, could begin without some kind of containment. That was just the way of it, and why all the books and TV shows had the heroes drawing out pentagrams on the floor or creating circles of salt.

All good fictions held a grain of truth.

"He's strong," the demon said. "Stronger than I am. Stronger than most of us. And when he claims a soul…it's dangerous to even try to take it away from him."

I paused, the vial tipped. I hadn't let the oil drop to the final compass point. "Dangerous I can handle. Tell me how to do it."

She bit her lip and stared over my shoulder like someone was going to come through the door to save her. Not a chance. It was February, wet, cold, and in the middle of the week. No one was going to choose this roadside bathroom when they could stop in at a Starbucks or the McDonald's in town and use the facilities.

"I have everything with me to banish you for good," I said. "And it will take next to nothing to close down this crossroads."

That did it. Her gaze snapped back to my face. A light sheen of sweat glossed her forehead.

Demons, all of them, had the ability to change their appearance to whatever pleased them—which was usually whatever they needed to be to manipulate marks into selling their souls.

I'd never seen a demon sweat.

She might be putting it all on—making me think she was nervous, panicked. Or there might be enough on the line if she told me Bathin's secrets that she was legitimately terrified.

My gut said she was terrified.

"It's a spell," she said. "Not everyone can do it. I don't…I don't even know if you can."

"Let me worry about that. Tell me how it's done."

"Swiftly, snip by snip, ruby and black blades in a loving hand."

I knew the poetic words were just a cover for what one needed for the spell. Double-speak to confuse the ingredients one needed to gather. "Specifics."

She pressed her lips together. "It's…it's all I can say."

"Is this a spell in a book? Text on a stone? Tell me how to follow through."

"It is written. One page in one book."

"I want that page. I want that book."

"I can't."

"You will. Bring me everything I need—blades, hands, snips, and that one page of that one book."

"You don't understand how dangerous it is. I can't. I *can't*." She was visibly shaking now.

A tiny part of me felt sorry for her. But she was the first lead that pointed me at a specific spell, a specific way to break Bathin's hold on Delaney's soul since I'd started looking months ago. I was not about to apologize for doing everything I could to keep my sister safe.

"By tomorrow, midnight," I said, "I expect to see a package on my doorstep, otherwise—"

The door swung open and her eyes flew wide.

"Myra," a man's voice rumbled, low and rich, lava over gold. "What a surprise to find you here."

CHAPTER TWO

I DIDN'T have to look over my shoulder to know who had just walked in the room. The scent of him—maybe cologne, maybe the fragrance of his skin—was warm with cloves and notes of something too masculine to be sweet, like aged brandy and smoke and warm candle wax. His presence burned like the sun cleaving a clouded sky.

He was heat; he was strength. He was a force that washed over me, prickled against my skin, drew me to him with a pull that left me shivering. A pull I had never felt with any other person or creature before.

"And here we are. Together," Bathin said.

Heat kindled deep in my chest and spread down to my fingertips, to my feet, pooling in slow, lazy eddies low in my stomach.

It annoyed me that he brought that kind of reaction out of my body, that kind of want. Annoyed and confused me.

I didn't like him.

Liar.

He had held my dad's soul captive, tricked my sister into selling her soul for Ordinary's safety. He had tricked us all into letting him stay here.

I could never like anyone who was that manipulative and thought only about his own desires, his own pleasure.

Liar.

He had done nothing to redeem himself in my eyes.

He saved Ben. He saved Ryder. Brought a bottle of wine on Christmas Eve and spent the night talking with me. Not pushing, not manipulating. Just a few hours of comfort, not being alone for once, if only for a short time. It was nice. More than nice. It was balm over a hell of a year. It was comfort. And so unexpected.

So needed.

I forcibly pushed those memories aside. He was a demon. Everything he did was for his own gain. Wasn't it?

The doubt in the back of my mind remained no matter how much I ignored it.

I was attracted to Bathin. Had been from the moment I'd first seen him with Delaney. Well, second moment. At first I'd wanted to kill him for taking my sister's soul, no matter how good looking or sweet talking he was.

Letting him into my home on Christmas to talk the night away had left me even more confused about who he was and what he was trying to do here in Ordinary.

I had, for a few hours, forgotten he was a demon. Had forgotten he was my foe.

Had forgotten I shouldn't want to want him, shouldn't like to like him.

That night had almost, disastrously, ended on a kiss before I'd remembered that the handsome man he appeared to be was a facade over the very unlikable creature he actually was.

"Bathin." I didn't turn toward him. "Women's restroom. You're not allowed in here."

He chuckled, and I shivered as it set off sparks under my skin.

"Oh, this is not the first women's restroom I've ever been in. They are so useful for certain kinds of secrets, after all."

"Are you here to share your secrets, Bathin?" I asked with my bored, but slightly threatening cop voice.

His footsteps came nearer, hissing as they scraped across the sand-covered concrete.

"I have nothing to hide," he said. "But you? Here you are, talking to a demon. A crossroads demon. Who is doing work where she isn't welcome and will not be tolerated."

Zjoon made a little *eep* sound and went from a healthy color to something that would make a deceased fish look chipper.

Bathin stopped next to me.

I sighed and glanced at him.

He had on a pair of jeans that were practically painted over his thick thigh muscles, long legs, and narrow hips. A lightweight Henley was unbuttoned at the collar, the sleeves pushed back to reveal tanned, defined forearms. The shirt clung to his chest and flat stomach like a well-choreographed advertisement for men's fashion.

It was the first time I'd seen him in something other than slacks and a button-down. Yes, it looked good on him.

Dark hair slicked back, a strong nose and cut jaw, Bathin was every heartthrob of my fantasies rolled up into one lickable package.

Not that I was thinking about licking him. Or about his package.

"Prince Bathin." Zjoon's voice sketched a bare whisper. "What an honor—"

"Now, now, let's not fall so quickly into falsehoods," he said. "I know you, Zjoon. I know your clan. And this"—he shrugged—"has nothing to do with honor."

I opened my mouth to tell him that he didn't know jack about what was happening, because this had been working out just fine for me before he showed up.

But a hard glint in Zjoon's eyes reminded me, once again, that demons were not to be trusted.

Maybe me being here was less a part of my family gift, and more a part of being manipulated by a crossroads demon. Maybe demons had decided that now that they had one Reed sister soul, they might as well claim another.

"This crossroads is my territory and well defended." Zjoon's tone was deferential, but not meek. "It cannot be dissolved by you."

"Is that so?" Bathin asked, just as evenly.

A demon staring contest wasn't what I'd signed up for. I had a bottle of oil that could lock down this whole game. But I still needed an explanation for how to get Delaney's soul out of Bathin's clutches.

"Not even you can remove me from my land, Black Heart," Zjoon spat. Her eyes were stony challenge, her lips a sneer. What had seemed beautiful about her before twisted into a parody of human features.

"What's your play here? What game do you think you can win against the Reed sister?" Bathin crowded closer to the demon, his boots a spare inch away from the edge of the invisible circle around her.

"This is no game," she said. "This is my job."

"As long as you are alive," he agreed.

Even I couldn't mistake that threat.

The last thing I wanted to deal with was a dead demon or a war in a bathroom.

"Okay," I said, "very impressive. Both of you. Now settle down." I tipped the vial up and plugged the opening with my thumb.

"You"—I pointed at Bathin with the vial—"are currently a citizen of Ordinary. That comes with rules you are required to follow. One of those rules is that you will bring no harm to others."

"No harm to those who live within Ordinary's boundaries," Bathin corrected me while he held Zjoon with a steady glare. "This crossroads and this creature are clearly outside of Ordinary. Isn't that convenient?"

"You have no right to stand in my way," Zjoon said.

Bathin smiled and pushed one foot forward, straddling the line between Ordinary and the outside world. "Try me."

And this was the point where I had to decide to either step in and separate them, which would only be within my jurisdiction for another foot or so of ground Bathin had yet to cross, or let him go at it, get rid of her, get rid of this crossroads, and close down a soul-trading post none of us had even known about.

The good for all would be to banish the demon—well, both of them, but for sure the crossroads demon—and close the crossroads.

But I didn't have the full information from Zjoon yet. And after months of looking for a solution to Bathin's soul deal with Delaney, I didn't want to lose the first real lead I'd had in weeks.

And, okay, there was a third way to look at this. Bathin and Zjoon could have planned it all out to make me do something they wanted me to do. It was a little extreme and complicated to suspect that, but underestimating a demon's ability to use a person's emotions, coupled with a demon's willingness to play the long game, was disastrously foolish.

This was my decision. Stop the fight and give myself a chance to get more info out of Zjoon, or let Bathin kick her out and shut down this soul hole for good?

I knew what I should do. What would keep the citizens of

Ordinary safe. I should let Bathin get rid of Zjoon, and close this shop down.

I reached over and pressed my hand on Bathin's arm. He instantly fell still, except for his breathing, which seemed to suddenly go quick and light. All his muscles tensed, coiled, as if he were trying very hard to hold back some kind of reaction to my touch. As if he were trying very hard not to do something.

"This isn't Ordinary," I said. "Not where she's standing. It's not our job to police beyond our border."

And yes, hearing that fall out of my mouth surprised me too. I could feel the flush rush over my face, pooling hot across my collarbones. Had I seriously just suggested that we allow a crossroads in the middle of a public bathroom where a demon tricked people out of their souls to remain open?

Bathin turned his head, his gaze heavy and sharp. "Not *our* job to police beyond *our* border?" he said. "What deal did you make with her?"

I opened my mouth, but apparently didn't start talking fast enough. His arm snapped out of my hold so fast that I didn't even see it move until his hand tightened around Zjoon's throat. "What deal did you make with her?" he asked the crossroads demon.

A wheezing squeak was the only sound she made, her lips trying and failing to shape a reply.

"Bathin," I said. "Let her go."

He didn't let her go; he didn't even loosen his grip. But he did look at me. "You still have your soul, so you're clearly not as gullible as your sister."

"Watch it."

He didn't even smile. His gaze was dark, piercing, as if he could see deep inside of me and read the pages of my mind. "Your soul is your own. It is whole. In place. Lovely." He drew his free hand upward, the fingers relaxed as they brushed the air.

Except it felt like he was brushing my soul, his touch torching a liquid thrum beneath my skin that was not painful. At all.

"That's not going to work," I managed without my voice cracking. "You are not welcome here, Bathin, nor are you invited in this situation. Leave and let me handle this."

"Does that tone of voice usually work on…anyone?"

I narrowed my eyes and thought through the things I'd packed in my jacket, wondering which one would hurt him the most when I threw it at his head.

Luckily, I had my gun on me. A nice, heavy gun.

I reached for it.

"Put her down." This time my tone was nothing but business.

Bathin chuckled, his perfect white teeth biting down on the sound. The mood rolling off him shifted again. Going from angry—*protective?*—to nonchalant in an instant.

"Well, well," he said as his hand loosened and he leaned incrementally away from the demon. He did not release his hold, not yet. "I never thought I'd see the day when Myra by-the-book Reed shows mercy for demon kind. Isn't that remarkable?"

"It isn't remarkable," I said. "It's practical. We have no problems with demons who are outside of Ordinary because anything outside of Ordinary isn't our problem."

"Is that so?"

It was.

But it wasn't.

We'd engaged in a battle with an ancient vampire who was outside of Ordinary. We got letters and other communication from gods outside of Ordinary; we were more than willing to help the non-supernatural towns around us with any kind of police support they might need.

We weren't a closed-off, obscure little town that no one had heard of. We were one of the busy tourist destinations in Oregon, and to remain as such, we had a lot of contact with the world outside our boundaries.

So, strike that. It was not at all true that we ignored the outside world.

Bathin knew I was lying, knew that he had caught me at it. And he liked having the moral upper ground, the jerk.

"All right," I said, "let's handle this from another angle. You, Bathin, are a citizen of Ordinary. You worked *very* hard to make sure that you could live here, stay here."

He narrowed one eye, not liking where I was going with this.

And I hadn't even gotten started yet.

"If you step outside of Ordinary to deal with Zjoon, to commit *murder*, then I will assume you are revoking your claim to citizenship, along with your claim to Delaney's soul."

"That's not how it works."

I pointed at the badge on my hip. "Who you going to go crying to?"

The air went heavy and hot. Humidity popped high enough that the skylights clicked and settled in their frames from the heat change.

Huh. So an angry Bathin was a hot Bathin. Good to know.

"No matter where I am in this world, or any other plane of existence," he said, "I will still own your sister's soul."

"Not if I have anything to say about it."

He knew I was trying to find a way to free her, had known it since the beginning. It was some kind of game to him. He enjoyed watching me spin my wheels while I tried to track down his secrets.

I liked the idea of finally rattling that smug confidence.

I reached into my pocket, not the same one that held the vials and spell supply, but the hip pocket of my jeans. His eyelids dropped just a fraction, and he wet his lips.

I tried to ignore how dry my mouth went at the sight of that. Tried to ignore how much even that shift in his expression looked like lust, felt like desire.

Demons manipulate. Demons are never what they seem. Demons are chaos. My job is order.

I withdrew a slim packet, just a fold of stiff cloth with one thing pressed between its layers.

"Is that a ticket?" he asked. "To the movies? A play? I'd be delighted to go on a date with you, Myra Reed. How very romantic. And so near Valentine's Day."

I opened the cloth and carefully lifted free the dried flower.

Bathin's nostrils flared, and his jaw tightened. "Angelica."

I calmly pulled a lighter out of my other pocket, flicked and held the flame under the brittle flower.

"Myra," he warned.

Zjoon squirmed in his grasp, suddenly more afraid of the flame and flower than the demon who was stalled in the middle of choking the life out of her.

I raised an eyebrow.

"You shouldn't play with things you don't understand," he said.

"Like this?" I asked innocently. The flower had caught the flame, and the scent of anise and cayenne, along with burning angelica, filled the thick, hot air.

Bathin shook his head, but there was a small smile playing on the edges of his lips.

"Darkbane," he said. "Aren't you clever?"

The flame was almost at my fingers. I threw the flower at him.

He raised his free hand at the same moment that he released Zjoon.

One smooth parry of his palm, a pivot on the balls of his feet, and the air in the room moved. Like, really moved.

It was as if the air had suddenly turned into a river, a breeze, a wind, all flowing with his movements, and guiding the ashes of the flower, like a burning stick on a burning stream straight at Zjoon's face.

She snarled and swore, raising her clipboard up to guard her head. The ember and ash flower hit the clipboard.

It was like a lightning bolt breaking a storm.

A hard, cold shot of air sliced through the room, radiating ice so quickly that I heard the skylights crack. I took a step back, hand on my gun, though a gun wasn't going to do much in the middle of a demon banishment.

The cold spread fast, too fast. Ice slicked down the walls, devoured the stalls, and sped across the floor, clicking like a thousand claws scrabbling, like a thousand pincers snapping. Toward us. Toward me.

Ice swallowed the edge of the crossroads. Zjoon made a sound like a soft groan and exploded into a column of smoke, wafting with the scent of scorched dirt.

That ice was coming too fast. I wasn't a demon, so it might not do anything at all to me.

Or it might. The spell wasn't really clear about the strength. Nor did it say anything about ice being a side effect.

Well, hell.

The door was too far away, and the floor leading to it was covered in ice. I stood in an ever-shrinking circle of clear concrete. In about three heartbeats, either my boots were going to be covered in supernatural ice, or I was going to find out if the spell would turn me into smoke too.

Strong arms wrapped around me. A wide, strong body pressed against me.

For a second, just one strangely silent and clear moment, everything stopped.

I looked up into his eyes and saw…fondness? Something far too soft to discover behind a demon's bright gaze. He smiled, but it was slow, too slow for the fraction of a second I knew we both shared.

That smile hooked at my heart and tugged, gently, like a hand reaching out in the darkness, drawing me into the light, into the dance with a sway, a rhythm that settled the chaos in my heart, settled the silence into soft music, the *thud, thud, thud* of my pulse.

I couldn't look away from him. Didn't want to be anywhere else but here, in his arms, in his hands, in the calm of this first pause. Both of us poised for the first step, the first movement of this dance, this song.

His gaze asked a question. I didn't know the answer, wouldn't face the answer, even though everything in me chanted: *yes*.

He inhaled and…

…light: too bright, bone gray, blinding…

…rain: falling softly on my face, pattering against the sidewalk around us…

…wind: buffering and cold, stirring his hair, stirring mine, wrapping us in sea salt and the scent of green…

I exhaled, a little shakily. We were outside. It was quite a bit cooler here than inside that overheated sauna of a restroom.

Bathin's arms around me were warm, one low across my back, his hand almost, but not quite, touching my hip. His other hand rested on my shoulder, his long fingers pressed gently on the side of my face.

He had pulled me close, or maybe I'd done that myself. My thighs lined up with his, but there was enough of a height difference, even though I was in boots that gave me an inch or two, that my head only came to his chest.

I could feel the heat of him, could hear the steady, raging rhythm of his heartbeat.

He shifted his hand just enough that he could drag his thumb across my lower lip.

I trembled at his touch. And in that moment, I couldn't think of him as a demon, made of illusions and fire and lies. He was something more, something—no, someone—kind. Calm. Safe.

"All right, Bathin," Jean snapped. "Step away from my sister. Now." She paused for a second. "Or kiss her, if that's what she asked you to do."

I pushed out of his embrace and instantly missed his warmth as the wind nearly sucked the breath out of me.

Bathin squared off so he was facing both me and Jean, who was now standing next to me, her hand on my arm, possessive and firm.

"You two want to tell me what happened in that bathroom before the fire department gets here?" Jean asked.

"Fire department?" I glanced over at the concrete building. Sure enough, smoke was wafting out of it. "Huh."

It wasn't like concrete was going to burn to the ground in the middle of a rain shower. There wasn't enough flammable material in the whole structure to roast a marshmallow.

"You called the fire department?" I didn't know why I was stuck on that. Probably because the rest of my brain was filled with Bathin…

…his touch, so gentle. His eyes, so kind, wanting…

Illusion. Demon.

I clung to that fact, to that logic, and pushed away all the other chaotic thoughts. There was no room in me for confusion. I was calm, no matter the chaos. I was order. That gave me control.

And that was all I needed.

"There's no actual fire in the building," I said.

Bathin's eyebrows rose and he made a little *humph* sound.

"You have something to say?" I asked.

He crossed his arms over his chest, straining the material

of the Henley and showing the hard muscles of his arms and chest.

Those arms.

"Cayenne?" he asked.

It took me a second. He was talking about the angelica flower spell. "Yes?"

"And anise?"

Annoying. "Would you like me to write the spell down for you?" I asked sweetly.

A grin flashed across his face. "No, I think I know exactly how you made that spell. And really, Myra, you should have consulted an expert."

"I don't need your opinion."

"Next time," he went on like I hadn't been talking, "I suggest you use a little less anise. Unless you intended to burn down the entire building?"

"The bathroom is not burning down."

A *whump* of air sucked all the heat out of the wind for a second. Then even more smoke, now greasy and black, poured out of the building.

"Holy crap," Jean said. "What the heck happened in there?"

"Demons," I said.

"Plural?" she asked.

"There was a crossroads demon in there, waiting to make a deal."

"Tell me you didn't make a deal." She sounded worried. I tore my gaze away from the burning—well, technically only smoking a little bit—bathroom and gave her my attention.

Her expression was a mix of things: worry, amusement, maybe annoyance.

Jean was always full of emotions, living life with both hands reaching, and mouth wide open.

"I did not make a deal." It wasn't a lie, but it wasn't the full truth, either. I'd threatened Zjoon and told her I'd close the crossroads down if she didn't bring me the banishment spell. Since Bathin had trampled into the place like a bull elephant through a peanut field, I hadn't had the chance to close the crossroads.

If she came through with the goods, then I had, basically, closed a deal.

But at least my soul was not the currency.

And since the building was possibly going up in flames, maybe the crossroads was a goner anyway. Another dead end in my investigation.

I pressed both hands to my hips. It wasn't the first time one of the leads I'd followed dried up.

I'd find a way to get rid of Bathin. Crossroads demon spell or no crossroads demon spell.

"Did you know about the crossroads?" Jean asked Bathin.

He shrugged. So: yes.

"Why did you come here?" I asked him. "Was it about that letter? Because that wasn't funny."

The sound of sirens finally reached us. This viewpoint wasn't that far from the fire station. They'd be here any second.

"What letter?" Bathin and Jean said at the same time.

Both of them looked confused. And yes, Bathin might be faking it, but I had the feeling he wasn't. And if he didn't know about it, I wasn't going to tell him.

"I'll tell you about it later, Jean," I said. "Right now, I want to know why Bathin came here this morning. To a women's restroom."

"You were making deals with a crossroads demon who had set up shop right outside of Ordinary," Bathin said. "Where else would I be?"

I narrowed my eyes. "Were you spying on me?"

"Don't you think highly of yourself?"

A flash of heat hit my cheeks, but it was not anger. He just…he just made me want to shut him up. And not in police officer ways. In other ways that involved a lot of touching. Kissing.

Groan. Why did I have to want him? Why did I have to want this illusion of the man I knew he wasn't?

I pressed my lips together and shook my head. It had to be the smoke and near-miss with the crossroads demon that was messing up my head. I didn't fall for…whatever he was. Whatever I was feeling. I didn't fall for that.

Bathin waited for my answer, the soft expectation lit up his face. The wind tossed his black, thick hair, pushing a curl of it across his forehead. I wanted to reach up and draw that lock of hair clear so I could better see his eyes.

He raised one eyebrow and…did he just nod?

"If I find out you are doing anything," I said in a tone of voice that would freeze the core of an active volcano, on Mars, in the dead heat of summer, during a solar explosion. "Anything at all to actually read my mind, I will break your face."

"Whoa," Jean said. "Nice. Well, I see you two are getting along so much better than the last time I saw you together."

"Last time you saw us together," Bathin said to Jean without looking away from me, "she was locking me in a cell and threatening to disembowel me so she could use my blood to draw a spell that would turn me"—he did a little circle thing with his finger in the air—"inside out."

"Good times." I smiled.

"Do you see me complaining?" he practically growled.

The sound of his words set something off in me. Something like fire. I couldn't look away from his face, his eyes, his mouth.

Oh, hell nope.

I'd given up on that kind of relationship. With anyone. Too complicated.

"Maybe you should tell me about that letter," he rumbled. "Was it dirty?"

I couldn't talk because my mouth had turned into a desert.

The fire truck pulled off the main road and started through the parking lot toward the restroom.

"Thank goodness the firefighters are here," Jean said.

"There's no actual fire," I said again.

"Not in the restroom, there isn't," she said. "But you two? Whew." She waved her hand in front of her face and laughed.

And Bathin, damn him, laughed with her.

CHAPTER THREE

"SO, WE have a new god in town," Delaney said, adjusting the bundle strapped to her chest. "Well, not a new god. He's been here before, but he's back now."

I sipped my tea and stared across the diner table at my sister. She fiddled with the strap of the backpack she'd slung around so it hung in front of her and set the whole thing on the booth seat next to her.

The backpack squirmed, the lump of whatever it was inside it getting bigger, until it was…sitting up?

"What's in the backpack?"

She turned from waving down the waitress for coffee and stared at the pack.

"It's…you know." She reached over and unzipped the top of the bag. Two soft, pointed ears popped up into the air, followed quickly by a fuzzy pink head, darling bright eyes, and a little piggy snout.

"You're carrying the dragon in a backpack?" I asked.

"Don't even start. It's a long story. Ryder didn't have time to 'babysit my problem child.'" She did the finger quote thing, then dropped down on the booth seat next to the pig, who looked happy as a…well, a dragon pig in a pancake house.

"He was taking Spud to the vet and was worried pig dragon would get bored alone in the house and eat something. Like the couch. Or our bed."

I tipped my head, studying the pig. "Could he?"

She nodded, then shrugged.

The waitress, an elderly woman who moved like both knees had retired back in the Eisenhower administration, shuffled over and poured a nice, steady stream of coffee into Delaney's mug.

The heavy scent of fresh coffee mixed with the smells of bacon, eggs, and the hot apple crumble they baked from scratch every day.

It was only five o'clock in the morning, and the breakfast

rush, such as it was, hadn't hit the Blue Owl yet. The truckers who used the parking lot to catch some sleep had already rumbled out of town hours ago, and the commuters heading to the valley or up and down the coast wouldn't be here for at least another thirty minutes.

"You going to tell me what really happened at that restroom yesterday?" she asked me after she'd drunk half her coffee.

"You read my report."

"Yes, and I talked to Jean. And Bathin." There went the other half of her coffee. Down in two gulps. Somebody wasn't getting enough sleep.

I took a sip of my tea so I didn't immediately start grilling her on what Bathin said about what happened at the restroom. Because I didn't care what he thought.

"There was a crossroads demon," I said. "I asked her for information on how to get your soul back."

Delaney nodded. She was far calmer about having her soul in the hands of a demon than I was. I couldn't understand that about her, and honestly, it made me angry that she just accepted she'd have to give up something like that to keep this town, and these people, safe.

"You didn't make a deal?" she asked.

Again.

"I did not make a deal. I was blackmailing her, not trading cows for beanstalks."

She smiled briefly, then leaned her elbows on the table. "Blackmail. Why, Myra, I didn't know you had it in you. Naughty."

I waved her comment away, which signaled our waitress to return. Poor thing had barely made it back to the order counter behind us. At the speed she was ambling, we had time to talk about anything we needed to before she was in range to overhear our conversation.

"Then Bathin showed up. He knew the demon. Didn't like her much," I said.

Delaney rubbed at one eye. "Okay, about that. He told me she's dangerous."

"All demons are dangerous."

"We have one demon who is living inside Ordinary. If he tells me some crossroads demon who's been operating in a public bathroom none of us have ever been inside..." She shook her head. "I mean, how is it even possible we've never been in that bathroom?"

"It's technically outside Ordinary, or at least the circle she worked within." I glanced over at our waitress, who was still steaming along. "Don't you think it's amazingly coincidental that I happened to find that crossroads demon who happened to be susceptible to blackmail for information? Amazingly coincidental that Bathin showed up just as I was closing the crossroads?"

Delaney tipped up her mug, but the coffee was gone. She set it down and frowned at it. Her dragon pig had dug his way out of the backpack and snuffled over to sit next to Delaney like he expected a plate to be set for him. Probably so he could eat the plate.

She distractedly picked up her napkin and held it down for him. He took it in his little maw and just held it there for a second. Dragon pig with a clean white napkin hanging out of his mouth.

A tiny flicker of fire kindled in his little piggy eyes. Then he hoovered the napkin into his mouth, chewed, and swallowed, all in one blindingly fast motion. A tiny puff of steam curled up from his cute little snout, and his curly tail wagged.

"I just chalked it up to your family gift. Right place. Right time." Delaney dropped her hand and petted his head. The dragon pig arched up into each stroke, made a grunting sound, and then snuggled up closer to Delaney, still sitting like a perfect little dragon pig waiting for his breakfast.

Why did I get the sense that he wasn't just waiting for breakfast? From the way he sat, it looked like he was waiting for someone or something to do anything to threaten Delaney so he could eat them.

Dragons were like that.

"You think Bathin set it all up?" Delaney asked.

"I do."

"But he was on your side. He wanted to shut the crossroads down and get rid of the demon."

"Sure. That's what he said. For all I know, he made her show up there, created that crossroads, and did it all to feed me false information for how to save your soul."

The waitress finally landed on our shore, and we both ordered breakfast.

"Okay," Delaney said. "Don't eat the fork."

The dragon pig stood to its full, tiny height and carefully rested its head on the top of the table, snout almost touching the fork that rested near Delaney's elbow. "Why would Bathin go through the effort and trouble of making a crossroads, then shut down a crossroads? What's in it for him?"

The dragon pig opened his mouth and inched his little lips closer to the shiny silver cutlery.

"No fork."

"He wants to get on my good side?" I suggested.

Delaney took a moment to really look at me, my uniform: clean; hair: neat; makeup: on point. She might be under-caffeinated for the day, but she was no slouch in paying attention to the people and things around her.

"Do not eat the cutlery," Delaney warned the dragon pig.

The dragon pig closed his mouth, but didn't really move his snout away from the fork. He did give it a longing look.

"Bathin wants to get on your good side to what?" Delaney continued. "Keep you from finding a way to release my soul?"

"That's what I'm thinking."

"Okay, so why were you at the viewpoint? I thought Jean talked you into helping her pick out a Valentine's Day gift for Hogan."

"She didn't need my help. She just wanted someone to shop with her and buy her lunch."

"So why did you go to the restroom?"

"I knew I should be there. So I went."

"Then it was the family gift."

I nodded.

"We know Bathin doesn't have any influence over that," she said. "Where's the… Oh my gods. Where's the fork?"

The pig was still sitting next to her as if he hadn't moved at all, his snout pressed on the edge of the table so that only his little button eyes could peer over the top, his pink, perky ears straight up. There was a tiny puff of smoke wafting out of his nostrils.

He was fricking adorable, and I couldn't help it—I chuckled. "I think he ate it."

"Oh, for gods' sake. Really?" She scowled at the little pink menace. "Do you know how many spoons I have left in my house? Three. I have three spoons. And it's not like I ever see him climbing up to open the silverware drawer. I can't tell if he's convinced Spud to bury them, if he's eating them, or if he's hoarding them. Spud's such a doofus dog, he'll do almost anything to make Terrible here happy." She glowered at the dragon pig. His eyes rolled just enough that he could see her, but he squeaked like a good, terrible piggy dragon, and wagged his tail even faster.

Was it even possible for him to look cuter? Yes. Yes, it was.

"Check the backpack?" I suggested.

"I'll check the backpack, but you know what else a"—she lowered her voice—"a dragon can do? It can cloak things that it likes to steal. Ask me how I know this." She dug through the backpack. There were no forks.

"How do you know this?" I asked, playing along. She might be complaining, but I was pretty sure she wasn't upset that a dragon in the form of a tiny baby pig had adopted her and moved right in with her and Ryder.

While none of us knew why the dragon had decided to come into town—unless we wanted to believe a trickster god, that the dragon was a Christmas gift—the dragon had already proved useful.

Dragons could track down demons.

Much to Bathin's dismay.

And my utter, utter delight.

Anything that made Bathin dismayed was my kind of thing. Including a not-so-innocent cutlery-eating dragon pig, and yes, even questionable crossroads demons.

Our breakfast arrived on the much speedier knees of a younger waitress, who gave us both a quick smile, pulled bottles of ketchup and hot sauce out of her apron pocket, left a full carafe of coffee on the table with a quick "On the house, chief," and then was off in a flash to handle the small crowd of customers waiting to be seated.

"There was a fire hydrant in the middle of our bedroom," Delaney said.

I blinked. "A fire hydrant."

"Yep."

"A real fire hydrant?"

"Yes."

"As in, a functional fire hydrant that belongs to the city?"

"As in, a functional fire hydrant that not only belongs to the city but also belongs on Northwest Twelfth Street, and had been missing for a week."

"Week." I was trying to figure out why I hadn't heard about it. Also, how the hell did one steal a fire hydrant? There was water attached to those things. Water that gushed and flooded when the hydrant was disturbed.

She gulped fresh coffee then took a bite of her sourdough toast. "I didn't know it was gone. Nobody knew it was gone. No one called it in."

"Explain." I started in on my breakfast. I'd ordered the scramble with onion and mushrooms, fresh tomato slices on the side, and buttermilk biscuits. All made from scratch and with the kind of deft hand that would keep people coming back even if this wasn't the only twenty-four-hour diner in town.

"It looked like the hydrant was there. No one in the neighborhood thought it was missing. There was no water going anywhere. The only thing that was kind of weird was that dogs didn't like walking past it. That happened enough that a couple neighbors called in to mention it to us."

It had to be one of the creatures who lived on the street. Humans never paid attention to the supernatural unless it was right up in their faces and unavoidable. Most humans would just think their dogs were being quirky or acting silly if they shied away from a fire hydrant.

But those of us who kept the town's secrets knew that dogs—really most animals—had great instincts when it came to things outside the realm of normal.

"So you checked it out?"

She nodded. "Ryder and I drove by. Pinko here was with us." She tipped her head toward the dragon pig, who was now snuffling at the backpack. I wasn't sure if he was trying to find a way to crawl into it, or if he was wondering if it would make a good palate cleanser.

"Do not eat the backpack," Delaney said without glancing at him.

"You are sounding more and more like Mom," I said.

She chewed bacon angrily at me. "Shut up."

"It's uncanny," I went on just to needle her. "Have you and Ryder talked kids? Because it looks like you've got the scolding and annoyed face down."

"Shut your mouth." She bit down on more bacon, but this time she grinned. "And no, we have not talked about kids because we are taking our relationship slow and easy."

I raised an eyebrow. "Nothing about your relationship has ever been easy. You both ignored your feelings for each other for years before you sort of caught fire and exploded into love last spring."

"We did not explode."

"Like a fuel-leaking rocket."

"How's that flirting thing going with Bathin?" she asked between crunches.

"I do not flirt with him."

"Uh-huh."

"I don't." My face was heating up. Stupid face.

"Yes, you do, Mymy. All the time. And he flirts back. Constantly. Are you going to date him? Is that what you want?"

My brain was throwing out mayday signals, and my heart was jumping under my skin. I was *not* going to admit to my sister that I was attracted to Bathin. Because I wasn't attracted, obviously. I was just…

lonely

…interested in him so I could get rid of him. Or, at the very least, make him give Delaney back her soul.

"So that fire hydrant," I said. "That's so fascinating. How did you figure out it was missing?"

"You still haven't told me what happened on Christmas when you two had wine and 'talked' all night," she said.

"There was no flooding?" I said. "How does that even happen? The water main wasn't shut off."

"Is that what really happened on Christmas, Myra? You talked all night? Or was there something else going on between you two even then?"

"Illusions I can understand, but dragons don't have control over the elements. Well, most of them don't. You haven't seen any other suspicious water situations at home, have you?" I asked.

"Because even though I'm not sure falling for a demon is a good idea, I can see the appeal." She pursed her lips, thinking. "He's…well, not *nice*, but he's hot. And since he's here in Ordinary, he's going to have to abide by the rules, which could work for something short term? I just worry about you. I know you're not the casual dating type, and Bathin seems like the kind of guy who isn't really into settling down."

"I mean, a stolen fire hydrant is a pretty big thing. Have you seen any other strange water situations, like the toilet flushing counterclockwise? Or the sink flowing upward. Maybe tea evaporating before it hits the cup?"

"You know I drink coffee, not tea," Delaney said, breaking our not-answering-each-other standoff. "I'm worried about you, My."

"I know. I know how to take care of myself. And I'm not going to get involved with anyone."

Her eyes softened and she reached out and touched the back of my hand. "That's what I'm worried about. Not that you'll be careful—I know you'll be careful. You're *always* careful. You won't put yourself at risk. But…life is all about taking risks sometimes."

I made a groaning sound. This wasn't the first time she'd given me this talk.

"Just," she said, pressing her warm palm down across my hand until my palm flattened on the cool linoleum table, "listen."

When I said nothing, she took it as compliance. "You deserve all the love and happiness in the world, Myra. Not because you are hardworking and responsible and smart and dedicated. But because you're kind and hopeful and funny and just…you. You shouldn't close yourself away from all the good things that could be yours just because there's a chance something might go wrong."

"Are you calling me a coward?" It made me angry that she thought of me that way, but another part of me knew she was right. I'd risked my heart early, and been turned down, thrown away. I didn't ever want to feel that way again.

"No. Oh my gods, of course not. You're one of the bravest people I know. But when it comes to reaching out, to being vulnerable, no, that's not quite it either." She bit her bottom lip for a second. "When it comes to risking your heart, that's when you hesitate."

She pressed on the back of my hand and squeezed it gently. "And I get it. I know why you are so cautious. I'm not one to talk. It took me years to get straight with Ryder. With what I feel for him."

"Are you done?"

"You know Jean and I have your back. Anything you get yourself into, anything at all, we'll be there to handle it if you need us. No questions asked."

"Is this about me joining the roller derby team without telling you?"

"No." She lifted her hand and took another drink of coffee. "Maybe. You get pretty…insular sometimes. I'm worried you won't talk to us when you need someone to listen. Or someone just to bounce ideas off."

It still stung a little that she thought I wasn't brave or open enough to be trusted to handle my personal stuff on my own. But another part of me, the logic engine in my head that never stopped chugging, heard what she said, and did not deny she had a point.

I hadn't told her about that letter yet, had I?

I'd done my best to keep my family—my two sisters and myself—together and safe since Dad had passed away. That had included me stepping up as the family information resource. I had inherited all of the records, journals, and volumes and volumes of lore and legends—enough to fill an entire underground bunker—from Dad.

It was my job to understand the creatures and gods and beings who lived in Ordinary. It was my job to understand the creatures and gods and beings who lived outside of Ordinary.

When something went wrong, I was the one who did the research and came up with a solution to the problem.

My inability to date, my broken heart that had had plenty of time to heal back together but had done so crooked and wrong like a poorly set bone. It refused to open up to so much as look at someone much less actually feel something for them…

…*except Bathin*…

…wasn't something I could research and find an easy answer for.

"I'm just not in a place where loving someone—loving someone new—fits in my life," I said. It was honest. Maybe not what she wanted to hear, but it was not a lie.

She knew that too, my surprisingly wise sister, who carried the burden of allowing gods to set their powers down so they could store them and live here in our little tourist town. My sister who stood against the will of gods when they refused to follow the rules of this land, my sister, too old for her years, who faced down powerful beings without once complaining or backing down.

"I like what I do, Myra," she said gently.

"Are you reading my mind?"

"No. You just get this look on your face when you're worried about me and the gods. It's a different look than when you're worried about me and my missing soul, and an even different look than when you're all annoyed that I bring that kind of stuff up." She grinned, and her hand left mine so she could point a finger at me. "Just like that. That's the face. That's your annoyed face."

"So we're moving on from my lack of love life?"

"Sure. But that's not what this was all about. You get that, right? What this is all about is you not keeping everything to yourself. This is about you talking to me. I'm right here, Myra. I'm your sister. You know I love you. And you know I'm your boss, too. Which means you should be impressed that I haven't actually ordered you to do what I want. Because I am the best boss you've ever had and do not abuse my privilege."

I snorted. "Did you find the hydrant?" I asked.

She didn't press me about the subject change because she

was my sister and, yeah, the best boss I'd ever had.

"Nope." She leaned back, her gaze taking in the diner around us, like she had suddenly seen something or heard a familiar voice. There were more customers here now, and the ambient noise was made of friendly conversations that rose and fell just above the piped-in eighties tunes. I took a look around too. I knew most of the people in the diner, including my across-the-street neighbor who was eating alone in the corner, absorbed in a book.

Jonah was a nice enough neighbor. New to Ordinary, he used to live in a rental shack on the outskirts of town, but as soon as the little one-bedroom ranch style across the street opened up, he'd moved. It was closer to his work at the supermarket and to the beach, so it seemed like it suited him well.

He came across as socially awkward and prone to sweating, but otherwise hadn't done anything to stand out in the neighborhood.

"And?" I prompted her.

"Ryder tripped over it."

"In the street?"

"In the middle of the bedroom. Right where we walk to the bathroom every single day, except for yesterday. Blank air? Suddenly filled with a very solid, very heavy fire hydrant that almost very broke his ankle when he fell over it."

I chuckled. The dragon pig interpreted that sound as approval, and the dragon pig was not wrong. I'd done a lot of research on dragons, and this one in particular since it had trotted out of a sea cave and into my sister's life. This particular dragon had a knack for illusion. And like most dragons, he liked to hoard things.

But he was known to hoard unusual things. Gold, sure. But more often ancient texts, heart stones of long-forgotten civilizations, and, apparently, fire hydrants.

Maybe he'd left the letter. "Say…" I started, trying to think of how to bring this up.

Delaney's gaze fixed on whomever had just walked through the doors.

I looked over my shoulder and couldn't help but be a little

happy to see the man walking our way. Well, not a man, a god. On vacation.

Eros, or Cupid when he was a god, just went by Bo here in Ordinary.

Artists did not do him justice. Depicting him as a handsome man or a cute, chubby cherub missed the mark of the god himself by several miles.

Because the Cupid we knew, this man, whom we hadn't seen in years, looked like a hard-edged, fighting-fit old biker. He was bald and wore two gold hoops in his earlobes and a glint of diamond at the top of the right ear. His beard was really a long gray goatee topped by a mustache that almost, but didn't quite, make for handlebar style.

He wore black leather jacket, pants, and boots. Tattoos colored every inch of skin I'd ever seen—his arms, shoulders, his feet, back and chest, and his hands. I'd noticed most of that ink when he'd been in Ordinary for several summers, and could often be found down on the beach drinking beer and throwing rocks at seagulls.

"Where'd you stash his power?" I asked.

"Since he's the first god to come back to town, I just put it in the vault," Delaney said. "When the next god shows up, it will be his or her responsibility to keep the powers."

"How many years has it been since Cupid has been in town?" I was usually good at dates, but I was pulling a blank on this one.

"About a decade," she said. Then she raised her hand and waved him over, offering the open chair at the end of the table.

He clomped over and lowered himself into the seat with a grunt. "Isn't this cozy?" he said in his musical baritone. "Been a couple of years, hasn't it, my beauties? Police work agrees with you both. I'm sorry to hear of your dad's passing. He was a great heart of a man, with a will of thunder."

That was Cupid. Outside, he was a take-no-shit badass; inside, he had the melancholy of a world-weary poet.

I supposed if one was the god who could make people fall in love, make things come together—including, if his stories were to be believed, light and darkness, matter and energy, heaven and earth—and if one also had the power to rend all of those things asunder, to tear every note out of the harmony of the universe, one might have a rather unique perspective on the world and all who lived within it.

"Thank you," Delaney said. "Coffee?"

He nodded and shrugged out of his leather jacket, draping it across the back of his chair. He wore a plain black T-shirt, which revealed impressively muscled and impressively inked arms.

Delaney turned over the extra cup on the table, filled it from the carafe, and handed it to him.

The white ceramic looked tiny in his wide, calloused hands. Across the knuckles of his right hand was the word GOLD, and a dove in flight spread over the back of his hand and up his arm. The knuckles of his left hand were tattooed with the word LEAD, and an angry owl glowered across the back of his hand and arm.

"How's Ordinary treating you so far?" Delaney asked.

"Better now." He gave a little toast with the cup and gulped down half the coffee. He kept the cup curved in his hand, maybe for the warmth, and rested his other elbow on the table. "I see you've been up to no good since I've been gone."

"How so?" Delaney asked.

I finished my breakfast. Bo was one of the gods who took to humanity like a fish to water. I supposed working in the business of connections and separations, working in the business of the human heart, gave him an advantage.

"No soul," he said, nodding at Delaney. "Demon?"

Delaney nodded back. "He's in town. He's following the rules."

"Is he now? He got a name?"

"Bathin," I said.

Bo blinked once then took a drink of his coffee to hide his confused frown. "Explains the dragon," he said. "You find that?"

Delaney shook her head. "Gift from Crow. Or so he told me, and, you know—trickster."

Bo inhaled through his nose, long as a sigh. "Demons are a trick in and of themselves. Didn't know they were allowed in Ordinary."

"Ordinary is refuge and home to any creature, as long as they follow the laws and rules," Delaney said. "Even gods who are hiding out from the one day a year everyone pays attention to them."

He grunted.

"What are you doing here before Valentine's Day?" she asked.

He grimaced. "Can't a man just want some peace and quiet for no reason?"

"A man, sure," I said. "But a god tends to think out the reasons for wanting to put his power down for a while."

"I don't recall getting the third degree last time I came into town." He wasn't upset. If anything, his eyes had a twinkle in them.

It looked like he'd missed being here, maybe missed being among people who knew what his day job was, and didn't treat him differently because of it.

"Well, the new guard runs things a little differently," Delaney said. "We've had a rough year."

Understatement. She'd been shot—twice. Her soul had been taken. We'd had to track down a kidnapper, a murderer, and an ancient evil. Delaney's boyfriend, Ryder, had been drafted into service to a god—and not one of the nice ones who liked us.

That was a lot to cram into a three-sixty-five.

"Noticed all the deities are AWOL," Bo said. "Some story behind that?"

"I kind of died for a minute." Delaney looked embarrassed, like she was admitting she'd locked her keys in her car.

His eyebrows went up, sending wrinkles across his forehead and scalp. "Well." He nodded. "Well."

"Death was here," I said. "It's a long story, but turns out he doesn't like being denied a death he's been after for centuries. Not Delaney's, something else. But her letting go of the ability to allow gods into Ordinary was all part of his plan. Not that he let us know."

Bo relaxed at that. "Thanatos is quite a thing. Relentless." It was said with fondness, and not for the first time, I wondered exactly where in the ages and stories of gods Bo fit in.

Some said he was the first god; some said he was the son of Chaos and Darkness. Some said he was just a cute kid who happened to have War and Love as parents.

I had the lore and ancient texts that no mortal outside of Ordinary had ever had the chance to read, but no one had seemed to nail down Eros's origin.

"He opened a kite shop," Delaney said.

Bo laughed, the sound of it deep and delighted, and as Delaney added in the details of Death in Hawaiian shirts and expensive tailored slacks and Italian shoes, the laugh went hissy and got us, and a few curious people a booth over, giggling too.

He finally wiped the tears off his reddened face. "Ah, I miss this place," he said. "Can't believe I waited so long to come back."

"How long are you staying?" I asked.

"At least through to March."

"Can't handle another Valentine's Day in the real world?" Delaney asked.

"You have no idea. Love." He shook his head. "No thing more complicated than that thing."

I picked up the carafe and filled his cup. "Welcome to the club."

CHAPTER FOUR

I'D FACED down dangerous monsters, dangerous humans, dangerous deities. I'd been involved in "community-building" exercises that were primarily a test of sheer grit and willpower to get through. I'd done plenty of trust falls and faith climbs, and joined the roller derby so I could get physical and risk breaking a bone now and then—for fun.

But this? This was hell.

"It is not hell," Jean insisted, pointing her pink-and-white lollipop that matched her hair color at me. "This is what normal people call fun."

The bowling alley had been rearranged to make room for twenty small tables decorated with bud vases of roses, small mason jar candle holders wrapped in twine and wooden hearts, pens, notepads, a bowl of paper strips, and chess timers.

This was not a chess tournament. I wished it were. I would at least feel like I belonged there. This was…

"Speed dating is so passé," I croaked. It was like all the spit in my mouth had dried up and turned into the light sheen of panic sweat that covered my skin. "They make apps for this stuff now."

Jean chuckled. "We are a tiny little tourist town on the edge of the cold, cold Pacific Ocean. We're allowed to be behind the times in some things. Our internet provider can't even guarantee we have steady wireless if the wind blows too hard, much less that it will stay connected long enough to right swipe. And yet"—she grinned, the stick of the lollipop tucked against the corner of her mouth—"we endure."

People milled around. The clash and roll of pins and bowling balls took up a layer of noise in the place, grinding and growling over the music that was supposed to be romantic, but sounded like opera keyed down and played too slow.

The usual stale smells of beer, hotdogs, popcorn, and the weird off-brand disinfectant spray Jacques used on the shoes was mixed in with the heavy scent of vanilla candles, and two chocolate fountains burbling along somewhere near the pool tables.

"You look fantastic," Jean went on, checking out my outfit.

I wore black slacks and a light blue button-down shirt. Nothing fancy. Nothing speed-date-appropriate. Because when she and Delaney had called me to meet them for dinner and bowling, I'd expected dinner and bowling.

"Here we go." Delaney handed each of us a beer. "I could see you panicking from clear across the room. Thought a beer might help a little. You know, this is just for fun, Myra. You don't actually have to date any of these people."

I was starting to itch. I was allergic to this. Allergic to dating fast, slow, or at any speed.

"Why don't you do it, then?" I said.

"Because," she said patiently as she tipped the beer in my hand toward my mouth, encouraging me to drink, "I am already in love, and so is Jean. Bertie needed one more single woman to round out the list of people who signed up, and it counts as a community event, so she insisted someone from the police force be here to represent us."

"Why not Hatter?" I said. "He's single. Why not Shoe?"

"They're on duty. Someone has to keep an eye on this town while the rest of us take the evening off."

"You suck," I said.

She scowled. "Fine. Next time, I'll let you tell Bertie no."

She had a point. Bertie was the town's one and only Valkyrie. She didn't take no for an answer. Over anyone's dead body. Ever.

"So I just have to sit at a table and listen to someone talk for five minutes?"

"Three," Delaney said.

Okay, I could do this. I could. It wasn't a real date. I'd hauled lots of people into the station and made them talk while sitting across a cold, hard table from them. This was more like that: an interrogation.

My shoulders started to relax a little at that idea.

I could interrogate someone. Easy. All day. Fast or slow. No problem. I could even have a little fun with that.

"Reed sisters," came a far-too-familiar and far-too-annoying male voice.

Not male. Demon.

I glanced up. Bathin was sauntering our way, his gaze locked with mine.

He wore a deep red button-down shirt that was unbuttoned at his neck, a small charcoal square of cloth in his pocket. The shirt stretched like poured silk over the muscles of his chest, shoulders, and flat stomach. It was tucked into a pair of tailored gray slacks that looked like they'd been made for him alone.

His dark hair was pulled back, not long enough for a band, but longer than it had been when he'd first showed up in town. A curl of it fell artfully over his forehead, and I clenched my hand to keep from brushing it off his face—or slapping it off his face for being so annoyingly perfect.

Could go either way.

He looked gorgeous, dangerous, dark.

Chaos and trouble. Heartbreak and hope.

I took a long, long pull of my beer.

"Bathin." Jean popped the candy out of her mouth and pointed it at him. "Don't you clean up nice?"

"I'm even better at getting dirty." He waggled his eyebrows at her.

Jean barked out a laugh. How could she think he was charming or funny? How could she fall for that?

How could anyone not?

"I just bet you do." She grinned.

"You already have a boyfriend, Jean," I blurted, maybe a little too quickly and a little too loudly.

Kill me with a crowbar.

All three of them turned to look at me, surprised.

"What are you even doing here?" I asked. "Like that?" I waved my beer in his general direction then decided another drink sounded really dandy right about then. So I drank.

"Well." He drew that word out a little too long, as if he were trying to figure out how to talk to a toddler about sex. "I'm in Ordinary because of a business deal I made with first your father, and then your sister. I'm here in this bowling alley because I am single and ready to mingle."

And then he winked.

Winked.

There was no way my heart fluttered a little at that. There was no way I found him charming despite all the terrible things I knew he actually was.

Liar.

"So Bertie forced you into this too?" Delaney asked him.

He nodded, his eyes a little wider than before. "I have faced down many formidable opponents. But Bertie takes her battles to another level."

"Never argue with a Valkyrie," Jean suggested. "Not if you like breathing."

"Quite," he agreed. "And you, Myra? Are you offering your virgin neck upon the dating chopping block this evening?"

"Nothing about me is virgin," I grumbled. "Not even my neck."

Delaney choked on her beer and coughed hard enough and long enough to bring tears to her eyes. In between her coughing fit, she managed to gasp out, "Don't even want to know what you meant by that."

Bathin opened his mouth to say something, but Bertie showed up and rang a little bell to get everyone's attention.

Bertie was a petite, spry woman who appeared to be in her eighties, her white hair short and styled in a blunt, businesslike style. She wore a flamingo-pink jacket, a white pencil skirt, and heels, all trimmed by a thin line of gold that should have made the whole thing look ridiculous, but instead pulled it all together.

Her gold nails glinted with tiny diamonds and rubies set upon them.

"Thank you all so much for coming to the first speed-dating event in Ordinary. We have a suggestion box near the shoe rental counter. If you have a suggestion for how we can improve or grow this event, or if you'd like to vote on what we should call this event going forward, please drop a note in the box before you leave.

"You have each been given a number when you arrived. There is a corresponding number on a table. Please find your table and take a seat. If you have a red card, you will remain seated at the table. All those with green cards will move from table to table after the three-minute bell rings. This is the three-minute bell."

She rang the little crystal bell in her hand that appeared to have a drop of blood, or maybe a heart, in the center as the clapper.

Everyone glanced at their cards and got moving with nervous laughter and excitement—seriously, *excitement?*—toward the tables.

"You're table four," Jean said from way down a tunnel somewhere.

I lifted my beer to my mouth, but it was empty. Had Delaney swapped my full beer out for an empty one? Not funny. Not funny at all. I glared over at her, and she had this ridiculously amused look on her face.

Of course Ryder had shown up and was standing behind her, his arms wrapped around her waist, their bodies pressed close together. He watched me over her shoulder and looked pretty amused too.

What was wrong with these people?

"Myra?" Jean said, touching my shoulder. "Table four." She pointed.

I looked away from Ryder's stupid smiling face just long enough to notice he had a fresh, cold beer in one hand.

"Beer me," I demanded.

Ryder tipped his head a little to the side, his lips pressed down against a laugh. He leaned into Delaney and stretched the beer out for me.

Delaney, the traitor, was laughing.

I nodded my thanks to Ryder, and he nodded back. The acknowledgment of a fellow soldier who knew just how bad things were at the front. I knocked back another deep swallow or two of beer, turned, and marched to table four.

Let's get on with this.

CHAPTER FIVE

First Guy:

"Dustin, is it?" I asked with a bored glance at his name tag. "Is that your name?"

"Ha-ha, you've known me since high school, Myra."

"Just answer the question, sir. Is Dustin your name?"

"Um, yes? Why? Did you expect it to be something else?"

"I'll be the one asking the questions today. When you speed on the highway, do you have your cell phone in your hand?"

"I don't... I haven't. I have a dash mount for my cell phone," he finally managed.

"So you admit to speeding?"

He groaned. "Oh, God, this is going to be debate team all over again, isn't it?"

Second Guy:

"How long have you lived here, Stan?"

"Four years." His hands were folded on the table in front of him, his gaze steady. He must have seen Dustin's frantic escape and had steeled himself for the next three minutes.

"And before that?"

"Texas."

Short, jury-ready answers. I approved.

"You work at a chiropractor's office, is that correct?"

"Yes."

He *was* the chiropractor. I was surprised he hadn't given me that detail. Most doctors couldn't wait to brag about their degrees and specialties.

"What did you do before you came to Ordinary?"

"I was a divorce attorney."

Ah, well, that explained some things.

"Is there a reason you chose to move halfway across the country to a small town almost no one and certainly no news agency has heard of while also changing your career and your lifestyle?"

He grinned like he was enjoying this. "No comment, officer."

THIRD GUY was a gal:

"Look," Mindy said when she dropped into the chair, "I'm gay, and I'm in a committed relationship."

I knew that, and I knew her. She was a tax accountant. She was *my* tax accountant.

I was surprised she was here tonight. Tax season was underway, and her schedule had to be insane.

"This is a speed-dating event, Mindy. Do you think Tiana would approve?"

"Oh, I *know* she will." Mindy pulled a binder out of her bag and slapped it down on the table between us. "We have three daughters. Three. The minimum order is five boxes. Take your pick."

I glanced down. It was a Girl Scout cookie order form.

"You could have sent out an email. You know I'd place an order."

"Nope. I'm taking care of all our orders now. Tonight."

"How many do you need to sell?"

"Two hundred boxes."

"That's not so bad."

"For each girl."

"Oh," I said. "Oh."

She slid the pen over to me, a steely look in her eyes. "Less time I spend selling cookies, the faster I'll get through tax work."

"I don't think it's legal to blackmail clients with cookies," I grumbled.

"Not blackmail, just letting you in on the facts. And they are *delicious* cookies, which you will get whole and not crushed, like all the fancy cookies at the grocery store and gas stations."

"The cookies at the grocery store are crushed?"

"Everyone's been complaining about it for the last couple months. You hadn't heard?"

"No. Are you telling me the Girl Scouts are literally

crushing their competition?"

She looked startled by that. "No, not at all! That's against everything the organization stands for. We just noticed that the bags of fancy cookies are all broken up. Could be a shipping issue."

"Hm."

She shook her head. "You can strap me to a lie detector. None of the girls in the troop, or anyone involved with Girl Scouts, is going around crushing cookies. Because we don't have to. Our cookies are delicious and addictive. They sell themselves."

She was not wrong. I picked up the pen and filled out my order. "Put me down for ten boxes, and say hello to the girls for me."

THIRD-TO-last guy:

"Have you ever lied to get out of jury duty?"

Tom had lasted a whole minute before breaking out in a sweat, his eyes darting around, looking for escape.

"N-no. Why would you? What do you mean?"

"Remember you're talking to an officer of the law, Tom," I said. My beer was long gone, but I was having a surprisingly good time speed interrogating.

"Is that a question from the little bowl?" He reached for the bowl of paper strips with suggested icebreaker questions printed on them. "Maybe I should…uh…ask you something now?"

"Have you ever broken a packaged cookie?"

"I… Maybe?"

"We've had cookie-crushing incidents in the grocery stores and gas stations. You buy gas, don't you, Tom? Shop for food?"

He pawed through the paper like there was a door to salvation at the bottom. "Yes?"

"You've broken a cookie once or twice—I mean, who hasn't?"

"Yes—I mean, no! Only mine. After I buy them?"

I stared at him and made a little note in the book they'd given us for just such a thing. Okay, not for this, but for whatever people who were good at dating would want to make a note of.

"Are you…um…writing down something about me?"

I just kept writing. At this point it was a doodle, a little monster throwing cookies in his huge mouth and *I hate Delaney and Jean* carved into an anatomically correct heart.

"I did…I saw…a guy," Tom said into the silence I'd refused to break. "He was behind me at the grocery store? He was standing in the aisle, blocking it so I couldn't get my cart by. And he picked up those bag cookies, the expensive ones, in both hands and snarled at them. Held them up to his face and sort of growled."

Really? I hadn't actually expected to get a lead on this. I was just using the cookie line of interrogation to pass time.

The only action I was going to take on the cookie petty crime was to suggest the stores get a camera on the aisle and send employees down there more often to monitor the damage.

"What did the shopper look like?"

"Uh, short? Just under five foot, I'd say? Wore a hat. I didn't really look at him that closely."

"Short? Not a child?"

"M-maybe? No, I don't think so. He was wearing a suit under a coat."

"Did he look like a tourist?"

"What does a tourist look like?"

"Like someone you've never seen in town before."

"Oh. I didn't look that closely. He wasn't wandering around like he'd never been in the store before."

"Age?"

"Fifties—no, sixties?"

"Race?"

"Caucasian."

"Tom," I said with a smile, "you have just given us our first lead on this case. Thank you."

Everything about Tom relaxed. He looked like a man who had just walked away from the firing squad with a glass of champagne and a smoke.

"Let me get your name and number in case we need to talk to you again," I said. "Is that all right?"

"Sure," he said. "Yes, sure."

Tom was a cable installer, and a nice guy. Although that whole "never lied to a jury" answer was a load of bunk. Everyone lied to get out of jury duty. We had a file full of the best excuses and pulled it out on slow days for a chuckle.

"Do you have any questions for me?" I asked.

Tom looked down at the strip he'd pulled out of the bowl. "Uh, yeah. Dogs or cats?"

I raised one eyebrow and leaned back in my chair, putting on my "good cop" face. "I prefer cats. How about you?"

"Dogs. I mean, cats are okay too? I think?"

"No, no. You don't have to say that. It's clear this wasn't meant to be. I do appreciate your sharp attention at the grocery store, though. Good work there."

I smiled. Tom smiled. We both smiled.

See how nice this was? See how well I could do this?

"Here," I said, reaching for the stash of cool, unopened beers Jean had given me. She probably thought I'd need them to get through the event, but I'd found they worked like a charm as a peace offering.

I didn't have to give out my card or my number, or deal with anything even slightly emotionally messy. Just interrogate a person and hand them a beer.

This was neat. This was orderly. Plus, I actually got a lead on a case without having to go knock on doors.

Not a bad way to spend the night.

I offered the beer to Tom. "To get you through the rest of the event," I said with a smile.

"Thanks, officer." He took the beer and uncapped it. "This was…uh…good?"

"Sure, Tom. Real good. And good luck out there. I noticed Trish has had her eye on you since you first walked in. Have you met her? She works in the pediatric wing of the hospital."

He swallowed beer and then nodded. "Once at a block party. We talked. She seems terrific. She's been watching me?" And yes, that was pure, happy hope in his voice.

I smiled, giving him an encouraging nod. "She has."

"Well," he said with relief and a bit more starch in his spine. "Well. Our three minutes is almost up, right?"

"I think so."

Bertie rang the bell, and Tom ran a hand through his hair, and set his smile in place before strolling over to Trish.

Trish lit up like a lighthouse when she saw him coming her way.

Aw. It was cute. Nice. I liked romance. At least for other people.

I glanced at the clock. The speed-dating part of the event should be almost over. Only a couple people left.

Jonah, my neighbor, settled down in front of me. He was sweating hard, his dark hair slicked up into curls across his forehead, his stubbled jaw glinting with little drops of moisture.

He gave me a hesitant smile that he immediately tamped down. He wiped under his eyes several times. Was he crying?

It was possible he was having an even worse night than I was.

After the Tom thing, I was feeling generous.

"Hey," I said. "Are you feeling okay, Jonah?"

He swallowed, nodded once, then clenched hands together in his lap and stared at me.

Just stared.

It was possible he was even more socially awkward than I'd assumed from watching him come and go across the street.

"Beer?" I pulled out the last one. He took it, careful to keep his fingers from brushing mine, and, after three tries, got it open.

His hand shook a little as he took a drink, then went back to staring.

All right, then. Not a man of many words.

"Your yard's looking nice this year," I said.

He blinked a couple times, and a small, real smile curved his mouth.

Finally.

"Thanks." His voice was bristly and low. I'd always assumed he was human, but now I wasn't so sure.

"How are you liking the new house?" I asked.

"It's…" He nodded, took another drink of beer. This time he looked over his shoulder, as if expecting people to be staring at him.

I took a gander around the room. No one was staring at

him.

"Nice?" I suggested.

"Yes," he agreed. There it was again, something in his voice that told me this was not a human in front of me.

"You haven't been in town for very long," I said amiably. "Where did you move in from?"

His throat worked some more and his eyes went a little wide. "Pennsylvania."

"Ah," I said. "Pretty place to live."

He shook his head, then stopped and shrugged one shoulder. "I like it here. Quiet. I like the rain."

Yep. Definitely not a human. I did a quick rummage through which kinds of creatures might come out of Pennsylvania. It could be anything from an abominable snowman to a vampire.

But this guy wasn't something I immediately recognized. Dark hair, square face, deep voice, bristly. Wart by his left eyebrow, strong teeth. Sweating hard, even though it wasn't all that hot in here. And crying? He wiped under his eyes again. Maybe not crying, but his eyes were watering.

What did that add up to?

I could ask him, but it was a rude thing to do. Now that he was here in Ordinary, he was just one of us, monster, human, or deity. I scanned the crowd to see if Hogan was around. Jean's boyfriend could tell who was what, could see through the outside that gods and monsters projected. But Hogan wasn't around.

I'd just ask him later.

"Flowers." Jonah pointed at the vase. I waited. "Do you like them?"

"Yes, I do."

"Your yard is full of them," he said. "Roses."

Well, this was going better. He seemed to have found a subject that didn't leave him tongue-tied.

"I enjoy gardening," I said. "Do you have a hobby?"

He shook his head, ducked it a little, and gave me a sideways glance. "That's, that's a lie. I, um, write. I like to write."

"That's a nice hobby, Jonah."

His smile went full-wattage brilliant.

"I like it. I'm…head over heels for it." He chanced making eye contact to see how that had gone over.

I smiled. "I'm head over heels for things too."

"What things?"

"Well, my family. My friends."

"Oh," he said, like a light bulb had finally screwed down tight and bright. "Head over heels."

This conversation was ambling off into nowhere.

Luckily, Bertie rang the bell and Jonah bolted out of the chair, heading straight over to Trish and almost colliding with Tom, who was taking his time with his departure.

"Okay then," I said to no one. Jonah was socially awkward, but didn't seem like a bad guy. Maybe once I knew what kind of creature he was, I could make a better connection with him.

"Ah, yes," a deep voice rumbled. "Finally, we are alone."

I closed my eyes for just a second, wishing Bathin would go away. But instead, I heard him settle into the chair in front of me. I could hear him breathing too, steady and deep, could feel the heat of him and smell his cologne.

"Still here," he murmured. "And I won't be leaving for at least three full minutes."

I rubbed at the bridge of my nose, wishing I didn't like the sound of his voice. Wishing I'd found a way to break his hold on Delaney and exile him from Ordinary.

"I brought a gift," he said.

I opened my eyes. He stared straight at me. Smiled.

"I don't want a gift," I said.

"Now, now, Myra. This is a friendly gathering. I'm being friendly. With a friendly gift." He tipped his head down toward the object on the table.

It was a box of tea. A box of very expensive tea that I could only get from one specialty tea shop in Eugene. I loved this tea. It was my favorite.

"What is that?" I asked.

Bathin leaned forward, getting comfortable. "That is tea."

"I don't want it."

"Oh, I think you do."

"Did you bring a gift to every person you speed dated?"

"Would that make you jealous? Are you admitting you have

feelings for me?"

"I don't get jealous and I don't feel anything for you." My heart was pounding too hard, and that little voice in my head was calling out my lie.

I ignored that little voice. Ignored the heck out of it.

"Is that so?" he asked. "I will remind you I am a demon and I can sense when people lie."

"It's not a lie, and because you are a demon, I don't believe that you can tell when a person is lying or not."

"Why would you doubt me?"

"Demons lie."

"We also tell the truth. Often, and to great effect."

He was derailing this conversation and leading it to places I didn't want to be. This wasn't a real date. For me, this wasn't even a speed date. This was a chance to interrogate people.

And Bathin was in the hot seat.

One eyebrow raised. He must have seen my change of attitude. He liked it.

Well, he wasn't going to like it in a minute.

"So demons tell the truth?"

"Yes."

"Good. Think you can tell the truth for the next two minutes?"

"Will you accept the tea if I say yes?"

"Fine. Yes."

"Then my words shall remain pure and true. And honest," he said when I opened my mouth.

"All right. Did you have any part of the crossroads demon being there yesterday?"

He blinked hard. "No. I'm curious as to why you think I might have. I did try to kill her, as you'll recall."

"Don't be so casual about that. Killing someone."

"So now you're a defender of demons? I'm on board for that."

"Do you know what she and I were discussing?"

"I can assume it was how to get rid of me, and that she promised to bring to you a means to my end. Which: hurtful." He winked. "I also assume you were looking for a way to make me give your sister's soul back. But you know I can't do that,

Myra."

"Won't do it, not can't do it."

"That's true. I won't do it."

"Why?"

That question seemed to catch him by surprise. "The possession of a soul isn't a one-way street," he said slowly, as if he were picking his way through the concept.

"Are you saying Delaney owns a part of you? That she owns a part of your soul? I don't believe you. Demons don't have souls."

"No, that's not what I'm saying."

He didn't elaborate. I waited. Time ticked down.

"Are you lying about that?" I asked.

"No."

Which could be a lie. But from how steadily he held my gaze, from what I could see in his eyes—interest, humor, and something more. Something a lot like sincerity. Maybe he wasn't lying.

"Explain how a demon possessing a soul is a two-way street," I said.

"No."

All right, then.

"I'll find out how it works," I said, "you know I will."

"If anyone could, it would be you, Myra Reed. But it is not knowledge found anywhere in this world."

"That won't keep me from finding it."

He spread his hands, looking calm and unconcerned. "Then you will."

"Why don't you just give this up?" I was frustrated, and I knew he could hear it in my voice. "Why don't you just give her back her soul? It would make everything easier. It would make everything better."

"Not everything," he said softly.

"What do you mean?"

The little crystal bell sang out in Bertie's hand, and Bathin sat back and bumped the tea toward me with his long fingers.

"You don't need to give me your number," he said. "I know where you live."

"That doesn't sound stalkery at all."

He grinned. "If I were stalking you, trust me, you'd know."

"Because you'd be sending me creepy poems in the mail?"

He frowned. "No. Why do you ask? Is someone sending you creepy poems?"

"No."

And here was the test. Could he tell I was lying?

His eyebrows rose. "I see."

He could tell. Well, crap.

I looked away, unable to hold his gaze any longer. I covered that by reaching down for an ice cube out of the cooler.

"Is that for me?" he asked.

"Nope." I popped the ice in my mouth.

"Fine, good," he said. "Because I've already gotten what I wanted."

"Uh-huh." I crunched down on the ice, bored, hoping he'd catch a hint and leave me alone.

He stood. "This has been very educational, Myra. Don't you think?"

Something about his words gave me goosebumps. As if he had just gently but firmly wrapped an arm around me, offering me his heat, his strength, his solid presence against all the worries and doubts and fears of the world.

It was a subtle but alluring illusion, and it was very, very tempting to fall into that.

He chuckled softly. "So stubborn." And then, with one last smile, he moved on to the next table.

I found I couldn't look away from him. I found I didn't want to.

CHAPTER SIX

IT WAS over. I resisted the urge to cheer in relief. Several of the participants stayed to play pool or to bowl, which made Jacques happy to have the extra business. People also lingered to exchange numbers.

I got out of there as quickly as I could.

Right past Tom and Trish sitting at the corner table, holding hands and smiling at each other. A lot. It looked like the beginning of something wonderful.

I was happy for them. I was happy for all of them.

I was happy I'd never have to do this again.

My traitorous sisters had hightailed it out of here half an hour ago, because they were not idiots and had caught on to my increasingly threatening glares and gestures.

Bathin was gone too.

I didn't want to think about why I'd paid attention to him all night, but I couldn't stop thinking about him. I wanted that to be because he was a puzzle I hadn't solved yet, a cipher I hadn't broken.

But he was more than that to me. Even if it was just easier to think of him as the obstacle I had to overcome to save my sister from a bind she'd thrown herself into willingly, but not wisely.

I made my way out of the bowling alley and into the rainy, cold February night. It wasn't going to freeze tonight, but it felt cold enough for it. I was sober, had been sober for hours.

The parking lot was well lit and empty. I opened the cruiser door and paused.

There was a small heart-shaped box on the passenger seat.

The only people who had a key to the car were my sisters. If they thought a box of chocolates was going to be enough for me to forgive them for throwing me to the wolves, they were wrong. There was revenge to be had. And I would have it.

Eventually.

I preferred my revenge stone cold and startling. So it'd be weeks or months before I got them back for this. And all the while, they'd be wondering what I was going to spring on them.

I tossed the tea on top of the candy box and drove home.

With the tea and chocolate in my hands, I closed my garage door and walked into my house.

Home.

My shoulders dropped, that tightness that lingered beneath my breastbone easing up with the first step into my own space.

This was my safe place, my happiest place. This cozy house filled with the things I'd dug out of antique stores, pillows I'd made, gifts I'd been given. This was where I cooked and baked, trying at least one new recipe a week.

I could be myself here. Not the middle sister who had a library of arcane information and data stuffed in her head. Not the cop who was fair, if sometimes a little stern. Not the newbie roller derby teammate who still didn't feel like part of the team.

And not the last Reed sister who was still single and not dating.

I placed the boxes on the kitchen counter and started the kettle for tea. Maybe I'd bring the candy to bed with me and eat all the best pieces while sipping tea and watching Netflix.

I pulled off my coat, hung it. Went through the mini-ritual of measuring out the tea leaves and pouring water.

Letting it steep, I turned to the box of candy.

I should leave it here in the kitchen. Otherwise I might be tempted to eat the entire box in one go. Maybe just one piece while I waited for the tea.

I reached for the lid and stopped.

Just stopped. My hand lingered just above the box and all my cop instincts were ringing. There was no plastic wrap on the box.

For a moment, I wished I had Jean's family gift. That I could tell if something dangerous was about to happen.

No. I was being ridiculous. If something dangerous were in the box, I would have noticed it while it was on the car seat next to me. I would have noticed it when I carried it into my house. I would have noticed it when I put it on the counter top.

I flicked the lid off the box.

Worms wriggled and squirmed in damp, fragrant black soil.

Okay, that was…

Creepy

…not funny. I reached over without looking and pulled my mug to my lips. I sipped tea and stared at the little wrigglers poking around in the bed of loose dirt.

Would Jean do this? Would Delaney?

No, I knew my sisters. Giving me a box of worms and dirt after they'd set me up for Bertie's date-o-rama was not their style. They weren't that mean. Also, they knew I could kick their butts.

So who would leave me a box of worms?

After tonight and my hard-line interrogations? Probably every one of the people who had sat at my table.

Bathin?

He'd brought me the expensive tea. But why add worms to the offerings?

I sighed, pulled out my phone, and took a few pictures of the box, then carefully dumped the worms out onto a piece of cardboard and sorted through them to make sure there wasn't anything else in there, like a body part.

Nothing but dirt and worms. That was something, at least.

I grabbed a bucket from the garage and put the worms—which I had rehoused into the box—into it. Then I covered the whole thing with a lid with a couple holes for air. I wasn't going to kill innocent worms just because they'd been part of a terrible Valentine's event.

I washed my hands, wiped down the kitchen, then took my tea and a box of cookies I kept stashed behind my pancake mix into my bedroom.

Should I report this to my sisters?

Yes.

But it could wait until tomorrow. I was tired and a little wrung out from the event. I wanted to be alone. To have some time to turn off my brain.

To recover.

My sisters may have had the best intentions throwing me into the speed dating, but they didn't see it from my perspective.

Each person who had sat down in front of me was a

reminder of what I didn't have. What I'd never have: someone to love.

I shuffled into my bedroom, turned on the light.

"Are you kidding me?"

Right in the middle of my bed, placed neatly on top of three red silk hearts, was a pair of golden scissors.

I blew out a breath and stared up at the ceiling. "All I wanted was a quiet night at home with tea and cookies! But no! I had to do fake dating. And worms. And strange crafting implements. On. My. Bed!

"Whoever snuck in here and left scissors on my bed, I am going to break your arms, because now you've made me feel unsafe in my own damn house, and that, I will not forgive!"

The ceiling, the room, the house around me remained silent. There was no one in the house with me, but there were plenty of people or creatures who could get through any sort of locks I had on the place.

It didn't even have to be a nefarious break-in. Lots of friendlies didn't realize they'd overstepped a human custom until they'd done so. Sometimes a creature new in town took a while to get accustomed to societal norms.

Like not breaking into other people's houses.

But why scissors and hearts?

I shoved a cookie in my mouth and chewed. I wasn't taking another step without some sugar fortitude.

I gulped tea and glared at the bed a little more. "Fine," I said to no one. "I'll do some more work. Totally how I wanted to spend my evening."

For the second time tonight, I took pictures of a possible crime in my own home.

The scissors were small enough that I could fit them in my pocket. Made of gold metal that might actually be gold, covered in symbols and runes scratched along the handles and down the outside of the blades.

Those runes and symbols blurred and danced as I tried to focus on them. They carried a power. Maybe a curse.

I opened my nightstand drawer and put on a pair of gloves knitted from thread that had been blessed and purified and warded against all magics.

I also pulled out a little black bag made of the same thread and woven with thin strands of gold and silver. Whatever was placed in this bag was nullified for a short time. Enough time, I hoped, to figure out what the scissors were, what they were used for, and who had left them for me.

I held my breath then picked up the scissors and the heart cloths beneath them.

Sparks of red and black and silver surrounded the scissors, dripping like melting wax.

There was no heat, no sound, no smell.

But there was knowledge. Sudden and clear, as if someone had whispered it in my ear.

I knew what the scissors were for: cutting Delaney's soul away from Bathin's hold.

Or, more precisely, cutting Bathin's hold away from her soul.

They were a wicked, evil instrument. They would cause him pain. A lot of pain.

There was only one person who would have known about them, and known to bring them to me. Before midnight, just like I'd asked.

The crossroads demon. She had just handed over the way to get rid of Bathin.

I opened the scissors carefully, making sure the cloth stayed wrapped on the handles. The inside of one blade was ruby red, slick as a polished jewel. The other blade was jet black, bottomless as obsidian.

It was beautiful. And very, very dangerous.

Swiftly, snip by snip, ruby and black blades in a loving hand.

I slipped the scissors into the black bag, and then just stood there trying to decide what I wanted to do and where I wanted to be.

The warm tug in my chest indicated I didn't need to be here in my bedroom right now. I knew it was going to take hours before I fell asleep anyway.

I glanced at the tea, cooling on my nightstand.

I needed something stronger. Much stronger. And I knew right where I should be.

CHAPTER SEVEN

MOM'S BAR was owned by Hera, but she, along with all the other gods, had left town several months ago. Luckily, all of the gods who owned businesses while vacationing here had contingency plans in place.

Mom's was now safely in the hands of Niko, who was a Bakeneko, and didn't mind looking after the place until Hera came back to town. If she came back to town.

The low light and easy, bluesy rock made me glad I'd come here. The place wasn't very busy or crowded, and the people in the room were intent on minding their own business.

I strolled over to the bar.

The only god in town, Cupid, sat with his back to the room, more than happy to ignore humanity and all that went along with it.

Tonight, I could sympathize.

He wore a black T-shirt that showed off his muscles and tattoos, jeans, and old biker boots. The mirror behind the bar was covered by bottles, so I didn't expect him to see me coming.

"Myra," he said as I sat next to him.

"Bo," I replied.

The bartender strolled over and gave me a smile. "What'll you have, officer?"

"Just a shot of Jose, thanks."

He tapped his knuckles on the bar then turned to pour and set the shot in front of me. "On the house."

I nodded my thanks and pressed my fingers against the glass, turning it on the bar top.

"You look like someone who needs to talk," Bo said in his deep rumble. He still hadn't looked my way, but he raised his beer, something dark and rich I could smell over all the other heavy spirits in the room.

"I know you're on vacation," I said. "This is kind of a work thing."

He turned just a bit my way, angling his wide shoulders so he could better see me. I turned toward him too, planting my elbow on the bar.

"What's on your mind?" he asked.

I reached into my pocket and placed the black bag with scissors on the bar.

Bo stared at the bag a moment, then nodded. "You planning to use those on someone?"

"Have you met Ordinary's only demon yet?" I asked.

"Nope."

"If you had, you'd want to use them on him too. Right on his smug face."

"Bathin, right?"

I nodded. Turned the shot glass by half again.

"So you hate him?"

"I didn't say I hated him."

"Those scissors in your bag are very old, very hard to find, and very dangerous. They are not something you should carry if you care at all for the demon."

I grumbled something about demons and just exactly how much I didn't care about one specifically, and most of them generally.

Bo made a humming sound and drank beer.

"You don't think I like him," I said.

"I think you need to be very clear what you feel for him before you do anything with those scissors."

"He took my sister's soul."

"I've heard."

"He had our dad's soul trapped. Did you know that?"

Bo tipped the bottle again, then set it down. He signaled to the bartender to bring him another, and to bring me a second shot.

I hadn't even had a sip yet. Yes, I liked to sip tequila, no lime, no salt. I liked the taste. Liked to savor the burn. Had always preferred my drinks raw and hot.

When fresh drinks were in front of us, Bo finally answered me.

"I did know."

"You knew that Bathin trapped Dad's soul? Why didn't you

tell us about it? I thought you were our friend."

He gave me a tolerant look, the look of a god who had bigger concerns than a few gifted mortals policing a tiny beach town.

"My power is an old one, Myra." The neon behind the bar cast soft blue and red glow on his shorn head. The diamond in the top of his ear glittered like a single star. "Have you ever read the original records of how Eros began?"

My pulse sped up a little. This was information I wasn't usually offered. "I have not. But I would love to."

"Lots of people would. But if it's ever been written fully or accurately is not the point." He winked.

"My beginnings are lost to memories so long ago that even I wonder what is the truth and what are dreams. I am old. Very old. I am harmony; I am binding; I am the connection between light and darkness, heaven and earth, life and death. All that is separate, I join together.

"Or I rend it apart as I see fit. I am love. I am hatred. I am alliance; I am destruction. When your father chose to give his soul to the prince in return for keeping Ordinary safe, I knew about it. That was an agreement, a joining. Your father gave his soul into Bathin's care."

"More like Bathin tricked him into it," I said.

"Perhaps. Your father had a very great heart, a very great love for this town, and an even greater love for his daughters. He may have entered into the agreement willingly. As did your sister."

"She had no choice."

"We always have a choice," he said. "She chose."

All right. That was true. "You bring things together," I said. "Including demons and souls. That means you can take them apart."

He rubbed one hand over his mouth and then tipped his head so he could hold my gaze.

In his eyes were universes, sorrow, laughter, love, fury.

Darkness and light.

"All things joined fall beneath my powers."

I shivered. He might not be carrying his power right now, but there was still a godliness about him. A presence that gave his words weight.

"You could make him give Delaney's soul back to her."

"Probably."

He eased back on the bar, his gaze drifting across the room, lingering a moment on the door, then coming back to me.

"You aren't going to do it, are you?"

"One"—he held up a finger—"I am on vacation. To do what you ask, I'd have to pick up my power, and that is not going to happen. Not until…not until I decide."

Another shadow crossed his face, and I had a moment to wonder why he had chosen this time, of all time, to put his power down. I wondered that often about the gods. Did they come here because they were bored, or tired? Or did their choice to step away from their power, no matter how temporarily, have nothing to do with emotions a mortal would understand?

If I had to guess what had brought Bo here to sit in this little bar in this little coastal town in the middle of almost nowhere, I'd say it was sorrow. I'd say he'd been on the road too long, and was looking for a place to rest his bones, lick his wounds.

It wasn't something I'd ask him. And since my family gift was being in the right place at the right time, I was pretty sure he was getting as much out of me being here at the bar on this dark and lonely night as I was.

"Don't you think Delaney gives enough of herself to this town?" I said quietly. "Don't you think it's time for someone to give up something for her? Give something back to her. To keep her safe. To make her happy?"

"I do think all those things," he said. "Are you the person to make all that happen for her?"

"I'm the one with the libraries of knowledge. I am the one Dad left with that responsibility. She's the only one of us who can bridge the god power into rest here. She's important. To all of us. And it's my job to take care of her when she does something like this—gets herself tied into things that are going to hurt her."

"Bathin's a thing you think is going to hurt her?"

"He already has. He's a demon. They thrive on pain."

Bo took another drink, then placed the beer carefully down

on the bar, heavy fingers caging it.

"Bathin isn't like most demons," he said. "Or he isn't now."

"Now?"

"Not since he made that deal with your father."

"Okay. I don't follow."

"Your father had a very great heart. He stood in Delaney's exact position, gateway for the gods. Holding that soul, his very specific soul…that can't be without consequence."

"What consequence?"

He flicked at the nail of his thumb with the callous on his middle finger. "That's not my story to tell."

I slugged back my first shot. "Not nice, Bo. Teasing me with information. Not nice."

"It's not my job to be nice."

"If Mercury were here, he'd tell me the story."

"Oh, he'd tell you a lot of stories, I'm sure." Bo smiled, a light of delight in his eyes. "Some of them might even contain a word or two of truth."

I laughed and lifted the second shot in a toast to a god I hadn't seen in years. We both sipped.

"Do you like him?" Bo asked.

"Mercury?"

"Bathin."

"No."

He made another humming sound around a swallow. "Do you want to?"

That surprised another laugh out of me. "I thought you weren't willing to pick up your power."

"Oh, I wasn't offering. I'm just curious. If you had just met him and hadn't known he was a demon, if he hadn't taken your sister's soul, would you give him a second look? Would you like him?"

It was probably the bar, the music, the familiarity of the god beside me, and the tequila (definitely the tequila), but I took a moment to really think it over.

"He's complicated. Mysterious. I love solving a mystery. He likes the chase, and doesn't give up easily, so…I like that. He's done some really…decent things. Heroic things when we didn't have anyone else to turn to. He might not seem reliable, but when the chips were down, yeah, he was there. Every time."

I stopped and rubbed a fingertip over the edge of my shot glass. That was a pretty long list of positives. I needed some negatives to balance it out. The only problem was that no negatives were coming to mind. There were tons of things I didn't like about him. Weren't there?

"I don't trust him. Not at all."

"I didn't ask if you trusted him," Bo said. "I asked if things were different, if he had never touched your father's soul, or your sister's soul, if you would want to get to know him."

The answer floated there, somewhere in the warm tug in my chest, in that same part of me that held my family gift. The part of me that always knew where I should be. The part of me that knew where I belonged, where I fit in, like a puzzle piece pressing into place.

The part of me that was never wrong. And it knew where I fit. Who I fit.

Yes.

And that single, shining truth startled the hell out of me.

"Oh," I said, reeling under the immensity of that truth. "Oh."

Bo's eyes were kind and endless.

"Thing about the heart? It is never wrong. It might be inconvenient—damned inconvenient." He lifted his beer to wash away whatever memory that statement drew up in him. "And it might be foolish," he continued. "But it is honest. It feels what it feels. The trick to living with a heart is figuring out how much you listen to it, and make decisions on its counsel."

"That's such an easy trick," I grumbled. "Thanks a lot for that."

"And the thing about the scissors?" he went on, a little like he was enjoying turning this screw. "They will extract a cost from anyone who uses them."

I groaned. "They're made by a demon, aren't they?"

"Yes."

"So I have to decide if I'm going to use the scissors to free my sister's soul, harm Bathin, and pay whatever price comes along with the things. Do I have that all right?"

"Yep."

"I don't suppose you know what the price might be?"

"Nope."

"Fantastic. Here's to impossible decisions." I held up my glass he clinked it with the neck of his beer. Then I slammed back the shot.

CHAPTER EIGHT

I SLEPT like the dead. In my bed. After I'd pulled off the comforter, blankets, and sheets and replaced everything with clean linens from the cupboard.

The scissors had been stashed in my closet in a box Odin had carved for me when I was a little girl. It was smooth, beautiful wood, silky soft as it shifted into whorls and angles that made the whole thing look like an ocean seen from between the branches of a great tree. Here and there in the water, fish jumped. The back of the box was dominated by anemone in full bloom, three tiny hermit crabs playing between them.

He'd told me the crabs were my sisters and me.

The box was blessed and warded against darkness. He had told me it was big enough to hold my favorite things, and for years I'd locked my diaries in it, mostly to keep Jean from reading them.

But after I grew up, the box had remained empty except for a few small prizes. I'd recently added the flyer from my first game on the roller derby team and newspaper clippings of cases we'd solved to the bracelet Mom had given me, and the tarot card from Jules.

And now, a black bag holding a pair of golden scissors—that could somehow free my sister's soul, but at a cost to me and extreme pain to Bathin—filled the space.

There wasn't a rule book or journal that could tell me what I should do.

But there were my sisters. We'd figure this out together. Now that we had the weapon—the scissors—we could decide on the right way to use them.

Of course, we still needed that one page from that one book that explained *how* to use the scissors.

Still, today felt like a victory, except for the whole worms and stalker poem thing.

I packed the black bag, the letter, and the worm bucket,

which I did not open, because: ew, and drove in to the station.

I considered stopping by the bakery to get some donuts, but then I remembered that my sisters had thrown me at Bertie's mercy and made me sit through speed dating in a bowling alley.

No donuts for traitors.

"Morning!" I said as I strolled through the door. "What fresh joy do we have on the docket today?"

The first thing I noticed was the boxes of cookies on the counter. Six boxes of Girl Scout cookies, all open. Looked like Mindy had done pretty well for herself and her daughters last night.

Delaney leaned on the counter, half a Thin Mint in her hand, coffee cup in the other, talking to Jean. I was here early, but Jean should have finished her shift already.

"Switch with Roy again?" I asked her.

She took a huge gulp of whatever iced coffee/extra Red Bull/ice cream monstrosity she'd talked the drive-through coffee shop to Frankenstein together for her.

"Yes. Trying out a few mornings in a row. See if I like it."

I raised an eyebrow. She was a total night owl. Always had been. I figured she'd changed hours so they more closely matched up with her baker boyfriend's very early morning schedule.

"Look at all those cookies," I said to Delaney with a sly grin. "I wonder where you got them."

She rolled her eyes. "Mindy talked me into a dozen. I figure I'll keep them in the cupboard here and we can bring them out when things get really stressful."

"There are six on the countertop," I said. "How stressful has the day been so far?"

"I only put one box on the counter." She contemplated the lineup. "Mindy must have hit up the entire town last night. We've had a few people stop by to thank us for our service." She tipped her head at my hand. "What's with the bucket?"

"Worms." I crossed to my desk, set the bucket on the floor, and draped my coat over my chair. "So there are a couple things I need to fill you both in on." I pulled out the plastic evidence bag with the letter, then the black bag, and placed them both on my desk.

I did not sit down, but Jean and Delaney came over to stand and stare at the items with me.

I went through everything. From receiving the letter on my doorstep, to the crossroads demon and her intel, the cookie-cruncher suspect, right on through to the worms, the scissors, and my conversation with Cupid.

"How do you even do so much in two days?" Jean asked me. "Two days, Myra. All I got done was dyeing my hair and wrapping Hogan's gift. And why didn't you tell me about the letter or the crossroads deal—"

I opened my mouth to argue.

"—fine," she said, "the crossroads *intel* when it happened? I was right there."

"So was Bathin."

She blew out a breath and squeaked her straw up and down in its plastic lid. "Right. He was. And then the fire department, and then we went shopping. Still. You could have said something."

"I didn't think she was going to actually bring me anything that could save Delaney's soul, since she disappeared before I could really pin her down."

We all stared some more at the black bag and the golden scissors that glinted on top of it.

"Okay," Delaney said. "The only information you have on the scissors is what Bo said, right?"

"Yeah. I haven't gone through the records to see if there is a mention of them that I missed, so all I have to go on is what Bo told me."

"And he said they will cause Bathin pain, free my soul, but all at a cost to the person who uses them?"

"Yep."

Silence, except for Jean slurping her drink.

"You are not using those things," Delaney said.

"Delaney," I said, "be smart about this."

"I *am* being smart. Those scissors are dangerous, probably deadly, and they are of demonic origin. We do not just willy-nilly start snipping away with a magical weapon to see what happens. Do you understand me, Myra? I am officially ordering you not to use these until we have hard data on what they can do—what they will do when used."

Okay, she was making sense, but I didn't like it.

"Promise me you won't use them, Myra."

"I won't use them."

She held my gaze for a moment, my sister who could face down gods and monsters without flinching. My sister who was following so closely in our father's footsteps that I wondered if her life would end the same way: suddenly and too soon.

"Good." She took a sip of her coffee, then pointed at the letter. "Let's see if we can find out anything about this, since it's our ground zero, okay? I can get Jules in here and see if she can get any vibes off it."

"I'm on it." Jean skipped over to her desk, snapping her fingers on the way.

"How much sugar and caffeine was in that thing?" I muttered to Delaney.

"All the caffeine and sugar. We should make her clean out the evidence room." She grinned. I grinned. It was great to have a younger sister on the force.

"We should," I agreed.

"Lock those up, okay?" Delaney pointed to the scissors.

"What about the worms?" I asked.

She sighed. "They're just going to stink up the place. Let's get some more pictures, then shake them out, seal the box, and store it. The worms can go in the bushes."

"You got it, boss."

Maybe it was the tone of my voice, but Delaney paused and pressed her hand on my arm. "I love you, Myra. Thank you for looking for a way to get my soul back. This might be the way we go. I just don't want any of us to pay any more prices for this situation, okay? Not me. And not you."

"I know. It's just...we're so close. I want to see this done and over. I hate that he's holding your soul."

"Me too. But it's a lot better than it was. I couldn't feel anything when he first took it; now I only notice it when things get too quiet, when I don't have anything to do."

"What's it like?" I asked her softly enough Jean wouldn't hear. I hadn't talked to her about it for a while. But each time I had asked before, she'd given me a different answer.

"It's like I'm missing something, or forgot something but I don't know what it is. It's like colors are more faded and there's a sense of…knowing I'm broken. Knowing that at some moment when I might need my strength and determination the most, it won't be there. It feels like I'm not enough."

I placed my hand on her shoulder. "You will always be enough. Even without your soul. But I want you to have your soul back, so you can be whole."

"Me too." She smiled. Did it look like it was a little faded? Did it look like she was trying to fake her way through not having a soul? Was there more to it she didn't want to tell me?

"Good," she said. "Now get rid of the worms." She walked off to pour herself another cup of coffee, and then check on how Jean was doing rounding up our local witch.

I got busy dumping out the worms and bagging the box they came in. I thought about dumping the worms out back, but decided I could take them home and put them in my rose bed. Worms were good at aerating the soil, and these were nice, big, healthy worms.

So instead of going out back, I walked out the front door with the bucket and over to my cruiser.

There were pictures tucked under the windshield wipers. Photos of my sisters. With the heads cut off and stapled to their feet.

Dozens of them.

Creepy as hell. I checked the car—no one and nothing inside. Scanned the parking lot and greenery around it. Nothing. Opened the trunk and put the bucket in it.

Okay. I wasn't going to touch those photos without backup.

I started back to the station, keeping my eyes peeled for any movement.

But it was a sound that stopped me. A soft sob that I would expect to hear at a haunted house, or foggy forest. Not out here in the cloudy February day.

I turned.

There was a human-sized cat standing just a few feet behind me. Or rather, standing behind me was someone in a cat costume, like a mascot for a sports team, except creepier.

A lot creepier.

"Hello," I said, aiming for calm and cop-like. "Can I help you?"

The cat pulled out a gun. Since when did cats have pockets?

"Easy," I said. "Easy, now."

The cat lifted its left hand, and a single photo dangled from its bulky paw.

A photo of me. With my head cut off and stapled to my feet.

That warm tug in my chest went hot. Great. Being in the right place at the right time meant I had to stare down the barrel of a weaponized feline.

My life. Just…unbelievable sometimes.

"I'm right here and happy to listen to anything you want to tell me," I said, keeping my voice friendly. "How about you put the gun down, and then you and I can talk?"

The cat head wobbled on the human shoulders. The cat made a couple gestures with the photo, but I had no idea what it wanted me to do. Pick up the picture? Turn around and get the photos off my car?

I lifted both palms up, so it could see I didn't have my firearm in my hands. "It looks like it's going to rain. Would you like to go somewhere? Sit somewhere out of the cold?"

The cat made that muffled sobbing sound again and swung the gun toward its own head.

"Easy. Hold on. Just a minute. Let's take a deep breath, together. Let's talk, okay? You have my picture. I see you have my picture. Is there something you want to tell me?"

Don't ask me how, but the cat looked sad. Its shoulders slumped, even as the gun pressed harder into the comically round and furry side of its head.

"Hey!"

That shout, hard and commanding, set several things into motion.

The cat startled and spun toward the shout, arm jerking and oversized fingers swinging the gun up and out, pointing at the source of the sound.

Pointing at the demon, Bathin, who was storming our way looking like he was about to have cat for dinner.

The cat aimed at Bathin.

And I…I don't know what came over me. Training, I guess.

I'd spent years of my life protecting people. Protecting the citizens of my town. The idea of anyone pointing a gun at anyone else made me want to intercede.

It wasn't that my heart froze silent and cold seeing Bathin barreling toward a loaded weapon. It wasn't the sudden fear and hot sting of adrenalin that poured through me at knowing he was putting himself in the line of fire.

For me.

That wasn't what he was. That wasn't who he was.

Or maybe…it was.

But dealing with a gunslinging Garfield was not his job. It was mine.

I launched myself at the fluffy menace.

The cat went down in a heap of fur, yowls, and stuffing.

I leaned my weight onto its back. It squirmed under me, trying to throw me off.

"It's over. Just settle down." I dragged the cat's arms up behind its back and got my knees planted on either side of its torso.

The cat went boneless and still.

Bathin was there, had been there a second after I'd jumped. He loomed behind me, made a sort of primal rumble that might have been a curse or a threat. I glanced over my shoulder.

His hot gaze was fastened to me, straddling the cat. He was angry. So furious that I could feel the heat rolling off him.

"Oh for gods' sake," I grumbled. "Go inside. Get my sisters."

Bathin's gaze met mine. Instead of the fire I was so used to seeing there, I saw ice. "Maybe you should go inside, Myra. I would be happy to…contain the assailant."

"That's not happening. Go get Delaney."

He hesitated.

"This is my job. This is my town," I said. "And this is what we do when someone pulls a gun in Ordinary. Go get my sisters."

Everything about him sharpened, and for a moment, he

was too hard to look at—too much fire, too much rage. And then the edges of him softened again, and he was just Bathin.

He glared over at the gun, thrown off in the bushes and out of reach.

"Don't touch it," I said. "Don't mess with it. That's evidence."

His nostrils flared as he turned and strode into the station, fists clenched, shoulders stiff.

I pulled out my handcuffs, which were not going to work with the bulky paws on this costume.

The gun had fallen off into the bushes far enough away that neither of us were able to reach it.

The cat/person/creature beneath me was unmoving and quiet, except for an occasional sob.

"Okay, so we're just going to take this slowly," I said. "I'm going to take off your cat head, so you and I can talk, all right?"

I let go of the cat's left paw so I could carefully pull off the costume.

The man—it was clearly a man in a cat suit—was familiar to me. Very familiar.

"Jonah?" I asked, unable to hide my disappointment. "What is this all about?"

He squeezed his eyes shut and refused to look at me. Even though he clenched his mouth shut, another little sob escaped him.

"It's okay, Jonah. Let's go inside where we can figure this out."

He seemed to relax a fraction at that suggestion.

Voices and footsteps were coming our way. My sisters here to save the day.

CHAPTER NINE

WATCHING JEAN and Delaney question Jonah was a weird experience. I stood in the cramped, dark space behind the two-way glass while Delaney and Jean both sat at the table with my neighbor.

They all had fresh cups of coffee. Jonah had agreed to take off the rest of the cat costume, and sat in his Steelers sweatshirt and jeans. He looked mortified.

Bathin had refused to leave my side. I got tired of arguing with him that I was fine and him ignoring me, so he had taken up a position next to me, arms crossed, glaring through the glass like he wished he could melt it with his mind.

Jonah had explained his actions leading up to the cat-costume confrontation. He'd spoken in fits and starts, in a very soft voice, and without making eye contact.

Jonah was my stalker. Or, rather, he was a very awkward fellow, a relatively new supernatural in town, trying to make friends.

He had sent me the poem as a valentine. That whole "coming for you" line was his way of saying he'd like to come over and have coffee someday.

He'd gifted me with a box of worms because he knew they were beneficial to my rose beds, and were the same worms he'd been raising in his basement and using to make his own yard thrive.

He'd cut off my sisters' heads in those photos and stapled them to their feet because he knew I was head over heels for my family.

And the picture of me with my head cut off? His way of saying he liked me a lot too.

With anyone else, I wouldn't believe those explanations.

But it turned out Jonah was a squonk: a creature that usually lives in the hemlock forests of Pennsylvania. They are known to be shy, ugly, and capable of dissolving into a puddle of tears when cornered.

Oh yeah, and the gun? It was a squirt gun. Jonah had been carrying it to use it on himself in case he became embarrassed. A couple squirts of salt water, and he could just puddle out of an uncomfortable social situation.

He was telling the truth. I could see it. Jean could see it. Delaney could see it. He hadn't been in town long enough to make many friends, and this was just his disastrously bad way of going about it.

"He's lying," Bathin grumbled.

"You're lying," I replied.

Neither of us looked at each other; we just kept staring through the glass.

"Okay, I am. But I still don't like him," Bathin said.

"You don't have to like him. You just have to promise not to hurt him."

"And if I don't promise?"

"I will personally throw you out of Ordinary."

"And let me take your sister's soul with me to the underworld?"

"No. I would not let you do that. Ever."

He turned his head. "Myra Reed. Do you have something up your sleeve?"

I didn't say anything. I didn't have to. He could read my mind. He'd proven that.

"I thought I sensed something different here in Ordinary." He reached toward me, his strong fingers gently turning my face until I was looking at him.

I didn't fight him.

Let him know that I had something he didn't know about. Let him guess at what knowledge or weapon I had hidden from him.

Let him see the victory in my eyes.

He met my gaze, searching for answers.

He inhaled, a short, soft gasp. "You have the scissors."

It was my turn to be startled. My eyes went a little wide.

"You do," he continued. "I can feel them near, can feel them on your skin." He lifted my hand, brought it to his lips. Not close enough to kiss.

Almost close enough to kiss.

I found I could not look away. Did not want to. Did not want to pull away. To lose this touch—his touch.

He did not look away either. I saw the question in his eyes. I nodded, slightly. He pressed his lips, hot as a brand, across my knuckles.

Suddenly there wasn't enough air in the room. Suddenly it was hot, and every inch of my skin was aware of the slightest motion of my own breathing, the slow, languid beat of my pulse.

"Beautiful Myra. How clever you are. To find the one weapon even I could not locate." His lips pressed against my knuckles again.

I shivered, as if the heated air in the room was suddenly too cold compared to his kiss.

"Will you give it to me?" he asked, every word wrapped in silvery oil and candlelight.

"No," I breathed. Everything in me strained to say yes. To give in to him. To be taken.

But a no was a no, and he lifted his face away from my knuckles, then shifted his hold on my fingers.

He gripped firmly enough that I was aware something had changed.

His expression was serious and intent.

"Promise me," he said, a command and plea I had never heard from him before. "Promise me that no matter how much hate for me is in your heart, no matter how much fear for your sister is in your thoughts, promise me you will not use those scissors."

"Why?" I asked.

"Because they will change anyone who uses them. They will…maim. The scissors were a gift. Given to my worst enemy. And you would not want to know what they will do to a soul as sweet as yours."

Okay, *that* snapped me out of whatever dreamy state I'd been in.

"I don't care what they would do to my soul." I snatched my fingers away. "I want my sister free." We stood so close that there was barely an inch between us. When had that happened?

I took a step away from him. And another, until I could

think again. Until I could breathe again.

"The price is too high," he said, taking a step toward me.

"Really? Suddenly you're worried about me and the price I'll pay if I use a pair of magicked scissors on you? I think you're scared, Bathin."

"Am I?"

From the look he was giving me, from the arms, once again crossed over his chest, no, he was not the least bit frightened.

"Free my sister's soul."

"No."

"I'll use the scissors."

"No."

"Then make me a deal, demon. You seem to be fond of those."

"The deal is you don't use the scissors."

"No," I said.

"This is for your own good. For your own safety," he said. "Why aren't you listening to me?"

"Because I don't like you."

He smiled, a hot curve of his lips that narrowed his eyes. "Did the crossroads demon give them to you? Did you promise her you'd let her steal souls right out from under the eyes of Ordinary if she gave you the scissors?"

"Who is your enemy?" I asked.

He tipped his head, shook it slightly. "Oh so many people."

"Who made the scissors?"

His jaw clenched, loosened. He huffed out a breath and ran his palm over his hair. "My mother."

Hold on. "You have a mother?"

He shot me a puzzled look. "Did you think I walked fully formed from lava and hellstorms?" At my look, he rolled his eyes. "Of course I have a mother."

"And she gave your enemy a pair of scissors that will damage the user *and* damage you, her own son?"

He shrugged. "She thinks she knows what's best, even if that's what I think is worst. It's a complicated relationship."

I couldn't help it. I laughed. That was such a...*normal* thing to say about a parent. I slapped my hand over my mouth, trying to hide my chuckle.

"Don't," he said fondly as he gently drew my hand away from my mouth. "I love your laugh."

I shook my head. "This is ridiculous."

"Oh?" He hadn't let go of my wrist yet. I hadn't made him let go, either. He stepped up close to me again. "What is ridiculous?"

"This. All this. Us."

He nodded. "It is, isn't it?"

"I don't like chaos," I said. "I don't like messy. I don't like…whatever you are."

"I know. You've said so. Several times. And yet here we are, right where we keep ending up. As if we were meant to be here. Just at this right place. Just at this right time."

He paused, and I let that sink in a bit.

I did keep ending up here, with him, in his arms, alone.

And it did not feel wrong.

Bo's words came back to me: *the heart is never wrong.*

But was this the right time to trust it? To listen to my heart instead of my head?

I lifted up on my tiptoes. Bathin was over six feet tall, and I only came up to his shoulder.

He held his breath, and everything about him stilled as I inched closer to him, my face tipped up.

He knew what I was asking. And that mountain of a man, of a demon, bent toward me, swaying downward to meet my need.

For a moment, we were caught there, teetering on the edge of someplace we had never been before. Teetering on the edge of possibilities.

No, my logic reminded me. This demon was chaos, and chaos was not what I needed. Not what I wanted in my life.

Yes, my heart urged. This demon was loyal, calm, intelligent, precise. Everything I wanted in my life.

Yes, my heart shouted. And I could no longer find a reason to ignore it.

The door to the room swung open with a whoosh of cold air and Jean already mid-conversation. "…get most of that? Because pressing charges for epic social naiveté is gonna be a tough one."

The spell was broken. The mood vaporized.

I stepped back, two full paces. Bathin straightened, and the passion in his expression banked like ashes beneath a mountain of stone.

Jean paused, just inside the door, holding it open to let the air, and apparently the good sense of the rest of the world, into this cramped space.

"Oops," she said. "Should I call the fire department? Or would you two like a little more time alone?"

"I'm not going to press charges," I said, still looking at Bathin.

He grunted.

"We're going to recommend him into the orientation class," Jean said. "Get him a buddy to help him navigate the rules in Ordinary so this sort of thing doesn't happen again. He's beside himself with embarrassment and remorse."

"Okay," I said. "So I guess we're done here."

Bathin raised one eyebrow. Challenging.

"Are we now?" he asked.

Into the silence that stretched between us, Jean chuckled. "So I'll give you two some time."

"No," I said. "We're done."

"We are not done," Bathin said. "We are just barely beginning."

"And that's the way it's going to remain," I said. I meant that. Most of me meant that. Okay, some of me was wishing I was just brave enough to follow through. To find out what it would be like to let a little chaos into my life.

Bathin exhaled through his nose, making his nostrils flare. Then he smiled and shifted the weight on his feet, his shoulders angled toward me. Closing the space between us without taking a single step.

"It is Valentine's Day," he said.

"Yes?" I had no idea where he was going with this.

"Do you have plans?"

Oh. *Oh.*

From the smug smile on his face, he knew I didn't. But even with no plans, even if the alternative was spending the day alone, I didn't have to tell him that.

"She does," Jean piped up. "Lunch. With Delaney and me. Sister's Valentine's lunch. So you can just slow your roll there, buddy."

He frowned, and I beamed. That was my sister, jumping in when she knew I needed backup, one hundred percent on my side.

"But she doesn't have anything going for dinner, so you should get on that."

"Jean!" I yelled, utterly betrayed.

She cackled and bolted through the door. "Super busy. Gotta take care of a lot of paperwork. So much paperwork!" she said over her shoulder as she sprinted down the hallway.

I sighed, closed my eyes, and rubbed at the headache my sister had inspired.

"So…dinner, is it, then?" Bathin's voice was gold and honey.

I was trying to formulate an answer, one that didn't involve me wanting to murder my sister or ask him if he'd like to be my accomplice.

I let my hand drop from my face and looked back up at him. "We are not dating."

"I see."

"We are not going to dinner tonight."

He hummed.

"We are not valentines."

He waited a moment. "Then what are we, Myra Reed?"

And oh, the answers could be endless. But I chose the truth.

"I don't know."

He was silent. If he were judging me for that omission, he made no comment as to what he decided.

"So, now if you'll excuse me," I said, "I have to commit sororicide."

His lips curved in a wry smile. Then he bowed slightly, gesturing to the door, through which I followed my soon-to-be-dead sister.

BATHIN DIDN'T get in the way of my argument with Jean. Didn't get in the way of my Valentine lunch with both my sisters, who were, when they put their minds to it, pretty amazing sisters to have.

They explained to me that Jonah had wandered into town a while ago and had been too shy to ask anyone about which particular rules he should follow. They'd already informed Bertie, who had reached out and found Jonah a buddy to help him navigate our customs, without coming across as a stalker.

As for the cookie crusher, we didn't have any other leads yet, but Delaney had gone by the store to talk to them about it, and she'd gotten them to set up a closed-circuit camera. With a little luck, we'd find out who was hating on the goodies.

They both invited me to join them for their Valentine's dinners.

I refused. Adamantly.

Because seriously? Being the third wheel at either of their evenings? No.

We talked about the scissors. Delaney was ready to threaten me into seeing it her way again, but she didn't have to. I had already decided I wasn't going to use the scissors.

Not yet, anyway.

I didn't have the one book with the one page that was the actual spell—the operating instructions. Without that, I didn't want to go forward.

My sister's soul was involved in this situation. I wasn't going to put her in danger just because I was eager to save her.

Bathin didn't get in the way of the rest of my work shift either, which meant I spent Valentine's Day doing what I did best: looking after the people in the little town I called home.

Dinner was just how I liked it: alone in my cozy house, a nice pot of strong tea and a successful bowl of the udon noodle recipe I'd wanted to try.

I wish I'd picked up a dessert after work, or stolen one of Delaney's boxes of Girl Scout cookies from the station. But I'd been in too much of a hurry to lock myself away from the happy couples walking hand in hand everywhere I looked to think that far ahead.

It wasn't that I hated people who were in love. I just hated how lonely I always felt on this particular day.

Still, my after-dinner tea was sweet and strong, I had a pile of novels I couldn't wait to dive into, and one of my favorite playlists filled the house with music I loved.

Not a bad way to spend the holiday.

Long after the sun had set and I had plowed through half a Regency romance, there was a knock on my door.

I wasn't expecting anyone. Didn't want to see anyone. Any problems of a criminal nature could be taken up with the cops on duty tonight—any other problem, I didn't want to know about until tomorrow.

I glanced out at the front stoop. Sighed.

I unlocked the door and stood in it, arms crossed over my chest. "What do you want?"

Bathin held up a bottle of wine in one hand and a box of truffles in the other. "Since dinner was out, how about dessert?"

"Dessert?"

"Wine, chocolate. An after-the-meal treat. Dessert."

"Just you and me?"

He glanced over his shoulder at the empty street, then back at me. "Looks like just you and me."

I leaned on the doorjamb. "Why?"

He could take that question a million ways, since I had a million "whys" I'd like answered. Why was he here? Why did he want to spend time with me? Why couldn't he just give Delaney back her soul so we could be done with this?

Why had he made me promise not to hurt myself when trying to get rid of him?

He leaned on the other side of the doorjamb, facing me, the wine and chocolates held low in his hands. "Maybe I don't want to be alone tonight."

I frowned.

"Maybe I like your company, Myra Reed. And maybe I'd like to spend some time with you. Just…time. An hour or two of conversation, before we go back to…whatever this thing is that we're doing." He pointed at me and at himself, the bottle of wine swaying as he moved.

I waited to see if he was going to push. If he was going to deal and cajole. But he seemed just as content as me to stand there with a doorway of space between us, even though he could be at any other place in this wide world.

And my heart? Oh, my heart was happy he was here, warm and content in a way that would have spooked me if I hadn't seen it coming. That feeling was a truth I couldn't ignore.

"Come on in," I said. "There's no reason for both of us to be lonely."

He looked surprised and relieved by my answer, the edges of him softening, as if I'd just seen him shivering and offered to bring him in out of the rain.

"Myra?" he said as he stepped into my house and held out the chocolates for me. "Even though I hate this holiday, happy Valentine's Day."

"Happy Valentine's Day, Bathin," I said. "I hate it too."

He chuckled and made himself at home in my kitchen, opening the bottle of wine and pulling glasses from the cupboard. I got comfortable in the living room, tucking my feet up in my favorite big chair, my fuzzy throw blanket over my legs.

It was nice to hear him working in the kitchen, nice to have someone here. He sang along to the song on my playlist: Etta James's "Sunday Kind of Love."

I leaned my head back and listened. His voice rolled along with the slow, swaying blues. He had a nice voice, low and easy and true.

I sighed, content. Whatever this was we were doing, this, tonight, felt right.

We were both right where we belonged.

Here.

Together.

And when I opened the chocolates, extra-dark chocolate truffles from Euphoria Chocolate Company, I was not at all surprised that he had brought me my favorite kind.

ACKNOWLEDGEMENT

THANK YOU to Dejsha Knight, Sharon Thompson and Eileen Hicks for your beta reading, copy editing, and proof reading. Another big thanks to Arran at Editing 720 who came to my rescue when I was losing a deadline battle. Huge gratitude to Skyla Dawn Cameron, formatter extraordinaire, and cover artist Lou Harper. You have all helped to make these stories sharper and shinier than I ever could have managed on my own.

To my family: thank you for keeping the holidays fun and joyous. It is the fond memories you crazy, wonderful people have given me that made me want to write stories like this.

Big thanks to my husband Russ, and sons Kameron and Konner. You are the joy in my life. Thank you for letting me be a part of your world. I love you. An extra shout-out goes to Kameron, who came up with the "zombie accordion" line. See? I told you I'd give you credit.

Lastly, but never leastly, I want to thank you, dear reader, for giving these stories a try. I hope you enjoyed this taste of Ordinary and that you will come back again soon to catch up with the creatures and gods and people in Oregon's quirkiest little beach town.

ABOUT THE AUTHOR

DEVON MONK is a national best selling writer of urban fantasy. Her series include Ordinary Magic, House Immortal, Allie Beckstrom, Broken Magic, and Shame and Terric. She also writes the Age of Steam steampunk series, and the occasional short story which can be found in her collection: A Cup of Normal, and in various anthologies. She has one husband, two sons, and lives in Oregon. When not writing, Devon is drinking too much coffee, watching hockey, or knitting silly things.

Want to read more from Devon?
Follow her online or sign up for her newsletter at:
http://www.devonmonk.com.